The Bridge - *a love affair*

The Bridge

a love affair

Allan J Organ

The Bridge - *a love affair*

Copyright © Allan J Organ 2014

All rights reserved.

allan.j.o[at]btinternet.com

Cover illustration: the bridge seen from upstream.

Image by Gothick from Wikimedia Commons, re-used under terms of Creative Commons-Share Alike 3.0

The Bridge - *a love affair*

To Lígia

Muse with the beautiful mind

The Bridge - *a love affair*

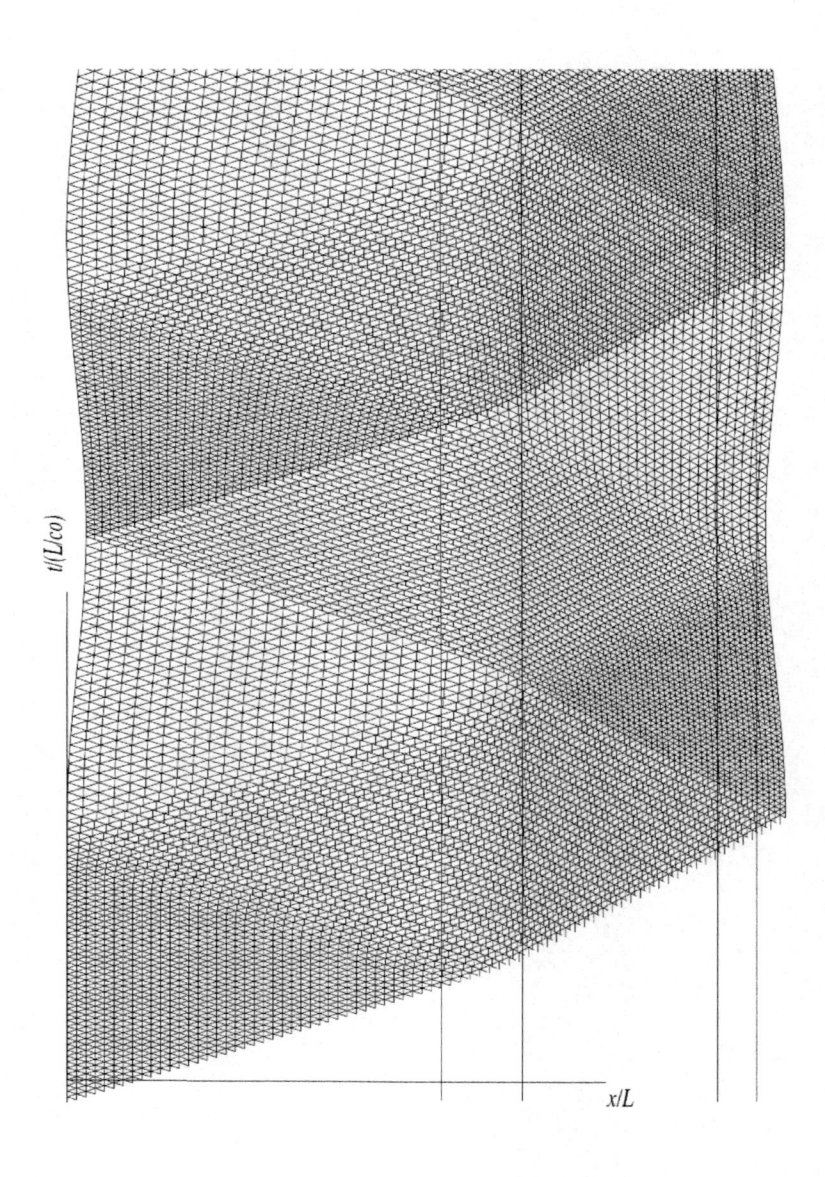

Graphical display of the solution to a problem in cyclic, unsteady, compressible flow with friction and heat transfer.

4

Contents

1	27th September 2016	7
2	Tornado	29
3	Coffee in Whitehall	47
4	Yes, Minister	63
5	Tropical island	81
6	Less steam, more traction	101
7	Bolero	115
8	Energy Research Unit	121
9	Fire escapade	133
10	Lígia	145
11	Musical interlude	169
12	Hitch-hiker's guide to the Atlantic	187
13	Call-up papers	207
14	Night op.	223
15	Expect the unexpected	239
16	Walk to paradise garden	245
17	A question of solace	255

The Bridge - *a love affair*

1

27th September 2016

Two objections to pyracantha came to mind immediately: In the first place they had spikes - long, hard, sharp spikes. Secondly they had territorial ambitions. This particular specimen occupied a location from which it increasingly interfered with full opening of the side gate. Sewell resolved on the spot that the top priority on his return would be that the bush should get its come-uppance. Just for now it was still possible to squeeze the bike through by using his buttocks to ram the gate against the bush while pulling in his stomach and half-lifting, half-wheeling the machine sideways over his feet. This accomplished, he held it by the saddle and followed it onto the gravel of the front drive to its accustomed waiting-place against the wall of the house.

The second test of wills with the pyracantha was won by a more comfortable margin. Once back through the gate, he swung it closed, shot the upper and lower bolts into their hasps and re-entered the house by the kitchen door.

Then it was into the lounge to check on his husky. Storm was the fourth Siberian husky in his life. A husky was intelligent and, above all, enthusiastic. For good measure it understood every word in the Oxford dictionary it opted to. Storm was on the sofa, curled into a compact ball that belied his size, his nose buried in that handsome tail. Sewell administered a vigorous scratch behind the ears. Being not yet daylight, it was a bit early in the lupine routine, so Storm enjoyed the bonding ritual as part of his husky dreams.

During the short absence Storm would be safe in the care of Mrs Hawkes. She occupied the flat, and was one of those unique friends with whom he would trust the number of his Swiss bank account (if he had one), let alone with the key to the house. She had once owned - and single-handedly managed - boarding kennels, for cats as well as dogs, capitalizing on the fact that she possessed an uncanny way with creatures of all types from hens to ponies: never had it been necessary to tell a dog more than once that it should not chase her cat or chickens: that dog never again sneaked a glance at either.

Sewell had taken the property partly on account of the spacious - if neglected - garden: a husky was an escape-artist, but previous owners had, for their own reasons, maintained an impenetrable perimeter fence. This had been achieved by reinforcing weak points with those damned pyracantha. While cat or rabbit might squirm through, no self-respecting husky would take its chance against one of those wretched bushes.

At over ninety, Mrs Hawkes - Violet - was not up to walking Storm, but had lost none of her magic: un-supervised, Storm would jump up and knock over an unsuspecting adult - but not Violet, with whom he communicated by telepathy. She was happy to take charge during short absences. Storm would doze under the apple tree, one eye half-open for his particular hobby - bumble-bees.

Sewell isolated the electricity supply at the distribution board. With mains power off more often than on, this had become essential: the fact that a cooker was not cooking no longer meant that it had been turned off. Isolating the gas supply was even more vital. He walked to the hall where a sturdy hold-all stood waiting. With the aid of a pocket-torch he looked down his pre-take-off check list by the side of the front door. Satisfied, he turned the hold-all endwise-on, lifted it across the threshold and set it down carefully beside the bicycle. Pulling the door shut against the night latch as noiselessly as possible, he gave a robust push to check, and straightened up.

It was morning - early morning. Five-thirty to be precise - not quite beginning to get light. And it was September. Of course it was September: didn't everything just *speak* September? You could feel it; you could smell it: that paradoxical mix of maturity and freshness.

The early start had meant dressing in the dark. This particular morning there had been help from moonlight entering the bedroom. But with or without the aid of the moon it was not that difficult: you just laid out your stuff the evening before. And after half-a-century of daily shaving who couldn't shave in the dark? Nevertheless, after eighteen months of draconian power rationing, he still found himself turning on a switch and expecting light - only to marvel at the power of habit - and at his own absent-mindedness.

He righted the bicycle and reached down for the hold-all. The lop-sided load conspired with the shifting gravel beneath the wheels to make for an inelegant shuffle towards the road. He crossed, setting the hold-all down on the raised verge to make for an easier reach from the saddle. Weighing up the best - and safest - way to carry a 25kg hold-all by bike in the dark, he found himself thinking back to shaving: it was beyond his power to do so except in the context of a memorable Atlantic crossing by the SS Homeric in 1962. He had been travelling to Canada on an immigrant visa and sharing a four-berth cabin with a sculptor from Ottawa, an American war historian and an un-memorable fourth party. The American's mission, which he broadcast throughout the ship with a good-humoured and infectious passion, had been checking on the 'kill' claims of World War Two fighter aces. To this end, his visit to the UK had taken in Adastral House, London headquarters of the Royal Air Force. Barely a sentence had he uttered which was not pithy, disarming or witty - or all three. One morning in mid-Atlantic, and with remnants of shaving-soap adorning nostrils and ears, he had paused in front of the mirror to observe: 'That's one reason why no man should fear death: he'll never have to shave again'.

The Bridge - *a love affair*

Sewell looked back at the house. He could not actually see Violet in her darkened front room, but the dear lady would surely be watching discreetly, working out what mission he might be on. Acknowledging her invisible wave, he swung his right leg over the saddle, reached down for the bag and pushed off from the kerb.

The initial fight to keep his balance prompted him - not for the first time - to question the wisdom of taking a 25kg load to the station by bicycle - and an awkward load at that. The answer lay in an acute shortage of alternatives: He had held on to his car while fuel prices had rocketed, but when the price at the pumps reached £10.50 per litre, it had joined the rest at the well-stocked re-cycle centre. The streets of Bristol were now a cyclist's paradise - at least during daylight hours when the pot-holes were visible. A skeleton bus service - all that remained of the once-proud Bristol Omnibus Company - was obscenely crowded, but at least ran to schedule on empty streets. On the other hand, the daily schedule did not start until seven o'clock.

A moon in its last quarter had risen just after midnight and still hung high in the clear sky. North Road sloped helpfully downhill, enabling him to coast while getting the measure of the balancing act. He knew the locations of these particular potholes intimately, and was soon sufficiently at home in the saddle to allow his thoughts to wander.

It was the sort of morning which invited reflection - demanded it - so why not? The bramble patch opposite the junction with Bannerleigh Road was just visible in the half-light. Two seasons ago he would have dallied to sample the blackberries. Nowadays, following Melt-down, every marginally-comestible fruit and seed - elderberry, rowan, bilberry, sloe, hawthorn and chestnut as well as blackberry - was picked the instant it was ripe - frequently before. The food shortage had been quick to sort those who could digest acorns from those who could not - or would not - and virtually the entire surviving population was suddenly knowledgeable to university degree level on the matter of edible fungi.   Resigning himself to the likelihood of never again seeing a real live blackberry, let alone eating one, he rolled past the bramble patch, testing the front brake in preparation for a stop at the junction with Bridge Road.

What a voyage that trip on the Homeric had been! Was there ever a *Strictly Come Dancing* challenge like doing the foxtrot on a dance-floor heaving and rolling to the Atlantic swell? And would his first James Bond film, *From Russia with Love* - the best Bond by a wide margin - have been as memorable for having been watched in a cinema set on boring concrete foundations?

With the aid of gravity he was soon rounding the bend onto the bridge approach. There would be no vehicular traffic, so it would not be necessary to negotiate the narrow pedestrian walk-way carrying the hold-all. The latter was getting heavier, and his left arm would shortly be demanding a rest. Changing hands was not an option, because a rear brake is less effective than the front. He would stop at the Clifton end of the bridge and flex his muscles while seeing what moonlight could add to the magic of Brunel's structure.

Rolling to a halt near the disused toll-booth, he lowered the hold-all to the ground. Dismounting stiffly, he pushed the bike a few paces further, leaned it against the railing and stretched indulgently. Atmospheric pollution from vehicles and industrial activity was now virtually zero, and with no light pollution, the sombre silhouette of the nearer tower was picked out sharp-edged against a star-speckled backdrop. Stolid, muscular, masonry thighs straddled the roadway ostentatiously, the bow-legged stance echoing the down-thrust it was shouldering. The run of giant chains between tower-head and anchorage tunnel sagged under the self-weight of the massive wrought-iron links in defiance of the tautening effect of the weight of the road deck, the foreshortened view exaggerating the droop. Possibly remembering more than was actually visible in the moonlight, he looked along the row of slender hangers, each no bigger in diameter than your wrist, by which the deck was suspended from the catenery* above.

---

*from Latin *catena* - chain.

The Bridge - *a love affair*

Viewed from a distance - from downstream or upstream - these superficially disparate components harmonized into a whole which, prior to Melt-down, had drawn camera-carrying tourists from all corners of the globe. An engineer would assume as a matter of course that the size and shape of each structural member - stocky tower, robust chain, slender hanger - reflected the fact that it carried the same percentage - say 50% - of the load at which it was calculated to fail. On the other hand, the interpretation of the professional is not that of the average tourist. Put another way, what would be the outcome of a bridge design competition among graduates of a college of art and design? Towers, chains, hangers and deck doubtless elegantly 'in proportion' but in all probability, incapable of supporting their own weight.

So: functionality which was the outcome of dispassionate engineering reckoning could be high art. He mulled the idea while wheeling the bike back towards the hold-all. Bending to pick up the cargo he walked the bike to the start of the footpath running south on the Clifton side, swung his right leg over the saddle and let the bike roll forward far enough to allow another test of the front brake: the road would get steeper - and steeper. In terms of gradient - one-in-five or one-in-six - he had no idea. All he knew was that no bike had a gear low enough to enable him to cycle *up* the gradient - with or without hold-all.

What a man, that Brunel: he had designed and supervised the construction of railways, tunnels, stations, bridges and ships. Biographies made little mention of collaborators or assistants, and surviving drawings were in his own hand. Nowadays, any one such project would call for the resources of a substantial team of engineers and architects - not to mention computers. Had the man never slept?

From Granby Hill he coasted towards Royal York Gardens, applying a heavier squeeze to the front brake. The hold-all had already been pulling well ahead of the handlebars on account of the gradient, and now angled even more steeply under the deceleration. Slowing to a safe speed for the right-hander into Granby Hill he grimaced at the increase in pain. As the bike straightened up he promised the shoulder a rest on reaching Hotwells.

The Bridge - *a love affair*

Retirement had in no way diminished the pride he had always felt in his chosen career, not least because of the vicarious association with the likes of Brunel. He had known colleagues move to other professions out of disgust at the public perception of technology - or for the lack of appreciation as to how much the smooth running of daily life was owed to it. He challenged himself to think of a single aspect of material well-being (he emphasized *material* as distinct from spiritual) which was *not* owed to technology: the ball-point pen and Concorde; the paper-clip and the combine-harvester (on-board sat-nav receiver directing an auto-pilot), the tooth-paste tube and the cruise liner; the dentist's drill driven at 250,000 revolutions per minute by a tiny air motor, the Coke can and the washing machine; the space shuttle and the hypodermic needle with one thousandth-of-an-inch bore; the kitchen blender and the cement mixer . . . . The list was endless - and if a mundane artefact (the toilet roll; the toothbrush) didn't display much evidence of engineering and technology, then the machinery which manufactured it by the millions most certainly did.

And what about the bicycle - the humble bike? The steepening gradient of Granby Hill called for a tighter squeeze on the front brake, the telescopic forks responded by compressing through a further centimetre, the hold-all swung further ahead - and the bike duly slowed. His first-ever two-wheeler had been a three-speed Humber roadster with rigid, steel frame. 'Suspension' had been stiff coil-springs under a saddle of unyielding boot-leather. The braking system had involved rubber blocks mounted on stirrups pulled against rims by rods connected to the brake handles *via* crude bell-cranks and pivots. In dry conditions braking was indifferent; in the wet it was next to ineffective. One might have expected improvement as the chromium plate of the rims wore through and rust took over. Perversely, the reality was the opposite. Right now he was astride a machine with light-alloy frame and chain-wheels, titanium bottom-bracket, twenty-one speeds and full suspension - coil-spring at the front, pneumatic at the rear. In daylight - and without the hold-all - he would intentionally aim for selected pot-holes and drain covers just to savour the response of the suspension. The front brake which was keeping his speed - and that of a 25kg hold-all - under control down a precipitous side-road was a diminutive disc brake almost indifferent to rain. A *hydraulically-actuated* disc brake! How many cyclists made a mental link to the painstaking engineering research and development behind the transformation to the modern cycling machine? And was ever a healthy, environmentally-friendly technology more taken for granted? The only chance of its letting you down would be lack of maintenance.

Approaching the bottom of the hill he shelved his musings for long enough to come to a halt at the junction with Hotwells Road. If there were to be any vehicular traffic, it would be here. Indeed, as he reached the junction, headlights approached from the right, forcing a choice between the discomfort of the continued weight of the hold-all and the undoubted pain of picking it up again if he once set it down. He decided on the former - a bad bet, since the lone vehicle was approaching slowly. It would be a municipal, military or police vehicle, as they were the only categories with permits to draw fuel. Or it might be one of a very small number of multi-fuel conversions or hybrids, so this could be interesting. The aching left shoulder reluctantly took the strain as the truck passed, silent but for tyre noise, leaving in its wake the pungent aroma of biomass distillate and second-hand cooking-oil burning in an improvised combustion chamber at what was obviously the wrong temperature.

The engine would be one of some hundreds planned originally for a solar energy project in the USA. The project had failed to survive the challenge from p-v panels, and the engines had been dispersed, a few ending up in the UK post Melt-down - although goodness knows what had been bartered for them. They operated on the Stirling cycle - hence the quietness - sharing design and development origins with the 4-275 auxiliary power units of the Swedish Gotland class stealth submarine. What had been a suitable receiver for concentrated solar radiation was far from the best heat exchanger in the context of makeshift liquid fuel. Still, needs must when the devil drives, and the biomass ingredient had the compelling attraction that a mere fraction of a given distillation provided sufficient energy to distill the next batch: free energy, depending how you viewed it - and with a bonus: anxious not to deter development of a technology on which the future of land transport might eventually depend, the Provisional Government had refrained from the traditional impulse of imposing a tax.

It came into his mind that he was in an uncannily good mood: he had just crossed the most beautiful bridge in the world by moonlight; the bike ride was progressing to schedule, and plenty of time remained to get to the station. He was looking forward to the conference and to seeing his collaborator Charo again, and a major treat was in store before he even got there: to Sewell, nothing better articulated the contribution of technology to social evolution than did the steam locomotive. And he was about to travel to Didcot behind such a locomotive.

The skeleton rail transport service was operated with the aid of steam engines appropriated largely from preservation societies and fired by anthracite from a re-opened Welsh colliery. The service between Paddington and Bristol amounted to two return trips daily. The locomotive on this run was Tornado, famous for having been designed - and partly built - in the UK long after the end of the steam era. She was not considered a replica but, at the time of her inaugural journey in 2009, number 50 in the original production series of 49 which had ended in the 1960s. The Provisional Government had requisitioned her for the London-Bristol service partly on account of her reliability relative to other 'preserved' locomotives, and partly because of her ability to haul fifteen packed coaches plus a number of freight wagons. A journey by steam train! Who could ask for more? This was a morning on which you reflected on the good things.

Melt-down had few redeeming features, but it's an ill wind that blows nobody any good. Steam had dominated rail transport in Sewell's youth, and the remaining fascination meant that he had little difficulty in keeping up with developments in the skeleton service: With the aid of intensive, overnight maintenance - preventive and remedial - 'standard five' 73050 *City of Peterborough* operated a twice-daily return service between Cambridge and King's Lynn. One locomotive at a time from a small fleet of three Bullied pacific 'spam cans' ran daily between Waterloo and Portsmouth while the other two were serviced. A similar arrangement kept one of three Gresley pacifics (*Bittern*, *Sir Nigel Gresley* and *Mallard*) serviceable for a daily return between King's Cross and Edinburgh, where setting a workable timetable had meant re-installing the between-rails water-troughs removed decades previously.

With minimal assistance from gravity this time he pushed off to the right, shortly turning left into Cumberland Basin. Reaching the metal footbridge he lowered the hold-all to the pavement and straightened up. Now the scar tissue on his back was adding its protests to those of the muscles. No pain was more tiring than back pain. Pressing his shoulders back until the shoulder-blades touched, he repeated several times. Having gained some relief he mounted the steps of the foot-bridge, from where the westerly half of the span of Brunel's masterpiece was responding to the sun-rise with tantalizing hints of its daytime glory.

From a distance, towers, deck, chains and hangers were no longer individual components, but a spellbinding structural statement. How had this iconic shape emerged? Clearly as an engineering response to the imperatives of an un-remarkable basic function - spanning a gap while carrying a load, and reconciling conflicting priorities along the way. Did that mean that *any* structurally-efficient combination of wrought-iron, wood and masonry drew one to it as a work of art? The suspension cables or chains of every such bridge take up the shape of a catenary, and every such catenary is defined by the same mathematical function. But what, at first sight, could be more aridly functional and less evocative of emotional response than the hyperbolic function $y = cosh(x)$? Anyway, wasn't the world full of indifferent-looking suspension bridges. No! $y = cosh(x)$ was not the answer - at least not the whole answer.

The setting was undeniably part of the appeal - but the location for the towers had been selected by Brunel largely on the basis of engineering criteria. So what remained? He had provided for the Clifton-side abutment to be higher than the other '*to avoid the illusion of the roadway falling towards the Observatory cliffs'*. Now, there was genius: you built out-of-level so as not to appear out-of-level - by precisely the right amount evidently - by three feet. Nowadays the refinement - supposing it were anticipated - would be tackled with the aid of virtual reality - computer-generated images superimposed on photographs of the gorge. The first ever photographic plate of 1822 had not evolved into a commercial process - the Daguerreotype - until 1839, in other words *after* the laying of the foundation stone of the first tower in 1831.

Perhaps analyzing a work of genius should be left to genius.

The morning had grown noticeably lighter, but the old moon remained visible against a satin sky. Inanimate objects of unquestioned beauty - the moon, a sailing ship - tended to be referred to as 'she' - at least, in the tradition of the English language. He took a final look upstream. Illuminated by a combination of moonlight and a brightening sky the bridge was - well - she was *gorgeous*. Not an adjective routinely applied to a static engineering structure but, at that moment, the only one which served.

Stretching his shoulders several more times he walked back down the steps and re-positioned the bicycle so that the hold-all could be picked up with the left hand. Swinging a leg over the saddle he consulted his watch. Two miles now to Temple Meads, and more or less along the level.

There was still no traffic to contend with, and what was a cycle ride for if not for pondering. Anyway, it took the mind off the pain.

But why defer to genius? These matters touch us all. Judging by his beautifully-penned piece for a newspaper supplement *My seven wonders of the world* they had exercised Lord Clark back in the seventies. Sewell had owed it to Lord Clark's seventh wonder - Concorde - to commit it to memory:

There used to be an idea that, if a construction followed impeccably the laws of its own necessity, it would automatically become beautiful. This is true of a sailing boat, but manifestly untrue of a fork-

lift truck; perhaps one can say that, if a man-made object has to contend with the elements, then some kind of resolute economy that we call beauty may be the result. Nothing has defied the elements as Concorde, and the result has produced a kind of absolute, which is as far from the bi-planes of the brothers Wright as it is from a threshing machine.

Powerful stuff. If gravity could be considered an element, then here was an insight - and one which chimed with Saint-Exupery's *Perfection is achieved, not when there is nothing more to add, but when there is nothing to take away.* Lord Clark's 'resolute economy' again.

How far, he wondered, had the parallel between the aesthetic appeal of an inanimate object been explored in relation to the attraction between the sexes? The notion turned his thoughts - as they were bound to turn eventually on a journey of any consequence - back to his career. And since career and marriage had been so interrelated - uniquely so in his case, it seemed - back to his marriage.

Cumberland Road would be direct and level - but tedious. He checked behind for any further vehicles sneaking up in silence, pushed off from the kerb, and was shortly turning into Hotwell Road.

It had so far been unnecessary to turn a crank. Hotwell Road was essentially level, but the awkward load meant that the bike's suspension responded at each revolution of the pedals. Not such a bonus in the circumstances: the energy it absorbed soon had him puffing hard. He would press on with a view to a final break where another Bristol icon could be pondered - the cathedral.

Turning into College Square he went through the now-familiar routine with bag, bike and shoulder exercises, finally walking stiffly into the cathedral grounds.

With hindsight it would be true to say that his wife, Lígia, had been his first and only true love - but in terms of relationships of consequence, actually the second. The first had eventually faltered, but that had not stopped it remaining hard-wired, half-a-century later, into his daily attempts to rationalize the subsequent five decades of his mortal span.

Was any type of building more accustomed than a cathedral to looking down on the affairs of man? Had not the song *Winchester Cathedral* caught the mood of a generation? All that time ago, he had been returning to the bus station following a fruitless shopping expedition. A perfect autumn day had tempted him to extend the walk to take in the riverside. With the embankment around the next left turn he had been aware that the street leading to the cathedral had been unusually deserted, not only of vehicles, but of people - with one exception: a female figure approaching on his side of the road.

Even at a hundred yards this had been no ordinary figure. She wore a knee-length summer dress. Dark-brown hair hung free to the shoulders. She was not looking directly at him as they converged, but the faintest of smiles on the perfect face suggested she knew that she was holding his attention.

He had not previously been aware of that style of dress and what it could do to a figure - or, indeed, what such a figure could do for that style of dress: it appeared to have been wrapped around diagonally, while at the same time sitting everywhere in perfect contact. Even as she walked, one curve harmonized effortlessly into another, not a feature or movement over-stated - or under-stated. Perfection personified. With ten yards to go, here was evidently a potential problem. Sewell was the survivor of several teenage crushes, all un-requited on account of his native inability to make the first move.

Of all the life-changing moments (more were to come) he was later to judge this the most significant. It hit him like a train that this was not, after all, a question of bravado or lack of it. He was not even being called upon to take a decision! There was simply no way under the sun that he was *not* going to make contact! At about five paces she looked directly at him. Mona Lisa suddenly looked like a witch by comparison. 'Fabulous!' was uttered with total conviction. He was rewarded with the most beautiful smile he had ever seen - on or off the big screen - and a simple, genuine 'Thanks.'

He was rooted to the spot, but able to turn his head as she walked on. Would she look back?

No.

He reached the cathedral in a trance and sat for a while, but the peace of mind he had become accustomed to finding on previous visits did not come. Years later a work colleague would analyse his state of mind: temporary insanity. Well, maybe insanity had been a bit strong - irrationality perhaps. He had put a modest donation in the collecting box and, still in a daze, walked to the bus station.

The bus journey home had been spent contemplating how, if at all, such an encounter could be conveyed to friends. There would be, after all, the basic problem of adjectives. His feelings might not have differed greatly from those of his fifth-form English master of years previously who, judging by the number of allusions, had harboured a crush on a certain Marilyn Monroe. It had not been possible in those days to 'Google' Marilyn but, once aware, you kept your eyes open. Sure enough, a newspaper weekend supplement had eventually carried a feature, amply illustrating the ample icon in black-and-white. As a seventeen year old at the time, Sewell had judged her to be something of an over-statement of femininity - and an overstatement was not his idea of perfection.

So, at the level of physical appearance, this definitive woman must have been a projection of criteria of his own. The vision he had encountered *en route* to the cathedral had matched his personal check-list down to the last detail.

The returning awareness of his surroundings caused a sudden movement which in turn sent a sharp pain through the shoulder which had been taking the strain. If he walked for a stretch, braking would not be a consideration, and the right arm could do a stint. Refreshed to this extent, he walked back down the incline to Anchor Road, past the Aquarium into Anchor Square, and from there *via* The Grove to Redcliffe Way. A time-check revealed that the schedule had slipped, leaving nothing for it but to cycle. The remainder of the route was level, the rear brake would supply all the required stopping power, so he could re-mount with hold-all in his right hand.

Once up to a steady seven or eight miles per hour, his mind defaulted to the reassuring security of youthful memories. A second shopping trip some weeks later had been more successful in terms of purchases. Pacing his walk, he had re-traced the route of the previous encounter. However, the hoped-for sighting had not materialized. Rain threatened, so rather than spend time in the Cathedral and arrive at the bus station soaked, he would walk direct and kill time over a coffee in the cafeteria.

He beat the downpour by a narrow margin, walked to the counter and ordered coffee. Paying over a brief chat with the lady at the till, he looked around for a free table and . . . there she was - sitting alone too, immaculately turned-out as before, but this time in dazzling, figure-flattering white jumper and sharp navy skirt. She had not yet looked up, and he was able to get closer by approaching from her side. The cup was being held in both hands, elbows on the table and . . . no ring!!

'Fabulous!' She looked round with a smile which spoke recognition. This time he had a follow-up at the ready. 'What do you do in real life? - are you a movie star?' (At the time he had almost certainly said 'film star', but the gambit had served him subsequently, and had become engrained.)

'No' was the straightforward reply.

'Well, you could be - and by all accounts the pay's not bad.'

'Better than teaching. And if we're going to keep meeting like this, hadn't you better sit down? I'm Jean. Presumably you don't need help introducing yourself.'

'David - and never Dave if we are to get on.'

'Nice name. Why use the lazy version?'

That's how it had started. He was soon introduced to the family, consisting of parents and live-in disabled aunt. Jean travelled daily to attend a teacher training course. Contrary to her sophisticated appearance she was almost two years his junior. A hobby was clothes design, which she pursued with a passion and with the aid of a technological marvel - an electric Husqvarna sewing machine brought by

The Bridge - *a love affair*

an uncle who had worked at Stal-Laval in Finspång, Sweden. It had been a demonstration model, only one step removed from the prototype and, like many demonstration models, superior to subsequent production machines.

It had been a while before the parents had allowed her to holiday with him. In the meantime, she would spend three weeks with them each summer camping in France. The separation had seemed an eternity, and when she had returned, invariably lightly-dressed and sun-tanned, the initial sighting made the encounter at the Cathedral seem like a matter of indifference. He would never forget his physiological reaction - although it defied description: possibly a mixture of levitation, butterflies-in-the-stomach and (dare he admit it to himself?) something akin to salivation.

There had been plenty of day-long excursions - picnics, walks by the river with her border collie - and driving for the pleasure of driving which had still been an option at the time. His sideline interest in photography had extended to developing and printing black-and-white 35mm film. Jean had occupied reel after reel of 36-frame film - mostly head-and-shoulders. When they were apart he would print selected frames from the latest reel and pore over them. During one such late-night printing session it had hit him that this uniquely beautiful face was, in fact, several distinct faces. He placed three of the prints side-by-side. In different passports they could have been three different persons - but each stunningly beautiful.

He turned left into Temple Gate, then right into Approach Road where, at last, he was confronted by the façade of that other Brunel masterpiece, Temple Meads station. Now close to his physical limit, he pressed ahead, past the main entrance, finally coasting to rest at the pavement which bordered the down-slope opposite the old Passenger Shed. The bag, now feeling a good ten kilograms heavier than when he had left the house, was lowered thankfully to the ground.

Leaning back tentatively on the saddle he slowly straightened his shoulders. *'Not bad for a . . . . '.* He stopped. Breaking the habit of re-affirming his age was proving difficult - but it paid off: The majority

22

of friends and colleagues judged him to be fifty to fifty-five - and well-preserved at that: '*Why did you retire at such a young age?*' had been a recent query. No sound argument remained for insisting on his calendar age. Life was short enough: if you looked young, act young.

By tipping the face of his wrist-watch towards the sun-rise he could read six-fifteen. The train was scheduled to depart at six thirty. Made it! The hold-all would not be popular: it was not a typical high-street item, but slimmer and somewhat longer - half-way to being a cricket bag from his school days - in other words, big enough to accommodate two bats, two sets of stumps and pads. A whole lot heavier too. On the other hand, it was about to get lighter. Sewell prised up each of the over-centre clasps. Reaching inside among shirt, socks and a change of underwear he withdrew a massive cable padlock. Like the rest of the commuters, he relied heavily on retaining ownership of the bike for the return trip home.

Along about a hundred-and-fifty yards of the pavement the authorities had strung a length of heavy steel hawser, perhaps twenty millimetres in diameter, which passed at intervals through sturdy anchor points. The scores of cycles already secured there were two or three deep in places. Locating a gap allowing sufficient elbow-room to manipulate the lock, he passed the cable through front wheel, frame, hawser and rear wheel, and snapped the lock closed.

Reaching into the hold-all again he pulled out an envelope. This in turn yielded two large stick-on labels with an impressive hologram and OHMS in large letters. An over-zealous official at the Energy Research Unit had included a couple of tie-on labels with the distinctive black-and-yellow radiation hazard sign. Using them would have guaranteed plenty of space for both him and the bag. However, the train would be crowded, and no expectant mother noticing the signs would travel in the same compartment as one of those labels. And since the contents had never been near a source of radiation anyway, he peeled the backing from the OHMS labels, applied one to each side of the hold-all, simultaneously screwing up the radiation signs.

The Bridge - *a love affair*

The number of cycles secured to the hawser would be more or less in proportion to the crowding of the train. This morning the line extended past the sixth anchor point. Resigning himself to the inevitable scrum, he closed the bag and, flexing the sore shoulders again, gingerly picked it up. Without the huge cable lock the bag was reassuringly lighter, and he was shortly in the queue for warrant holders.

The ticket inspector was assisted by a man and a woman in uniform - both from Sewell's unit. When it came to Sewell's turn the former addressed him: 'See you on parade Thursday, sir'.

'Not this Thursday, corporal.' He indicated the hold-all. 'Away on Her Majesty's Secret Service. See you Saturday, though.'

The platform was already crowded for the first of the two daily services to Paddington. The electrically-powered information displays had long been out of operation, departure times being displayed instead in numbers painted white on black metal squares and hung on individual hooks. Those old enough to remember a village cricket scoreboard would feel at home with the technology. The carriages were waiting with doors locked, and he threaded his way towards the front of the leading carriage. Getting one of the jump seats in the vestibule would make him last off the platform at Dicot and at the back of the queue for ticket inspection - but a small price to pay for a leisurely look at the locomotive before she set off for Reading and Paddington.

He made his way to the edge of the platform and, out of habit and fascination, looked down onto the crushed-granite ballast and onto the sleepers, shoes and clips by which the rails were held precisely four feet eight-and-a-half inches apart. Why that irrational gauge had been adopted for sixty percent of the world's railways he would never know. On the other hand, he did know a thing or two about ballast:

In school holidays he would take casual work, not primarily for the money, but for the physical exercise it afforded. He has been endowed with a fine physique, which he would no doubt have developed using the facilities of the school gym - had it been so equipped. If there had been private gyms, Sewell had not heard of them. In any case, this was two decades before Arnold Schwartzenegger's film *Pumping Iron*

The Bridge - *a love affair*

had galvanized the fashion in body-building*. On the other hand, opportunities for hard physical work had abounded in the 1950s. One such was shovelling rail-track ballast, and Sewell was soon in demand with the Great Western Railway for his ability to throw a shovel-full from the track-side onto the floor of a truck above head-height. The effect on his physique had been the changing-room envy of the school rugby team.

Shortly after Melt-down the siding which had linked the Passenger Shed to the main line had been re-laid so that the steam locomotive on duty could be prepared under cover overnight. That cover was the other side of the recently-installed, galvanized-steel roller-shutter door which now lay just ahead.

The engineer on duty that morning would be sergeant Hulse of Sewell's unit. Many members of the military reserves had two jobs - not only because their skills were in demand, but also on the basis that, if a person had an occupation which paid an allowance, then he or she could, in the prevailing economic circumstances, hardly object to doing a second job without remuneration.

Set into the roller-shutter was a wicket gate. Sewell transferred the hold-all to his left hand, operated the heavy metal catch with the right and stepped inside over the raised metal cill.

Re-commissioning the shed had involved digging an ash-pit and installing lighting - electric lighting. In a Bristol otherwise subject to strict rationing it would be interesting to know the source of power supply. Before Melt-down it had been Sewell's experience that it was sometimes easier to obtain forgiveness than to obtain permission. Melt-down had turned a matter of chance into a general rule. At any event, there was light. It came from two lonely, low-energy bulbs dangling

---

*Under the assumed name of Charles Atlas and a claim to being 'the world's most perfectly-developed man', a body-builder in the United States had been advertising a 'dynamic tension' method of enhancing the physique of those whom he derided as 'seven-stone weaklings'

25

The BRIDGE - *a love affair*

from the roof, and it combined with brightening daylight to reveal Tornado. This handsome piece of engineering was the A1 Pacific-class steam locomotive requisitioned eighteen months earlier by the Provisional Government as part of the process of getting a skeleton rail network running again. Here was the ideal place to marvel at the one hundred and five tons of machinery - one hundred and sixty-six if you included the tender.

Anyone who has experienced it will know that there is no sound more penetrating and intense than that made by a metal wicket gate being opened - or, indeed, being closed. The sound had brought Sgt. Hulse from the far side of the locomotive to reprimand the intruder. The oil-can quickly changed hands to enable the inappropriate salute. 'Oh - it's you, sir. Sorry. Sometimes when I'm in overalls it feels as if I'm in uniform. Good to see you. If you're wondering whether there's a delay, the driver's taking her out any second. '

'Morning sergeant. Mind if I watch her start up?'

'No problem, sir. I always stand and watch myself. Fascination never wanes, does it?'

The valve gear was moving into the full ahead position as they spoke. The brake shoes around the wheels of the tender relaxed at the same time. 'They don't sound the whistle in the shed, sir, ... '

Any further explanation drowned in a deafening hiss of steam from the cylinder drains. Tornado was rolling smoothly and effortlessly forward before emitting the first of a sequence of gentle 'chuffs'. Sewell watched her disappear through the curtain of flexible plastic strips which kept out the worst of the weather, thanked the sergeant and returned through the wicket gate to the platform.

Reversion to steam haulage had called for a number of operational changes: The Bristol of 2016 had no turntable, so incoming services from London would stop briefly at Lawrence Hill. The locomotive would be un-coupled, run forward and reversed by running it round the triangular intersection of the lines branching north, west and east. In this way it arrived at Temple Meads tender first. Following the evening arrival it would be un-coupled and run ahead until it crossed the

26

points. These would then be switched and it would reverse into the shed, ending up facing the correct way for the journey to Paddington the next day.

There was the familiar sound of a steam whistle. Tornado had run forward from the shed, crossed the points to join the main line and begun to reverse. The movement drew Sewell's eye along the track - Brunel's track running the 120-or-so miles to London. It crossed his mind that the earlier mental eulogy had been woefully inadequate: what distinguished Brunel and his ilk was their mastery of *design as the art of the possible*: individual links of the suspension chains were stacks of iron plates - like toast in a rack. An isolated plate weighed a quarter of a ton - barely within the lifting capability of two strong men - and a typical link consisted of eleven such plates! There were about 52 links between anchorage points, so an individual chain (there were six) weighed about 150 tons. Just how do you string a chain heavier than a steam locomotive between towers 200 metres apart while working 70 metres above river level? Until such matters are fully resolved, design has not even begun! And Brunel hadn't stopped there! His link design embodied built-in means for replacement of individual plates in service!

The driver brought the hundred-and-fifty or so tons of steel, water and coal smoothly to a stop with the buffers of the tender less than an inch from those of the leading coach. As the driver applied the squeeze, the fireman climbed down from the cab onto the platform. Slipping down between tender and carriage, he swung the heavy link over the hook on the tender and wound up the screw thread with the pendulum arm. Service pipe connections were made and checked.

The doors opened and Sewell stood back while a couple of dozen passengers swarmed aboard, then lifted the hold-all, placed it on the floor of the vestibule and climbed in after it. Folding down the jump-seat he sat down, setting the cargo carefully on end between his knees.

Just as the whistle blew, a sprightly figure with a neat grey beard jumped aboard. Someone slammed the door after him. The locomotive gave an answering whistle and the train jerked into motion, throwing the new arrival off balance. Half-rising, Sewell steadied the owner of the beard with one hand and the hold-all with the other. 'Michael! It's you! Welcome aboard the six-thirty.'

2

Tornado

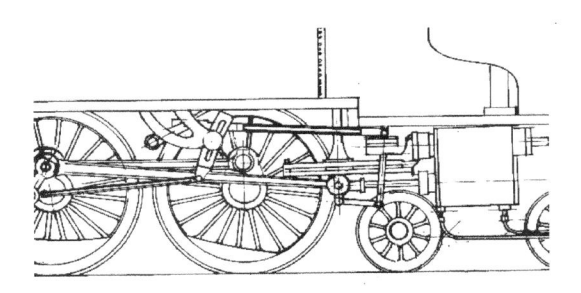

It was his friend and mentor, Michael or, to give him his full title, the Reverend Professor Emeritus Michael Langford. A sprightly young eighty-three, the professor allowed age to get in the way of nothing: he retained a mental agility which put Sewell in mind of a grey squirrel. Most Saturday mornings would find him teaching Aikido, which put his physical condition not far behind the mental.

Steadying himself, the professor folded down the jump seat opposite and sat down. 'Sally has given me the day off. I'm on my way to see a friend in Bath - the survivor of a family from our days in Newfoundland. He's come by half a bottle of vintage port. We're going to make it last the whole day with a little help from my home-made oat biscuits.' He waved a paper bag.

'Sally's just received another wodge of cash. That dictionary of hers has been our financial lifebelt: who on earth has been buying dictionaries during Melt-down and beyond I can't imagine - but it's a two-way, Chinese/English. Maybe the Chinese economy has settled down in a totally different way from ours.'

When in the mood to communicate Michael was unstoppable: 'Just finished a stint of memorial services. Some families prefer to call

The Bridge - *a love affair*

them funerals. I go along with that: it's their bereavement. There's still a backlog - some from the first winter. The saddest cases are those where there has been some sort of mistake - no record of cremation, for example. These were a real headache at first, but I've developed a routine for dealing with them.'

The first winter following Melt-down had seen huge mortality, the largest single element being at care homes where a combination of influenza and lack of heating had taken tolls close to a hundred percent. The majority of cremations and interments had already taken place - hastily, obviously - but churches were still working through backlogs of funeral and memorial services, with Michael doing his bit towards clearing them.

'How much are you doing?'

'Five days a week, Monday to Saturday with Tuesdays off. Just mornings. Somebody else does the afternoons. Half-an-hour per service, back-to-back. I'm exhausted when I get home - but it pays a lot of credits. If there were anything in the shops Sally and I could go on a spree.'

'Does the job give any inside information as to the size of the remaining UK population?' Massive migrations had taken place even as transportation by air and sea were winding down. Many of those whose liquid assets had not evaporated overnight, or who had contacts, had joined the exodus. Where they had gone, given that the problem was global, was not obvious. However, it was speculated that much of the movement had been towards locations offering scope for subsistence living - for coastal fishing in particular.

'Still estimating thirty to forty million.' was the last Michael had heard.

'I wonder whether one ever gets to hear the truth: A decade or so ago the official UK population figure was about sixty-five million. That must have come from the Office of National Statistics. Then two years after that a parliamentary colleague of Greg Hands MP had been told that the estimate at Tesco was closer to eighty million. Tesco fed the nation - at least at that time. And thanks to ClubCard they know the size of everybody's under-pants, so they probably knew what they were talking about. The world seems virtually empty - except when you're crammed into public transport.'

'You do your best with the information you've got.' was Michael's view.

'Anyway, how's the literary output?' (Having gained a reputation with books on theology, Michael had branched out into fiction.)

'The editorial board of *Grenzen der Filosofie* is still alive and kicking.' (So - he was back to papers on philosophy.) 'Just sent them my latest: *Is "a matter of fact" a matter of fact.* Obviously it's not going to appear in print until things settle down - supposing they ever do - but it's good to have it in the pipeline.'

Michael glanced at the hold-all. Sewell had not let go of it - even to steady the professor earlier. 'What's getting the free ride at public expense - one of your quiet, efficient, burn-anything, engines?'

'How did you guess? But not like one you've ever seen.'

'You are forgetting! You've never shown me one - except that table-top toy. And to call that an engine would be to flatter it.'

'OK, then, not like one you've *never* seen.'

'So you're off to a conference - or a workshop? Good sign: means things are moving again. Would a Liberal Theologian understand what you'll be talking about?'

'A Liberal Theologian such as yourself would have not the slightest difficulty: the meeting's at ERU Rutherford - the Energy Research Unit - on micro-scale power production. Starts tomorrow. MERGE set it up - Ministry for Economic Regeneration. They want to get the economy moving again - who doesn't - and that isn't going to happen without ways of powering industry, transport and the home using raw energy available within the UK. Melt-down has been ghastly, but at least it's forced a re-think that should have happened decades ago. There are opportunities for 'universal' heat engines - you supply energy in the form of heat, they deliver the power - not like the internal combustion

The Bridge - *a love affair*

engine and gas turbine. They are really picky about the fuels they will run on.'

'So you are giving a demonstration?'

'Yes - but there's a lot more to it: today it's 200 years to the day from the date of the patent on the original invention. Perfect excuse for an anniversary shindig. ERU shifted the date of the main conference to accommodate it. All our papers are in this afternoon's technical session. That's followed by an anniversary dinner tonight. I dread to think what the menu is going to be - soya burgers washed down with elderberry wine.'

Michael - an aesthete and an authority on wines - withheld comment.

'Two hundred years! What took you so long? Has there been a breakthrough?'

'The breakthroughs of popular press reporting seldom occur. It's more a case of technology finally catching up with the potential of a concept invented ahead of its time. This is more than just an anniversary: Robert Stirling's core invention - the regenerator - arguably speeded the Industrial Revolution. It led to the blast furnace, and the blast furnace gave us steel-making. Siemens adapted it to glass manufacture. The regenerator is central to cryogenic engineering - think of the MRI scanner! Not bad for a church minister in his twenties!

'The man was a genius and a visionary: he knocked off the engine design as 'merely' a specimen application of his regenerator. He languishes un-known and unsung relative to the recognized giants of the technology revolution - Trevithick, Watt, Boulton, Brunel, Stephenson: try finding the name Stirling in an engineering text-book. One of our sessions will discuss whether something can't be done. Not the ideal climate, a deep recession, but with so much being re-built from scratch, who knows?'

'Sounds as if the Revd. Dr. Stirling has had a raw deal. But you won't mind me pointing out that these things are seldom without reason. Even before Melt-down I wasn't aware of too many Stirling-powered cars, or trucks, or motor-cycles - or ships.'

32

'In some respects the Stirling engine is its own worst publicity agent. It's quietly successful: fitted to Swedish stealth submarines. AIP, or Air-Independent propulsion they call it. One of these subs., the Gotland, outwitted the US navy in exercises off the California coast - not long before Melt-down. The US navy never heard it coming. Technically it sank the carrier Reagan and killed one of their nuclear submarines.'

'But - forgive me again - there can't be a huge demand for submarine engines.'

'This is post Melt-down, professor! There is actually a bigger demand for military engines than for car engines - for the simple reason that the military are the only ones left who can afford engines. But even that's not the point: how many motor cycles, cars and trucks with internal combustion engines did you see this morning?'

'The re-cycle truck passed me. So I suppose I saw one.'

'Precisely. If life is to return to normality - and I am supposing we want the 'normality' we enjoyed before Melt-down - we need sources of raw energy and means to convert it - to electric power, to propulsive power. Otherwise it's back to horse and cart. The internal combustion engine needs highly-refined hydrocarbon fuel - liquid or gaseous - and the supplies we used to take for granted have dried up, at least for the foreseeable future. That leaves coal, wood and their derivatives and the so-called renewables - solar, wind, wave, tidal, hydro. ERU is working on micro-nuclear - one of the developments they will be presenting tomorrow. Before Melt-down, cars, trucks and buses didn't run on renewables. But if you can heat a Stirling engine somehow - any old how - it runs. Have you seen a modern domestic wood-pellet stove?'

'Only the other day as it happens. Impressive.'

'Then you'll appreciate the possibilities. To have a respectable operating range you'd probably need to convert the boot and the back seat to pellet storage - or maybe tow a tender like a steam locomotive. Some fuels which are otherwise suitable give quite a

The Bridge - *a love affair*

challenge in terms of exhaust pollution - but the official line is *get moving first, refine later.*'

'So you go to the submarine breaker's yard, get yourself a Stirling engine and install it in your car?'

'No. The submarine units are the first generation of the modern Stirling engine. Quiet, efficient and reliable, yes. But bulky and expensive.' He indicated the hold-all between his knees. We need the next generation: compact, low parts-count, oil-free operation, direct conversion from thermodynamic cycle to electrical power without mechanical connections - without connecting-rods, cranks and so on. Totally vibration-free, quiet and efficient, and with the power-to-weight ratio of a motor-cycle engine.'

'And you've done it? How?'

'Yes - and quite simply: teach thermodynamics to a micro-processor and control the gas process cycle in real time with that. The crucial work of chip design isn't mine - it's the brain-child of my collaborator in Spain. Did you ever meet Charo? She came with me to Violet's once.'

'Sounds like someone I would have remembered if I had. So it must be no.'

The train had been coasting for a while. The professor turned to look out of the window. 'Bath shortly. I wish you the best of luck: seems we're all relying on you - and on Charo! Do please convey my respects to the lady. And thanks for the chat. Time has flown. Now I'll let you get on with preparing your lecture.'

The brakes were being applied.

'Not much chance of writing in this crush. I still prepare hard copy, so it was all done-and-dusted a couple of weeks ago.'

Michael stood up. 'Forty years lecturing and you still read from a script!? My lectures are prepared the night before in a leisurely bath - sermons, too.'

'I know - I've caught a glimpse of the skimpy notes you preach from. But that's not what I said: I might read the first couple of sentences to get me started. After that I just talk to the overhead slides.'

'So why the written notes?'

'My life-belt - my hedge against mental blank. Haven't suffered one in two decades - but take away the notes and I'm hostage to fortune. Anyway, dispensing philosophy from the back of an envelope is one thing: working through the solution of a second-order, non-linear, hyperbolic partial differential equation is another.'

'I believe you. There's just time to tell me whether it's going to be possible to retro-fit one of your engines to my Peugeot. It's been standing there doing nothing since the price of petrol went through the roof. If so, please can I keep the cruise control. I love it!'

'Most unlikely. Cars - when they start to appear again - will be very different: much lighter, with a high percentage of re-cycled plastic. If they use our version of the Stirling engine they will be four-wheel drive, with compact electric motors on each wheel and regenerative braking. Those that run on liquid hydrocarbon fuels will do about 150 miles to the gallon.'

The train had stopped. With a 'Good to see you' and his trademark 'God bless' Michael left the train, as did a few others, allowing at least five-times that number to board. How many could the carriage take? Probably a whole lot more than you'd think: it was a British Rail Mk 4, somewhat hastily modified to increase total capacity at the expense of seating, and now reminiscent of rolling-stock on the London Underground. Sewell's mind turned to the many trips he had made *via* King's Cross on the way to meetings of the editorial board of his professional institution. When the weather was fine he relished the idea of the 45 minutes' walk, which took him past his old flat in Bloomsbury, down Charing Cross Road, past Nelson's column and through St. James' Park to the headquarters in Westminster.

A whistle sounded, the locomotive responded and they were off again.

On one such visit to the Capital, the main-line train had arrived at King's Cross in a downpour, so he would have to use the underground. The fact that the platform was packed was not initially cause for concern - until the train arrived already, he judged, full to capacity. Bodies nevertheless surged through the doors and, miraculously, he found himself on board, jammed just inside the door. His left hand clutched the yellow hand-rail while the right maintained a vigil over his back pocket. As the train pulled in to Euston it was evident that there were at least as many prospective passengers as there had been at King's Cross. Few got off - but against all expectation the train departed, leaving the platform - at least, that area visible to Sewell - empty of passengers.

Despite the human tide which had swept past, he had maintained his place near the sliding door. An open paper-back book and a matter of inches separated his face from that of a woman standing with her toes between his. Sewell pondered the possibilities of congenital short-sight *vs.* the same condition acquired as a result of years of commuting. 'Is it always like this?' he ventured. The book was lowered - just far enough for the two pairs of eyes to meet. The woman nodded without speaking, and raised the book to the original reading position.

A change in the exhaust beat of the locomotive brought his mind back to the present. If you had grown up with steam traction as the norm there was something reassuring - something trustworthy - about steam pressure being turned into tractive effort at the huge, iron-spoked wheels. He got to his feet for a moment to flex back and shoulders, and to stretch his legs. At six feet tall he could see the full length of the carriage. How many would be travelling to work in the capital - and how many would be going there to look for a job? Few if any would be on a shopping jaunt. He had not noticed a single back-packer, but the majority had entered the train carrying a small bag - in all probability a packed lunch.

If you were lucky enough to have regular work, then travel by public transport was free, subject to weekly renewal of a pass at your home station. If you could demonstrate that you were attending interview, then one-off return travel was also free. Having time and again been treated to his father's account of the search for work during early married life in the nineteen-twenties Sewell felt painfully sorry for those in the latter category: his father had been up at four-thirty each morning to travel to join the queue outside the Ford plant at Dagenham.

His own search for work, by contrast, had been effortless. Even before being awarded his master's degree he had been recruited to the position of research assistant by the new head of the engineering department from which he had originally graduated. The position had offered scope for submitting for a higher degree. Perfect.

The new head, Stefan Varghas, turned out to be a likeable slave-driver, who had been awarded the degree of ScD for work on the torsional vibration characteristics of automobile crankshafts published in Austria as a book *Verdrehungsschwingungen an Kurbelwellen*. His lecturing technique was to read from the book, translating into English while transferring equations and figures to the blackboard.

Between eight-thirty and nine-thirty the professor did the first of his comprehensive daily rounds of the entire department. The pace was brisk, and three or four junior staff were swept along in his wake in the fashion of a hospital consultant. The round, which accounted for the first two cigars of the day's unlimited allocation, was partly to check that no one was taking liberties with the flexible timetable of the academic environment. On the other hand, the inspection was easily thwarted: if an encounter was best avoided it was merely necessary to position yourself down-stream of the trail of smoke. If, on the other hand, you welcomed a brief exchange, you headed for a relatively smoke-free office or laboratory. The strategy did not become one hundred percent foolproof until one could reliably distinguish the current smoke trail from that of an earlier round.

It was one such round during early nineteen sixty-five that had found Sewell at his desk in the research students' room. There had been no pre-amble: 'Barber has resigned. You will be taking over his lecture course. It starts in October'. Deed done, the professor scanned the other desks for evidence of appropriate levels of research activity and swept out of the room leaving a smoke trail of finest Havana.

Apart from stints as demonstrator in the thermodynamics laboratory, Sewell had never taught. Moreover, he had been contracted as research assistant to the professor' rapidly-growing research team. There had been no mention of teaching duties and, surprisingly, no enquiry as to any teaching qualifications he might - or might not - have had. The start of the Michaelmas term was six months away. Apprehension, however, took hold immediately. Whether others had felt similar qualms, or whether a phased introduction would have suited his temperament better, he would never know. Looking back, he had wondered repeatedly what prospective undergraduates, or members of the public - or, indeed, the Ministry of Education - would have made of the career-development provisions of the era.

This Dr. Barber must be tracked down without delay. It did not take long to establish that he was already off the payroll, casualty of the professor's recent purge. With no immediate prospect of inheriting Barber's lecture notes, Sewell widened his enquiries. To his mounting consternation, it turned out that the course lay within the syllabus of the Graduate School. He was barely a graduate himself! Moreover, it was called Instrumentation. *Instrumentation*! - and taught as a theoretical subject *via* the blackboard. Was this not, by definition, hands-on laboratory material? Even if experimentation had featured, the sum total of his prior experience had been the use of copper-constantan thermocouples, the Leeds and Northrup type K2 potentiometer and standard cells. Things were looking increasingly daunting.

He sought an audience with the head of the graduate school, Professor Bannerman. No, there was no published syllabus, and no, a copy of the lecture notes of the recently-departed incumbent would not be forthcoming. In conspiratorial north-country tones the professor did, however, vouchsafe that '*All you need, Sewell, is a good set o' notes.*' So there it was: the sum total of his teacher-training.

Where now? Could he tell Varghas he was not man for job? Would he find himself the next instance of this 'resignation' euphemism?

It was not the norm for a member of the faculty to sit in on the lectures of a novice with a view to mentoring. Discussion in the staff common room over morning coffee or afternoon tea embraced every topic under the sun - with the notable exception of lecturing - and, indeed, of any matter related to teaching technique. What a system!

Unsurprisingly, the inaugural lecture had evolved into a harrowing experience - for him if not for the students. As the most junior, he had been allocated the least popular slot: Monday morning at nine o'clock. If he had slept a wink on the Sunday night, the period of unconsciousness had not registered. Having failed to invest in the elementary precaution of a dry run of his material, he was abruptly aware of a total lack of blackboard technique. Chalking up an equation so that it was legible from the back of the room would have merited at least an hour's practice. Where was the faculty handout *Notes for Lecturers*?

The performance rapidly became an experience of the surreal: aided and abetted by heat from a flush-panel radiator immediately below the wall-mounted blackboard set at maximum and with the Bakelite control knob broken, perspiration had run non-stop down his spine, intercepted initially by the waist-band of his trousers. This, however, was of limited absorbency and soon over-flowed. Having shed his jacket at an early stage he was in no doubt that tell-tale signs were appearing in the seat of his pants.

After an eternity of exponentially-increasing discomfort - and perspiration - his fifty-minutes' allocation drew to a close. He strode from the lecture room with all the dignity he could muster, drained and exhausted both mentally and physically, a self-condemned failure to face a week of apprehension about next Monday at nine o'clock.

Sudden pressure on his back and the sound of brakes confirmed that the train was slowing for its approach to Swindon. Yet more passengers! Could be the last chance to have a good stretch. He rose to his feet, pushing back his shoulders several times. Eventually, of course, he had come to terms with this lecturing business, and with his last-ever public performance looming it might not be a bad idea to allow a few positive thoughts to enter the soul-searching. The jump seat had flipped up. Turning to face it he re-positioned the hold-all, loosened his belt, straightened the front of the white shirt by tucking it deeper into his trousers, re-tightened the belt, straightened his tie and turned around

The Bridge - *a love affair*

again. The same belt did service with every item of clothing - jeans, shorts, suits - and for no shortage of reasons. It was a unique item: the leather strap was un-perforated, leaving it adjustable to a fraction of a millimetre or, more realistically, to any desired degree of tightness. It had been a presentation on the occasion of his retirement from the laboratory - the first of the two retirements - and celebrated the talents of a number of colleagues: the stress analyst, the solid-modelling specialist, the operator of the rapid-prototyping and NC machines - and as important as any, a self-effacing machinist of the old school, whose knowledge of cutting speeds, feeds *etc.* made the difference between achieving tolerances and fits - and having to start the job all over again. The buckle was machined from solid titanium alloy - no doubt somewhat under-stressed for its un-demanding daily task, but chosen for the unique surface finish achievable with the correct machining technique. While chromium plate would have been vulgar, and brushed stainless steel tastelessly bright, this particular alloy showed the subtlest hint of colour - pale topaz, perhaps. Moreover, the fine machining marks caught and reflected the light as do DVDs and holograms - except that the contoured surface of the buckle produced a more dynamic effect.

    The train had come to a halt. He stood up again allowing passengers to file past at the steady rate at which they managed to shoulder their way to the vestibule. This time, noticeably fewer passengers boarded than had left, possibly reflecting the fact that Swindon had returned to offering other rail connections. A stopping service to Paddington was hauled by whichever of two steam locomotives was serviceable - No. 7309 *Foremarke Hall*, or No. 2708 - both ex-GWR and on indefinite loan from the re-born GWR based at Toddington. An LMS-designed 8F locomotive 92203 *Black Prince* loaned by a private owner ran six days per week to and from Cheltenham *via* Stroud and Gloucester.

    He felt a strong connection with the 8F, the locomotive on which he had taken a one-day driver experience course based at Toddington. That had been long ago in 2010 - an outing unforgettable for more than the predictable reasons: as if the footplate were not hot

The Bridge - *a love affair*

enough, it had been a blistering day in early July. Scheduled training runs had been between Toddington and Cheltenham race-course. However, recent subsidence of the embankment at Gotherington meant stopping short at Broadway, where the locomotive would be run round to the opposite end of the coach rake for the leg back to Toddington. Closed for decades to main-line services, Broadway station boasted a spectacular display of flowers maintained by volunteers with the aid of a platform water supply. Never had flower water tasted as good as on that sweltering afternoon.

The door closed, and Tornado gave the statutory blast on the whistle. The vicious hiss of steam from the cylinder drains penetrated through to the compartment before being swamped beneath the succession of powerful exhaust blasts.

Next stop Didcot.

Although common-room chat had not included teaching technique - had perhaps even avoided the subject - it had abounded with anecdotes about lecturing disasters*. Any one of those embarrassments might have served to put his own self-criticism into perspective. However, any reassurance which might have been forthcoming failed to do so.

Not surprisingly, the relationship with Jean was suffering. If his problem reflected some deep character defect, a frank discussion would put at risk the admiration she evidently held for him. He had tried broaching the situation obliquely, only to feel betrayed by a reaction which suggested lack of interest, completely failing to recognize a perfectly reasonable response to the watered down account of his anguish. A mind beset by doubt on one front is a mind vulnerable to misgivings on another: was he being hypnotized by physical appearance into the illusion of a viable relationship?

He had begun to fret about how they would resolve family difficulties if children came along. The research side of the job had been gathering a head of steam: if he could only crack this lecturing business

---

*Example as footnote at end of chapter.

he could see himself climbing the academic ladder - possibly to a professorship. Like commissioned military rank, he reasoned, that would carry social responsibilities. Having talked himself - irrationally - around to the view that she was not inclined to thinking in the abstract, he was resigned to the conclusion that he would not get the support needed for such a rôle. (Had he asked himself instead how *he* could have supported *her*, the outcome might have been rather different.)

On the basis that doing something about it was preferable to doing nothing, he had identified a one-year, residential teacher training course (there appeared to be nothing directed at lecturers). Attending would mean resigning the research assistantship, but there was a small bursary, continuity of which would be dependent on his passing assessments, one at the end of each of the three terms.

Attendance would require re-locating by about eighty miles. Perfect: a bit of distance for eight months or so (the academic year was shorter than a calendar year) might be just the tonic the relationship needed. They parted a week or so before the course was due to start - and before reality struck: how on earth could he have failed to anticipate the queue of hopefuls waiting in the wings for him to put a foot wrong? The news, days after the start of the course, that a married man had stepped in hit him like a train.

Concentrating on the studies was difficult from the outset, and became more so as inability to sleep compounded the mental exhaustion. The first term assessment loomed, together with a choice: to sit the exams with a guarantee of being rusticated, or to quit forthwith. The latter offered less loss of face - but now two failures for the price of one! Not exactly a morale-booster. More than two, in fact: how on earth had he convinced himself that that the relationship had offered no support? What support could anyone of sound mind ask for over and above the loyal friendship of a patient, forgiving, serenely beautiful woman? He had well-and-truly blown it!

A violent, side-to-side movement of the carriage shook him out of his day-dream. By contrast with the care bestowed on locomotives, track maintenance had been reduced to inspection, wear and damage being dealt with by imposing speed restrictions. There were still sections on the line where Tornado could show her paces. It was evident that drivers made the most of them, and that firemen shovelled willingly. A bit fast around that particular curve, maybe!

A canal ran close to the track. Crofton, probably. He gazed at it absent-mindedly until the earlier train of thought inevitably took over.

His parents had welcomed him home for as long as things might take, but it took no more than a day for them to become deeply troubled at his listlessness. One weekend evening they had persuaded him to sit still for long enough to watch the opening acts of a television programme which had not yet become politically incorrect - the *Black and White Minstrel Show*. The troupe for that performance included two female singers. The taller of the two came forward for her solo spot. 'Isn't she just the image of Jean?' It was his mother - and wasn't she dead right!

It was some kind of last straw, and something snapped. He became aware that the room was in motion. The sound of the television receded into the distance - then returned overwhelmingly loud. He stood up, as if to check. The walls and ceiling moved away, and then came closer - just as he remembered from childhood fever that had accompanied mumps and measles. What a nervous breakdown might be he had no idea, but he was in no hurry to find out. He must hold on to his sanity at all cost - find something to focus on.

He rushed to the next room where his upright Model K Steinway piano lived. Flipping open the lid of the stool, he picked out a volume of Rachmaninov preludes, opened it at random, placed it on the music stand and forced himself to sight-read.

He reached the end of the first page and paused. The room had steadied somewhat. Encouraged, he pressed on. It was far from a performance, but he was later to reflect that he had never previously sight-read anything so demanding with such relative success. A page or two later he paused again - or it might have been ten pages. The immediate crisis was evidently over. Returning to the next room he

The Bridge - *a love affair*

found the *Black and White Minstrel Show* finished. 'That was the longest stint of practice you've done for a while.' This time it was his father.

Over the next couple of days, piano-playing alternated with long walks. He had moved from sight-reading to working on a single piece - *Rhapsody on a theme of Paganini* - just the eighteenth variation, the others were beyond his technique, but in any case the eighteenth justified the entire piece: The way Rachmaninov had inverted the original theme - an irritable, jumpy little ditty - into that great soaring tune . .

The exhaust beat fell silent. The locomotive was coasting towards Didcot. Time to begin manoeuvring towards the door. Then he would be perfectly positioned for a walk of a few steps along the platform for a close look at Tornado. What a lot you would miss if you had no interest in technology! Take the routine slowing of a steam train, for example. There would be two braking systems - three if you included the manual brake on the tender. The driver would shortly be activating the carriage brakes. In other words, the carriages would be slowing the locomotive rather than the 'obvious' way around.

Interesting how the landmark cooling towers had not merely been a feature of Didcot: they had *defined* Didcot until ignominiously levelled by controlled explosion a couple of years previously.

Another minutes or two and the carriage brakes had done their job. The race to the door got under way even as he leaned forward to pick up the hold-all, and he received a blow on the head from the runner-up. Waiting his time so that the cargo could be positioned within reach from platform level, he jumped down, hauled the bag out and surveyed the queue forming for ticket inspection. It would be quite a wait.

Footnote

Inevitably, subsequent years had brought insights confirming that his baptism-of-fire had not been altogether unique. There had been, according to common-room lore, the newly-appointed lecturer in an arts subject who proposed to deliver his material from notes - but who had neglected to read through out-aloud in advance.

Rather than lasting fifty minutes, the first lecture had stretched to a mere fifteen. A potentially embarrassing situation was averted by his having brought - but not rehearsed - the material of lectures two and three. Under the pressure of venturing into increasingly unfamiliar territory, he gabbled through lecture two in some ten minutes and lecture three in slightly less.

The possibility flashed through his mind of opening up the remaining fifteen minutes to questions and discussion. This, however, threatened to raise material he had not visited since reading up on it weeks earlier. He opted instead to gather his notes and to make a brisk exit through the nearest door. In the event, this turned out to be the cleaners' cupboard, which he then had to share with brooms and the asphyxiating smell of damp mops until students had finished filing out as they discussed his inaugural performance.

The Bridge - *a love affair*

3

Coffee in Whitehall

Sewell repositioned the hold-all away from the platform edge and walked towards the locomotive. He was rewarded with unmistakable reminders as to why he always took the time to do so: the fire doors were open and the incandescent glow of the firebox could be felt on his face. A steam locomotive is not merely a hundred plus impassive tons of steel, cast iron, phosphor-bronze and water. It is a simmering, living being giving off an intoxicating cocktail aroma of steam, coal-smoke and cylinder oil.

He paused next to the main driving wheels with their shining coupling-rods, connecting-rod and external valve gear. The elegant Walschaert's mechanism distinguished Gresley and Peppercorn designs from the arguably tidier-looking contemporaries of the Great Western Railway - the Kings - which had the sheaves of the conjugated gear out of sight between the chassis-frames.

The last carriage door closed, but there was no whistle from the platform. He looked ahead of the locomotive to the signal, which had not yet cleared. More than half the passengers remained queued at ticket inspection. He could either join the back of the queue without gaining a

The Bridge - *a love affair*

second on the time of arrival at Rutherford, or stay put waiting for Tornado to depart. He picked up the hold-all, walked towards a spartan, perforated-metal seat in direct view of the locomotive, and sat down.

He would know when she was about to go: the valve mechanism would be seen slowly re-setting to the starting configuration - full-ahead. There would then be a piercing hiss as the regulator was opened and steam drove condensate out through the cylinder drains.

Still the valve gear remained in neutral - and still a queue remained at the platform exit.

The team who had constructed Tornado had been forced to rely on help from Germany - a sorry reflection on the state of UK industry which had once built a hundred locomotives per year. The decline had been an early symptom of the shift from wealth-creation to the fad which had inevitably brought the global economy to its knees: betting on the market fortunes of bundles of 'securitised', anonymous debt.

A sound of escaping steam which had been simmering suddenly turned into an ear-splitting screech: the fireman would have been building up the fire needed to generate the steam for the heavy pull up to speed on the leg to Reading. The result of his premature success on the shovel was now venting furiously through the pair of safety valves.

Still the signal had not cleared. Even if nothing had gone horribly wrong it was clear that all was not right. He looked again at the handsome driving wheels and Walschaert's linkage. An ill-advised trivial pursuit-style challenge had been circulating which reflected badly on the challenger: *Name a famous Belgian*. Well, look no further: with the exception of designs for the GWR, every steam locomotive of any consequence had been equipped with Edige Walschaert's mechanism. Just how successful do you have to be to join the list of the famous?

And while on the subject, was this not grist for the mill which had been grinding earlier? The link between aesthetics and engineering functionality? The association had first been made for him in a short radio programme decades previously. Indeed, it had made such an impact that he could remember precisely where he had been when hearing it: at the wheel of his Rover 2000TC, leaving the A-420 where it joins the A-340 close to Bourton-on-the-Water in Gloucestershire. It was the sort of piece which could have been written by René Cutforth. It had been in praise of the very valve gear he was now looking at - Walschaert's valve gear. The essence had been that, if there were poetry in engineering, then it was epitomized by that very valve gear in motion. The piece was subtly double-edged: it achieved in prose the poetry it perceived in its under-appreciated subject.

Sewell had since trawled the internet many times in the hope of tracking down a recording, a hard copy - or even a mention. The odds against doing so post-Melt-down were now stacked far higher. How many gems had been wiped before the days of unlimited storage? - the first episodes of BBC Radio's *Dick Barton, Special Agent*, or those of Charles Chilton's *Journey into space*. And what about that priceless monologue by Donald Webster: *A-scrawmpin'*.

Still the signal not cleared. All that remained of the queue were three figures - and they did not appear in any great hurry to leave the platform. He would make a move: the chances of watching Tornado depart were clearly not improving.

'Dr David Sewell?'

'That's me.'

One of the figures stepped forward. 'I don't suppose you are carrying your passport?'

'Has Didcot declared independence?'

'No, sir. Any other form of identification?'

'Driver's licence. Nothing to drive, but it's come in handy a few times since Melt-down. Oh - and a little conference badge with my name.'

'These will do for the moment, sir. May I see?'

Sewell obliged. The man handed the items back, then extended his right hand in welcome while the left raised his own ID card to Sewell's eye level. 'McIntyre - John McIntyre, Deputy Secretary of State at the Ministry for Economic Regeneration, MERGE. Feel free to call me John - until we are with the Minister, that is. Then it will be titles or 'sir'.'

One of the other men made some kind of gesture. Judging by the blast from Tornado's whistle it had resulted in the signal clearing, and the locomotive exploded into life. Understandably anxious to be away, the driver had given an over-zealous pull at the regulator. With steam pressure at maximum, the superheater tubes roasting hot and the valve gear at full-ahead he had managed to spin the driving wheels. As the overdose of steam expanded through the super-heater the exhaust blasts slowed and died down. A more cautious attempt followed, and the train began to pull away to a succession of crisp, deep exhaust snorts. It soon became possible to resume the conversation.

'These two gentlemen are from the Diplomatic Protection Service. As a formality - and not as a threat - it is my duty to tell you that they are armed.' Un-smilingly, the duo proffered respective ID badges. Sewell thought he might as well take a look. 'May I?' Encouraged by a nod he took one of the credit card-sized badges. The picture could, indeed, have been that of the wearer - but equally of any other dark-haired male for that matter. There was a hologram, a stylized crown and the words *Diplomatic Protection Service*. Well, how far was he going to get by challenging it?

The ticket inspector waved them through as though they were old friends.

'Please be assured you are not involved in any sort of controversy. The very opposite, in fact: you and your work are suddenly in fashion. The Minister is aware that you are expected at ERU later today, and we shall see to it that you get there - but *via* Whitehall. Ministry first. You can ask me anything you like about it on the way to Town.'

'If it's about what's in this bag, you realize I'm only half the goods.'

'I do indeed, and the other half arrived from Spain by military transport overnight.' He stopped in his tracks. 'I'm sure you won't mind

50

me checking that you are carrying the goods needed to make this meeting work.'

Sewell placed the hold-all down, flipped open the over-centre clasps and removed his change of clothing and a layer of protective packaging. McIntyre signalled to one of the security men who drew something from a pocket - a photograph or, more likely since he was now unfolding an A-4 sheet, a screen dump of output from solid-modelling software. Kneeling, he peered at the contents of the bag and then at the print. Turning the latter sideways he repeated the comparison. 'Well, if it's not what we've been told to expect then I'm a Chinese laundry man.'

'Many thanks, David. May I, by the way?'

'Feel free.'

They walked through the station exit and towards a people-carrier parked on now-superfluous double yellow lines. 'Located enough diesel fuel to get us all the way to London, then.' Sewell observed. 'And back to Didcot?'

'Don't worry.'

'You make it sound as though there were no shortage.'

There was no immediate reply. One of the security men opened a rear door for McIntyre, closed it when he was seated, then opened the baggage compartment and beckoned to Sewell. The miming was beginning to become tedious. Sewell pointed to himself, then to the tiny compartment, finally drawing a question-mark in the air. The burst of laughter brought McIntyre's face to the window: perhaps it was a first for him as well. Still grinning ear-to-ear, the security man took the hold-all, placed it on board and closed the compartment door. 'This way please, sir.' He led Sewell to the other side of the vehicle, ushered him in next to the Under-Secretary, allowed himself another grin and joined his colleague in the front.

The road was empty, inviting a spirited pace. 'If I allowed myself to dwell on the privileges of this job I wouldn't sleep.' volunteered McIntyre, as if addressing Sewell's remark about the fuel. 'I console myself with the fact that, as far as I know, I was not involved in

51

any of the activities now carrying the can for Melt-down. The very opposite, I hope: my book got noticed. I'd been fired up by David Mackay - you must know his *Sustainable Energy -without the Hot Air?*'

'Certainly do. Got everybody thinking along the right lines. Earned him a well-deserved government appointment along the way. I like the common denominators he uses for comparing lifestyle costs. We've obviously got to move on from price-tag to life-cycle costing. But very few changes come without repercussions - something he seems to lose sight of in his recommendations for personal economies: 'Stop flying - and save 35 kWh per day'. If we all do it, Airbus and Boeing go out of business. That comes with its own cost. And assuming we don't stop travelling altogether, ship-building gets a bonanza. Travel by ship is about one third as efficient as air travel. So if you want to save - keep flying!'

'It's no bad thing to leave something for the rest of us to have a crack at: Einstein did it. One of my interests is the airship debate: there's barely a moment between one project foundering and another being proposed as the global solution to some transport problem or other. MacKay's take is in terms of *transport cost*, which, at 0.06 kWh per ton-km for a 400 m-long air-ship are, according to him, similar to that of rail - and to submarine! But it's obvious that rail and airship transport are not interchangeable - and that's before you consider resources and sustainability: there isn't enough helium in the world to support a significant fleet of airships, so the comparison's academic.'

Sewell took a turn: 'One of my beefs is with the popular economics of p-v solar panels: sure they look favourable if you're installing them with a government subsidy. But the reality is that you're being subsidized by all the other tax-payers who are *not* installing. My criterion has nothing to do with MacKay: wait until you see factories powered exclusively by p-v panels manufacturing p-v panels and making a profit. Then you'll know that p-v technology has arrived'

McIntyre again: 'Sounds as if we could talk for ever, but there's a little agenda to get through before you meet the Minister. You will be aware that there is no longer any such thing as credit for international trade - no official exchange rates.'

'Of course.'

'And that such international trade as does takes place is essentially barter: so many thousand serviceable, used vehicles for so many thousand tons of rice?'

'I knew that those of us who are left were eating somehow, and that we don't grow too much rice in the UK.'

'The barter business is working - and expanding fast. After two decades of selling each other financial 'products' it takes time to adapt to identifying barter opportunities. In the current climate, wealth is energy. Anything capable of alleviating the current energy famine is looked into very seriously for barter potential.

'Problem is that market value, if any, is tied in with exclusivity. Respect for patents held by foreign economies is at zero. And no country is interested in exchanging, say, a tanker of crude oil for a technology which some other country will copy the moment it gets its hands on it. This is the aspect the Minister needs to satisfy himself on personally if he's to sign a barter contract. I'd appreciate if you'd outline for me the feature - or features - which are going to make for exclusivity. Sir David will be asking similar questions himself - but if he realizes after you've left that he hasn't understood something he'll expect me to fill him in.'

'Simple enough: the engine has two distinct aspects: the hardware and the software. Manufacturing the hardware is a high-value activity, but could be replicated by anyone getting hold of an engine and reverse-engineering it. However, it won't work - or, at least, it won't be controllable - without the micro-processor - the engine management system. Each processor unit costs pence in volume production. It can't be interrogated or reverse-engineered. So the UK remains sole supplier to the foreign licensee. Pronto! Exclusive.'

'Sounds promising so far. We're not through yet - but that's the Harwell campus right ahead now. To save time we've arranged to pick up your colleague at security.'

The vehicle came to a halt a few yards short of a barrier. The DPS man whom Sewell had humanized got out just as the security man left his cabin. The two converged and conferred - and conferred.

The DPS man returned to the people-carrier at twice the speed he had left. 'Not here!'

'What!' McIntyre exploded. 'Did he say where the hell she is?'

'Already on the way to Whitehall. Transport are seething. Had to sign out the only other vehicle with sufficient fuel for a return trip plus the only other duty driver.'

'Didn't they know we were on our way?'

'Of course! Apparently it's the Minister. Reckoned he needed a guarantee of a chat with somebody on the project by this afternoon at the latest. He wasn't confident that David - Dr Sewell - would be on this morning's train - or that we would intercept him at Didcot if he had been.'

McIntyre was silent for a moment, then turned to Sewell. 'David, this is slightly awkward: I am under instructions to identify you positively before leaving Didcot for Whitehall. We were going to rely on your colleague for that: she's been collected from the Spanish consulate. I have to tick boxes, and it's more than my job is worth to miss a box. We understand that you had a serious accident at some stage.'

'I think you could call it that.'

'Would you mind showing us your back? I am sure we can go into the security office if you would be more comfortable.'

'Good grief, man! My back educated a generation of medical students while it was in the burns unit of the QE hospital in Birmingham.' He got out of the vehicle, took off his jacket and tossed it at McIntyre. 'Here, hold this.' The time had come to stop treating the man as a superior. He loosened the commemorative titanium belt-buckle and, reaching over his shoulders with both hands, pulled shirt and vest up to neck height. 'It's for you to decide whether that's make-up or the real thing.'

Without waiting for a reaction he let go shirt and vest, tucked everything back into place, re-tightened the belt and turned around. McIntyre was subdued. 'Thank you, David.' He looked at the others. 'Come on, let's go.'

The vehicle was back on an empty A417 before anyone spoke again.

'Do you ever tell people how you came by that injury?'

'Don't let it embarrass you. It was over half a century ago - on a night exercise with the TA. I was on walkie-talkie duty - the old WW-2 type you carried on your back. If you saw the film *Where Eagles Dare* I think it was the model Richard Burton used there - except that his was camouflaged white against the snow. Weighed about the same as half a bag of cement. I knew about the overhead power cable - you checked such things on the OS map before the exercise. You even counted the distribution poles as you went to make sure. I came to a gate more or less on schedule - tubular sort - welded steel, but a field gate - wide as the old-fashioned five-bar gate, and mistook it for *the* gate. I was listening out with the aerial at full extension, so even though the power cable was supposed to be somewhere else I went over the gate bent forward with the aerial almost horizontal.

'I was half-way over when the gate let go. I must have jerked upright and that's when the aerial made contact. I was unconscious for days - maybe with the help of an anaesthetic drip. I'd been face-down when they found me. The first thing they had done was to take the walkie-talkie off my back - without realizing how much of me they were taking with it: even the hospital never worked out which was electrical burn and which was chemical burn - the batteries had cooked and seeped.'

'That's one hell of an occupational injury. Did anybody sue anybody?'

'It was a totally different culture then. And I don't know who would be to blame - other than myself - if it were to happen now. Apparently somebody had filled a gap in the hedge by leaning a spare gate against it: there were no gate posts. Difficult to tell at night.

The Bridge - *a love affair*

Anyway it was just waiting to collapse. It was months before I was fully mobile again, and then it was time to let go and move on.'

A further period of silence followed. Signs to Reading came and went, and they took a virtually-empty A4.

'Does it hold you up now - the injury?'

'Not that you'd know. A back massage used to be a luxury before it happened. I wouldn't give a thank-you for one now.'

It had come to a choice for the driver between a near-empty M4 and a near-empty A4. He chose the latter, and the vehicle settled to an easily-maintained one hundred miles per hour - and presumably not very many miles per gallon.

'There's something I must tell you before I forget, and then I hope you will be kind enough to help with some non-essential inform-action: the Minister's full name is Sir David Valentine Wyatt. He likes 'Sir David'. Someone will be deputizing for the Chief Scientist to the Provisional Government - probably Dr Barbara Penrose. I hope so: she's as personable as she is intelligent and capable.

'You should assume Sir David understands engineering basics, and that he is familiar with any terminology needed to explain your power unit. He started as an apprentice with deHavilland at Hatfield: was part of the Comet saga from start to finish. Like a bear with a sore head last time I saw him: been in the office 10 - 12 hours a day. But there's always a good side: if he's in coasting mode you'll get a fascinating ear-full of the glory-days at deHavilland.

'What he's going to focus on today is this business of exclusivity. Trouble is, the first break he gets tomorrow he'll expect me to know as much as you. That's one of the reasons I was sent to pick you up and travel with you. Do you do a working man's guide to your technology?'

'Sort of! I think the best way is not to look at how this power unit differs from other types - petrol, diesel, gas turbine - but what they all have in common. At a certain level they all work by the same principle: they compress a gas (air, say) when it's cold, heat it, then re-expand it hot. Expanding the heated gas delivers back more work than it originally took to compress it. If it were not for losses - mechanical friction, for example - the difference is what is available as useful work. If it's a reciprocating engine the work comes out *via* a shaft. The way the excess work gets put to use in the aircraft gas turbine is less obvious - but amounts to the same. They are all called 'heat engines' - unless you are a boring pedant.'

'Simple enough so far. There must be a stage where it gets difficult.'

'Don't agree. In the IC engine and gas turbine the heating phase is achieved by reacting fuel vapour with the air - by combustion. Cooling is the cheap-and-cheerful process of exhausting the combustion products and taking in a fresh charge of cold air. The Stirling engine achieves both phases - heating and cooling - in a different way - by forcing the air through heat exchangers, one hot, the other cold. Means it can run on gases other than air.'

'And the reason these engines get called 'universal' heat engines is that it doesn't matter what you use to keep the exchangers at operating temperature?'

'You know as much about it as I do!'

'But your design has got to be very different. Otherwise we wouldn't be here right now.'

'It's different only in the way the gas gets shunted between the exchangers. The conventional way is to push it back and forth with a 'displacer'. The displacer's just a plunger, usually driven off the crank-shaft through a mechanical linkage. But if you design the gas path for high-enough speed the displacer can be thrown away: compression and expansion set up pressure waves which do the displacing at precisely the right points in the cycle. Much simpler engine - and one which delivers four or five times more power per swept volume because there are four or five times the number of work-producing cycles over any given interval of time.'

'So, in posh terms yours is a resonant system?'

'Yes - as long as you don't confuse it with the text-book resonance - like a weight bobbing up and down on the end of a coil spring. That's a conservative system. Ours is damped, which means it just peters-out to a halt if not forced, and it's the thermodynamic cycle that does the forcing.'

'The rest I think I already know: these rapid pressure changes, exchanges of heat and so on all interact, and it takes a microprocessor to monitor them and keep them in the right relationship to each other.'

'You should be giving the paper tomorrow.'

The discussion had distracted attention from the final stages of the journey. He saw the lions of Nelson's column pass to the right, and at last they were in Whitehall. The vehicle made a turn into a nondescript passage between high buildings and stopped. The driver's window was wound down, buttons were pressed and a substantial metal gate opened at a measured pace. They moved ahead again by a few yards and, with a sense of finality which was palpable, the engine was switched off.

'The Minister doesn't work from the Palace of Westminster, then?'

'He does. But there was nothing like enough time to get security clearance for your colleague - or you, for that matter. You can tell your friends this evening that the most important minister in the Cabinet came to see you rather than the other way around.'

Cards were swiped and further button-pressing followed. They entered a hall evidently for use by the lower ranks. If lifts were operating, the DPS preferred the fitness benefits of climbing the stairs. Decor and appointment improved the higher one ascended, a feature emphasized by the increasing depth of pile in the stair-carpet.

The hold-all was becoming noticeably heavier. 'If we are going much higher would anyone like to share the weight of this?'

The Converted One, whose face now bore a permanent expression of goodwill to all mankind, took one handle and, after equivocating briefly, his colleague signalled to Sewell to relinquish the other. A heavy wooden door giving off an overpowering smell of polish led to a corridor which had presumably been carpeted by choosing the most luxurious from the selection at Heales. They padded in deep-pile silence to a door at the far end. It responded to McIntyre's ID card by opening of its own accord into an ante-room, intimidating with the ponderous formality of mahogany and leather.

A smell of uncompromisingly good coffee coming from a side table competed with that of the polish - and scored a convincing win. McIntyre appeared to relax into his element: 'Help yourselves: it's real coffee - not the roast acorn stuff. If we drink standing we'll avoid the undignified scramble to our feet if the Minister decides to come out of his office.'

He carried his cup to a low table, placed it beside a small box and pressed a button. A light came on, the ID card was swiped, and a voice said 'Come!'

Could turn out to be a man of few words, the Minister. The card was swiped yet again and a heavy, leather-quilted door opened with a barely-audible hiss. If Sewell was expecting a glimpse of Charo already chatting with the Minister - and Charo would surely be chatting - it was not to be. He was treated instead to sight of a second door, again leather-quilted, and evidently not to be opened until the first had been closed to eyes lacking the necessary security clearance. A sort of quilted leather air-lock, mused Sewell. Following a brief delay, McIntyre re-emerged to a re-play of the discrete hiss. 'Your colleague's not here yet. They had to stop to deal with a puncture - but they are only minutes away.'

Well, she could take her time for as long as the supply of coffee held out. He helped himself to a second while McIntyre addressed the officers: 'Get the vehicle checked in, please, and sign off. Thanks for volunteering for the detail.' Then an exchange on the intercom: 'Dr Sewell, the Minister will see you right away.'

'OK to bring the coffee?'

'Leave it. Sir David gets a fresh supply delivered every half-hour. He gets the next higher grade of bean!'

Sewell set cup and saucer back on the table. Never turn down the chance of promotion.

The air-lock repeated its routine, and Sewell found himself in a room both spacious and at the same time claustrophobic: a massive, translucent lantern formed most of the ceiling and stood substitute for artificial lighting, but the daylight which filtered through fought a losing battle with the extinguishing power of dark mahogany and even darker leather. The sole feature made from modern materials was an engineer's trolley-head draughting machine standing within reach of the desk with an A0-sized drawing print clipped in place.

The Minister rose from behind the stolid mahogany. He stood out in complete contrast to the room: Distinguished metallic-grey hair. Neat moustache. Waisted, single-breasted jacket of light grey suit with slightest sheen was a perfect fit to the tall, slim figure. There was an uncanny likeness to the moustachioed Christopher Plummer in the film *The Arrow*. The high collar of the crisp white shirt hinted at the Edwardian - but the conventional neck-tie with perfect Windsor knot placed him firmly in the 21st century. White cuffs protruded a measured twenty-five millimetres beyond the sleeves of the jacket. The sole embellishment was the outline of a bird in flight on an otherwise plain, maroon tie - a swallow. A sharp dresser, indeed, adding to the difficulty of judging his age.

'Minister, this is Dr Sewell. Dr Sewell, Sir David Valentine Wyatt.'

The Minister held out his hand. 'Welcome. Did I notice you appreciating my draughting machine?'

'Allbrit Spacemaster, isn't it. Once made my living on one of those - exactly that model, too. Fine machine. If I . . . . '

A buzzer interrupted. 'Get that, John, would you.'

'Getting it' involved a deal of button-pressing. 'Dr Jiménez is here, sir. And they've picked up Dr Penrose as you instructed.'

'Show them in. Thank the crew from me and offer them coffee, but bring Dr Jimenez straight through - reassure her she's not missing anything.'

The air-lock obliged.

The Bridge - *a love affair*

Sir David pressed ahead: 'Got to admit the draughting machine will never make up ground lost to these solid-modelling packages that run on the computer screen. I've got nothing but admiration for people who develop the software. Means you can see your design in photo-quality image before you spend money having it made. But when it comes to understanding how something works I still get on better with the engineering drawing - the traditional orthographic. And another thing: I have yet to see the computer generate a dimensioned, toleranced detail drawing with anything like the sheer style and finesse that a good draughtsman gets into it.'

As Sir David was speaking Sewell had been composing a comparison between the Spacemaster and the Japanese machine which had superseded it, but again the intercom won the contest for the Minister's attention. A few button-clicks later the air-lock went through its routine, this time releasing a bundle of female energy with arms outstretched:

'Sewell!'

'Charo!'

The Bridge - *a love affair*

4

Yes, Minister

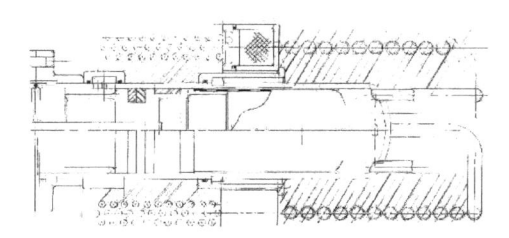

An instant was sufficient for excitement to take on a tinge of apprehension: How much less awkward if they had got their re-union over to schedule - at Rutherford - rather than in the office of a government minister. The Spanish, it immediately became evident, do not waste time weighing the pros and cons of hypothetical options. Ignoring the strangers in the room - of whom there were now three - she flung both arms around him, hugged like a limpet while administering the traditional Latin kiss, one for each cheek - and repeating for good measure. Well, the matter had been taken out of his hands. Mercifully, when he was finally released, the Minister was smiling broadly.

The second introduction was a markedly more sober affair. He was presented to Dr Barbara Penrose, standing in for Chief Scientist to the Provisional Government - a striking woman, thought Sewell. One of those over-sixties who have never put on an ounce of weight. Got to be a sports-woman. Probably played squash - and could give a bloke half her age a good thrashing.

The aroma of coffee was vying for attention. McIntyre gestured towards the source, and they converged on it. The Minister waited a few moments, then:

'Normally I don't let on when I'm relieved to see people: sign of weakness, they say. So the fact that I'm opening up to you now can be taken as an indication of the crucial importance of the next few hours.

'I take for granted our common awareness of the gravity of the economic situation. In a word we are at war: at war with shortages - not just of food, but of all the basic essentials - and, indeed, of ideas. The allocation of commercially-refined fuel has been meagre enough already: it's just been reduced to two litres per week - and that's for eligible operators.

'Any international trade is *ad hoc*, because there is no such thing as credit. When a surfeit of some commodity arises, it is disposed of in a one-off barter. Canada and Switzerland are the usual brokers. Foreign countries which were hosts to UK interests have nationalized them. Manufacturing licences for our products and designs are meaningless: Respect for international patents has evaporated. If we were to develop a car which ran on air, the maximum number we could sell abroad would be one: it would just be copied and put it into production locally.

'Traditional fiscal methods - tax relief, fiddling with the base rate, quantitative easing and so on - no longer have the slightest effect. It's back to basics - back to asking ourselves what is it that puts bread on the table when the chips are down. And the Treasury needs income as never before. Every one of my advisers says that the start point is energy - energy for agriculture - ploughing, harvesting, distribution; energy for powering industry; energy for construction, for transport, for hospitals, schools and home. I'm even hearing the technical people using energy and wealth to mean one and the same thing.

'You are here because you represent potential access not only to a new technology, but to a bartering opportunity - technology for grain. But it all hinges on our being able to offer exclusivity with the technology.

'I shall be the one who signs this deal - assuming it goes ahead. I'm fascinated by the technical side, obviously, but for the moment that's secondary: I need to understand what gives the exclusivity. Our trading partner doesn't want the market diluted with copies - neither, incidentally, do we: the export opportunity for ready-to-run units looks unlimited - even on the basis of barter.

'This engine that your development is based on - the Stirling engine - was considered obsolete when I was an engineering undergraduate. That was over half-a-century ago. First of all, is it a dodo, or isn't it?'

'Far from it, Minister. The Swedish navy operate Gotland class stealth submarines fitted with a pair of 75kW Stirling engines for power when operating fully-submerged. Just before Melt-down this sort of engine was under consideration for main propulsion as well.'

'Who makes them?'

'Kockums, sir. Malmö, Sweden.'

'Then why doesn't everybody just buy from Kockums?'

'They are fitted to subs. for one overriding reason: they are quiet - not silent - but well on the way to being undetectable. The military will pay way over the odds for that sort of power. And they have the money - or at least, they had pre-Melt-down. The engines cost a fortune - and specific power is not all that great: they are bulkier than a diesel of the same output. They are also complex, sophisticated and pressurized with hydrogen to about 110 atmospheres. Not much good for your smart-car.'

'But you have overcome these disadvantages?'

'We believe we have eliminated most of them, sir. One way of getting more power is by increasing speed: we run at 12,000 to 15,000 cycles per minute - the rpm of Formula One engines. And the engine is charged with harmless nitrogen rather than combustible hydrogen.'

'Give me what they call an executive summary. Then we'll go into as much detail as it takes. My Canadian counterpart will be standing by until eight pm GMT. We want to get over to Canada House before then. Jan Sernas: he's on the ball: PhD from U of T but a practical man too. Lots of advisers - but I've never seen him need to turn to them in an interview. I shall be facing some searching questions. What is it that can keep this technology exclusive? Put it in a nutshell.'

'The engine management system, sir. The UK manufactures the micro-processor exclusively in Cambridge. Any authorized licensee buys a single pre-programmed processor per finished engine and just plugs it in.'

'Alright, then. Why can't the licensee just copy the processor?'

'Because it can't be copied, sir.'

'May have to come back to that. Depends on the outcome of my next question. Why doesn't the prospective competitor design an alternative processor?'

'I'd like Dr Jiménez to answer that one, sir - after a bit of essential background: at any particular operating condition - charge pressure, working temperatures, load - there is a particular frequency the engine wants to run at: loosely-speaking it's a resonant system, like a weight hanging from a coil spring. Change the load and, without intervention by the processor, it either stalls or runs away. The processor is also necessary to make it self-starting.'

'And your prototype has solved this?'

'My colleague has solved it, sir.'

'Am I likely to understand how?'

'You could ask her, sir.'

'Dr. Jiménez? - and feel free to drop the 'sir' - it takes time.'

'It's been a multi-stage undertaking: analyse the wave mechanics of the thermodynamic cycle and code the analysis for digital solution in real time. Burn the solution onto a micro-processor. The processor accepts inputs from transducers in the running engine - pressures and temperatures - instantaneous values. To react fast enough, the code has to be predictive: amongst other things it changes the operating point of the linear electric generator in relation to changes in the external load.'

'Is there anything exclusive about your processor or the analysis coded into it?'

'The gas process analysis is old hat - a bit like the Stirling engine itself. The controller uses a computer-coded adaptation of a long-hand graphical method that once had to be done on a drawing-board - just like the one behind your desk, sir. It even has a name: the Method of Characteristics. The digitized version is obviously orders-of-magnitude faster - but that's not the whole picture: the chip design is optimized for parallel processing, and that's one of my specialities - optimizing code for parallel-processors.'

'Congratulations. But what's to stop the competition copying the processor as well as the engine?'

Sewell interrupted. 'That's where Dr Jiménez' other skill comes in: the chip responds to any attempt at interrogation by corrupting itself. It has been tricky working with the chip manufacturer: we had to tell them what we wanted in the way of hardware while disclosing the minimum about the software.'

'And how can you be sure it can't be hacked?'

'One can never be absolutely certain: obviously, the majority of development took place before Melt-down. But even in the depths of the present depression there has been no shortage of volunteers to keep the hacking trials going: those sort of people can't resist the challenge.'

'And . . ?'

'To date no one has succeeded. And every few months Dr Jiménez comes up with more sophisticated encryption.'

'So if micro-processor manufacture is confined to a secure facility in the UK, the engines themselves could be manufactured anywhere?'

'That's the way we see it, sir.'

'A couple of matters for my own interest. First of all, the Stirling cycle as explained to us needed a quarter of a revolution - ninety degrees - between the point of maximum volume of the hot space and that of the and cold. Your drawing -' he motioned towards the draughting machine '- has just the one moving component per cylinder

The Bridge - *a love affair*

separating the hot and cold spaces. To me this suggests half a revolution - or one hundred and eighty degrees.'

'Yes, sir. That would be the case at conventional rpm - speeds at which it won't, in fact, operate. But what actually makes things go is the ninety degrees between having maximum *mass of gas* in the hot space and maximum in the cold. In the traditional, low-speed version, maximum mass essentially means maximum volume. In our high-speed derivative the gas can't move fast enough to accompany the displacer - it lags behind. With the 180-degree difference in volume variations and high enough rpm in relation to acoustic speed in the gas we're back to the required mass distribution.'

'And the reduced parts-count combined with higher frequency has brought the size down? Just how compact is this thing - one-kW model for stand-by domestic power, for example?'

'That depends largely on the proposed heat source. With a clean distillate fuel, it's about the size and weight of a diesel engine of the same power. If you are going to burn wood pellets, then the combustor is bigger than the engine. Heated by solar energy the engine itself is compact - but the solar collector would need to be about five square metres in area at the most favourable sunlight conditions. Even more otherwise.'

'Engineering drawing?'

'Copy of my initial pencil drawings - cross-section.'

'I'm more than happy with orthographic views - first-angle even happier. But this is the 21st Century. You must have converted to CAD in the course of going to rapid-prototyping?'

'Certainly did: but this drawing shows the principle perfectly well, and if it gets stolen nothing is lost.'

'What do you mean - nothing lost? Can't our light-fingered drawing-snatcher build an engine from it?'

'Yes - but it won't work - even with the processor installed. Design of any consequence is a process of reconciling incompatibilities - and that's an iterative process. The engineering drawing is the designer's first scale model. This provides a feel for the number of exchanger tubes, length, diameter which can be accommodated. The tentative specification is fed to the simulation - which in all probability predicts depressingly low power output. The numerical specification is then modified and fed back to the simulation - with a more promising power prediction. Then it's back to the drawing board to coerce these changes into the engine. It can take many iterations.'

'You've dealt with my principal concern. Thank you. But Jan Sernas has raised another: an integral feature of the package we want to offer is potential - if any - for performance up-grade. Dr Penrose has seen the five development engines on test at the facility near Leamington. She confirms that all are delivering rated power - and from five different energy sources. But the prediction of future performance is based, I believe, on computer simulation. We are only too well aware of the track record of computer simulation in predicting the economic events of the past decade. So Dr Penrose has devoted the past ten days - and some nights, I understand - to studying your books and reports and to preparing some questions. Dr Penrose:'

'Ten days is a short time in which to become knowledgeable in a field having no overlap with one's own, Minister. So what I have done is to concentrate on the latest report and the most recent two books. This has left time to track down the other researchers' accounts of the subject - largely papers. I'm glad it worked out this way, because it has led to the sort of questions which should provide your assurances.

'Dr Sewell: you use essentially the same equations as everybody else to define the gas processes in this engine. But then you go about solving those equations in coordinate frameworks which no-one else uses - Lagrange and Characteristics. Presumably there is a reason?'

'Minister.' It was Charo. 'Assuming you are sympathetic to the pragmatic approach I can short-circuit the answer: If we were not using the appropriate algorithm and if we were not also coding correctly, the processor could not predict the gas process events sufficiently accurately and sufficiently fast to intervene in real time.'

'I take the point. But Dr Sewell?'

'I'll approach this by suggesting what a *solution* is - or should be. It should be an answer - or *the* answer - to the mathematical equation which it addresses - and that should be the case however well (or however badly) that equation represents reality. What's more, that fidelity needs to be verifiable. In the case of the Stirling engine, the equations are those of one-dimensional, unsteady, compressible flow with friction and heat transfer. The equations themselves do not depict reality - they define a drastic idealization, one symptom of which is that temperature and pressure events are clear-cut - too clear-cut:

'There is a view - not mine, by the way - that if the numerical machinations of the solution process 'fuzz things up' a bit, then the resulting 'solution' magically adjusts to the fuzziness of reality.

'The adherents never put the matter to the test - or, if they do, the results don't see light of day. The problem is that the gas processes inside the running engine - the interactions of varying pressure, temperature and velocity - are a thermodynamic pudding: they can't be separated out - even experimentally. To this extent, all of us face the same problem of verification.

'What there are, on the other hand, are physical situations which are far less complex, but *which are defined by the very same equations*. These *do* have solutions which are exact, independently verified - and known and respected for decades. So they can serve as benchmark tests for your solution algorithm. To the best of my knowledge we are alone in taking the trouble to verify numerical algorithms against them - and in going to print with the outcome.'

'Dr Jiménez.' Barbara Penrose spoke again. 'Please tell the Minister why you are so sure that the alternative algorithms - those you don't approve of - would not pass the same tests if their authors subjected them.'

'Because I have coded-up every relevant algorithm known to mankind - plus one not previously published - and tested the lot.'

'Allow me to congratulate you both.' It was Sir David. 'What do you think, Dr Penrose?'

'I have to say that I'm convinced.'

The Bridge - *a love affair*

Sir David again: 'What do our barter/trading partners get by way of specification and drawings?'

'Whatever they require: up-to-the-minute drawings generated by solid-modelling software - .dwg files and/or hard-copy, machining files - whatever.'

The Minister turned to McIntyre. 'Got all that, John? Jan Sernas will be asking.' And then to Sewell: 'Right. The moment of truth. You have been nationalized - and so has your engine, the microprocessor and all related technology, whether that technology be in print, in the form of computer software, or in your head. I'm not exactly issuing you with your 'double-O' status and a licence to kill, but you are under instructions to use any and all measures necessary to ensure that the Monarch's newly-acquired property remains the property of the Monarch - *any and all* measures. Obviously, how you implement the commission is up to you.

'The Monarch has agreed with the PM that any utterance or action willfully jeopardizing the barter contract I am about to offer to the Canadians will be dealt with as treason. You have heard of the new Official Allegiance Act?' He pushed a sheet of stiff paper across the desk. 'It commits the signatory to the use of physical violence as a measure of last resort. And, again, unreasonable failure to make use of all available means is an offence under the Act. Sign here, please.'

Sir David noticed Sewell's glance at Charo. 'Don't worry: foreign nationals can't be nationalized. Dr Jiménez has a few minutes to consider, and can sign voluntarily. You carry a mobile phone?'

'I do. Can't think why, though. The only function which might work these days is the SOS.'

'John!'

'Minister?'

'Take the professor's phone. Check it's fully charged. If not, fit a new battery. Set it up with our contact number - usual code-name - in his directory. And make sure his panic button is set to combined emergency services. Get both functions checked and drop this signed form off at Security. Be back in ten minutes.'

'Yes, Minister.'

Sir David turned to Sewell. 'You will find a new entry in your directory - *andorinha*: name of a bird in Portuguese. Not to be used for routine communication - but if you - or this project - come under threat, don't hesitate.'

'I know *andorinha*, sir, *swallow*. Beautiful word for a beautiful creature. Sleek, swift, rarely seen close-up. That's one on your neck-tie, isn't it, sir?'

'It is. And sounds as if you won't forget it, so it wasn't a bad choice of code word. Let's take it as a good omen. We'll get you back to your conference now. By the time that's over your travel arrangements will be in place. For the next twelve months you're property of HM Government.

'Ah, John - and the mobile. Good. Give the professor his ID card as well and let Security know they are ready to go. Dr Penrose, I'd like you to stay. John, have the visitors shown to the pick-up point and get back here as fast as you can: I want this portfolio ready for Canada House by late-afternoon.'

'Yes, Minister.'

McIntyre hurried them *via* the ante-room towards the earlier route. 'It's going to be quickest if I accompany you to the pick-up point.'

Charo insisted on sharing the weight of the hold-all. Their different rates of walking caused the cargo to bob up and down - but made for a sort of indirect physical contact which Sewell found pleasantly distracting after the recent tensions. She turned and smiled as if she felt the same.

The exit was duly reached. 'I need to pay a visit to the loo.' announced McIntye. 'All that coffee. You might think of doing the same: can't count on services en route. Help yourselves to the facilities. I'll get back to the office and send for the transport on the way. You may not recognize the driver - probably won't be either of the two who picked us up earlier. And you've got two travelling with you - a behavioural scientist Nick Stevens and his assistant. You won't get much change out of the assistant, but Nick will more than compensate.

'See you tomorrow for the grand opening. You've missed part of the paper session this afternoon, I'm sure your dinner will be a success.'

The people-carrier emerged from beneath the archway and stopped. The driver jumped out and opened the door. 'You've got company: two people for Harwell. Hope you don't mind sharing.'

There appeared to be little point in minding. The passenger compartment had two seats facing forward, two facing back. Charo sat down opposite a man who was the personification of relaxed, sartorial sophistication. The suit could have been collected new from his tailor that very morning. He lost no time in introducing himself, reaching out a hand first to Charo and then to Sewell. 'I'm Nick.' Then, indicating the powerfully-built man opposite Sewell 'And this is Bruce.'

The heavily-built one raised a right hand - perhaps as much as a millimetre - above the knee where it had rested - and lowered it again. Bruce and Nick might well have shared the same tailor - same material, same colour, same hand-stitched lapels. Not exactly ill-fitting in Bruce's case, but somehow incongruous around the muscular frame. If the man was not totally bald then he had treated his vast pate to a close shave that very morning.

Sewell broke the ice: 'On your way to Harwell too, then?'

'Yes. But on a different mission from yourselves.'

'Someone has told you about our mission?'

'Not at all: we are on a different mission from everyone else.'

'Fascinating. Tell more.'

Nick impressed instantly as one who welcomed a captive audience. The invitation was not wasted on him: 'I'm a one-man think-tank - geneticist turned behavioural psychologist. The Ministry have woken up to the fact that, if you want to avoid a repetition of Melt-down, then you analyze events leading to the occurrence - identify symptoms.'

'Well, one of the events which must be relevant was the mini-Melt-down of 2008. If you want the cause of either or both, I can give it you in a sentence,' offered Sewell: 'Those who should have known better mistook the financial markets for engines of wealth creation.'

'Sounds as if we come from the same direction - except for the presumption that it was a mistake. At the end of the day, market behaviour is human behaviour. My remit is to look at it in terms of epi-genetics - you know, inheritance of learned experience through alterations in the way genes are expressed. Like the discipline itself, we're at the early stages - calibrating the metrics.'

Of course, the *metrics*! Sewell had an allergic reaction to jargon. Is this man a quack - all wind and water? Well, they were stuck with him for at least another hour - and he was pressing ahead with the gratuitous lecture:

'More diffuse than engineering, so it's trickier to separate dependent variables from independent variables.'

Well, that at least appealed as scientific. It might be worth weighing in on this epi-genetics after all. 'I've had a very powerful experience which chimes with what I know of epi-genetics - so you've got yourself an audience.'

'Those who led us into this situation were of altered state of mind - psychotic, delusional.'

'OK for a barrack-room argument. But does it qualify as a government-funded research topic?'

'First off, let's be clear what is meant by *funded*: travel, accommodation and food are all pre-arranged. We merely subsist: there's no profit margin. Whether the project is worth anyone's while depends on how serious you are about heading off a recurrence. Obviously we weren't serious enough after 2008, so the situation deserves a more effective response than it got then. You remember, surely? The first searching question that was raised came from your queen: *Why didn't anybody notice?*'

Your queen, thought Sewell. Who and what are we dealing with here? He looked again at the sharp attire. Something didn't add up.

'The supreme irony is that the question arose on the premises of the prestigious London School of Economics - after the opening ceremony for a new building. It caught the Greatest Economists in the Land with pants down: all that the director of research at the Department

74

of Management could muster was that *at every stage, someone was relying on someone else, and everyone thought they were doing the right thing.*

'Not exactly the in-depth analysis designed to head off a re-run. Admittedly, a group of eminent economists eventually put together a three-page letter for Her Majesty. But even with time to reflect, they delved no deeper than to identify a *psychology of denial* and a *feel-good factor* under which the collective imagination of many bright people had failed to understand the risks. Can you believe it!? The Queen of Hearts had more substantive exchanges with Alice!'

'Be fair.' suggested Charo. 'If John Lanchester's eye-opening account of 2010 is anything to go by, it takes an entire book to explain the risks that modern banking had been exposing itself to - credit default swaps, derivatives and the rest of the so-called financial instruments.'

Sewell launched in: 'And doesn't Lanchester explain it well! I just wish he'd put greater emphasis on the overriding reality: that for all the trillions it has churned, that kind of trading has never directly - and I emphasize *directly* - created a penny of wealth.'

'One feels a bit churlish faulting the coverage, but I had been hoping to see his take on that aspect, too.' It was Charo. 'Couldn't find much in Stiglitz' 2012 account either.'

Nick took over: 'Well, maybe that leaves us to redress the balance: wealth is created by adding value. If engineering manufacture is not a value-adding activity then I don't know what is - but that's your bailiwick. My interest is in another aspect that Lanchester and Stiglitz didn't pursue - the behavioural and cultural. Look at it this way: a reasonable response to the 2008 collapse would have been a reining-in of the bonus culture. But no! In the face of outrage by treasury officials, the media, and the public, the response was the very opposite! The *opposite*! I ask you! By 2014, if you remember, the authorities in Spain had finally caught up with four executives of a Catalan bank, the Caixa Penedes, that had needed over €900 million in state aid. The four had awarded themselves €28 million in retirement plans *out of the bail-out money*!

The Bridge - *a love affair*

'Enslavement to a culture is usually excused in terms of losing sight of traditional values. What we're paying for is more like a psychosis - losing control - a chronic distortion of perspective.

'Remember the BBC payoff scandal? Deputy director Mark Byford left with a golden hand-shake £500,000 *over and above* his £495,000 contractual severance entitlement. But what you need to look at is how the Director-General Mark Thompson justified it to the committee of MPs: *that the way to get him to remain 'focused' as he worked out his notice was to double the incentive for him to leave*!

'Thompson went on to declare the £949,000 hand-shake to have been *value for money*. The *value* he is responsible for providing is to licence-payers, and the *money* in question was equivalent to 6,500 licence fees - a good deal of it paid by pensioners, the disabled and the un-employed. You might ask whether the words *value for money* could form in a balanced mind. How can the explanation reflect rationality when it was irrelevant, grotesque and insulting to Parliament and to every licence-payer in the land? *Culture* simply doesn't cover it. A spontaneous answer is a good indicator of state of mind. If there's such a thing as corporate autism, the symptoms are there.'

'And you are . . . Sorry, Charo. Your turn.'

'Aren't we just talking about greed? And hasn't greed been with us since humans grew hands? Symptoms are similar - greed feeds on itself .'

'OK, so if it's cumulative - self reinforcing - that would not be inconsistent with an epi-genetics view. If epi-genetics is a reality, then it's been around long enough to *help* humans grow hands - a bit like the Americas - there for quite a while before Columbus 'discovered' them.'

Sewell had been looking for an opportunity to catch up with Charo. Now he was having to accept that the ride to the Harwell campus was not going to provide it. Somewhat tetchily he enquired: 'And you are looking to prove a connection between epi-genetics and, say, collective greed?'

'Let us put it this way:' Relishing the new opening, Nick leaned forward, elbows on knees, hands free to make the necessary

The Bridge - *a love affair*

supporting gestures. And there it was again: something about this man found in those who spoke English as a second language - the constant need to demonstrate that he had perfected it. It went with the attire: the man would be in his element in waist-coat, spats and monocle. 'Let's put it like this: convincing yourself that behavioural reflexes can be passed on epi-genetically probably involves looking at extreme examples. But if verified in that context it can turn up elsewhere. Might be useful background for a fresh take on sectarian violence - or on persistence of religious myth. Do you know what is the single most frequently-used advertising prop?'

'The Coca-Cola can?' ventured Sewell.

'The gun!' suggested Charo.

'I regret to say that the lady is correct - although the mobile phone runs it a close second. A visitor from Mars would conclude that the gun is the preferred lifestyle accessory. Not long before Melt-down there had been a shooting at Sandy Hook elementary school in Newtown, Connecticut. The media reported *the worst ever massacre so far*. In other words, there had been massacres which had been more acceptable - *better* massacres, perhaps. Whatever has changed our tolerance threshold to that extent surely merits serious investigation.

'Mercifully the reality of the gun is irrelevant to the lives of the majority. But the image is used *daily* to entice us into everything from taking up playing the pipe organ to . . . . '

'Steady on, Nick. Did I hear *pipe organ* - the church organ?'

'I've been challenged before this point. So . . '. He reached between himself and Bruce for a slim attaché wallet, unzipped it, drew out an A-4 sheet and passed it across to Sewell. The copy, from Maclean's Magazine for 7th January 2013, reported a mission by recital organists Sarah Svendsen and Rachel Mahon to promote the study of the pipe organ. It pictured them standing in front of the console brandishing - Nick was quite right - a hand-gun!

'I suppose this sort of thing comes as a surprise to someone who has spent most of his time in senior common-rooms: not too many dons obsessed with fire-arms.'

'Don't you believe it! The dreaming spires illusion was blown away for me when you were still a teenager. Early nineteen-nineties, I think. Over twenty years ago, anyway. There had been a bit of a fad nationally for joint-honours courses - maybe not ancient Greek plus ballroom dancing, but that sort of idea.

'A certain university (tell you in a minute) had engaged a couple of press officers to edited a newsletter. It gained quite a circulation. One particular issue which found its way to me carried an announcement of a course combining Spanish with media studies - or with film studies - it's a while ago now. And the image of choice to illustrate a flagship university course? The gun: a driver being robbed of his car at gun-point.

'It was not a good time for me to be reminded of car-jackings: I'd not long heard from a former colleague in the US that his son, Ed, had been shot dead in Ann Arbor by a thug taking his car. Young Ed had been only six when I first got to know him.'

'You didn't keep quiet, I trust.'

'The Vice-Chancellor's office heard my views by letter. Told them that, for some people, being shot in the head is a reality rather than casual entertainment. I gave them a specific instance: Ed.'

'And they responded?'

'The letter back from one of the press officers administered the metaphorical pat on the head - she sympathised with my distress! Can't remember the exact words used to justify the image, but it was to the effect that the choice remained the ideal one.'

'You made no impact at all, then?'

'At the time, no. The Dunblane school massacre was in March ninety-six. Can't be sure, but I think that followed my protest. If she was still besotted by guns after that, I see no hope for the woman.'

'And the university which is - or was - blessed with her services?'

'Cambridge.'

'Well, there you are: epi-genetics - if it was a factor in her sad priorities - knows no class boundaries.'

The Bridge - *a love affair*

Nick forged ahead with his thesis. As he did so, a huge hand again stirred from Bruce's knee. It made its way to his jacket pocket at a rate calculated to conserve energy. They were kept waiting for some time before a plain, white packet was withdrawn. If Bruce proposed to smoke, then he had better seek approval so that Sewell could refuse on Charo's behalf.

For the moment the packet remained closed and its contents a secret. Nick was trying out his Spanish on Charo, looking intently into her eyes as he did so. As Nick's attentions had become increasingly less subtle, she had discreetly reached for Sewell's hand. He gave it a light squeeze as a show of support. Bruce turned to look out of the window, and Sewell took the opportunity for closer inspection. Hand-stitched lapels alright, immaculate white shirt, cuff-links and . . . massive shoes - a grotesque combination of shiny, light-grey imitation leather, velcro straps - and spongey-looking creeper-soles at least an inch thick.

But now there were developments on the smoking front: it was the left hand which was mobilized this time, and to the inside breast pocket. It was not clear whether the gesture was pre-planned, but Sewell could not fail to notice the shoulder seams open up, exposing the stitching as they struggled to contain the bulging muscles.

From inside the jacket came a lighter - the sort with transparent fuel holder showing the level of the liquid - but twice the size of any such lighter Sewell had ever seen before. It gave every indication of being full. If Bruce's smoking habits called for the services of industrial-scale ignition equipment, imagine the atmosphere they would shortly be breathing!

When, somewhat more than a year later, he would re-visit the events of 27th September 2016 as possible material for an auto-biography, he would remind himself of his maxim *Expect the unexpected* and enquire why he had not recognized the laboured slow-motion as a distraction.

A thump on his left thigh, accompanied by a sharp pain, was the last he would ever be able to recall of that journey along the Great West Road.

The Bridge - *a love affair*

5
Tropical island

Sewell's return to awareness took the form of a laborious journey - a fuzzy journey. A journey through jazz? No - *way* too largissimo. Incongruous associations - the QE2 dragging its anchor through a sea of Mars bars. A journey inside a fuzzy room with sides at unnatural angles - jazzy angles - angles which changed.

Everything would begin a slow rotation to the right - but then snap back to the original position with a metallic *ziiiing*! Now it was pitching forward continuously - but without ever tumbling. How was it managing that? Ah! One of those dreams - the sort where fear was experienced in the abstract - disembodied fear - the worst sort.

He was under water. The way back up to the surface was to locate those limbs - force them into action - shake your head - fight your way back to consciousness. Soon he would be awake, breathless, heart racing and sitting upright in bed - but awake.

To his relief he found he was indeed awake - sitting bolt upright, too. How did you know you were really awake after an experience like that? He was still in a room - a bare room, and it was indeed in motion - but the motion was steadying. Well, when you are part of reality you recognize reality. So this pale, blueish-white light, which could well be second-hand - a reflection maybe - and which played on the ceiling, was real - real enough to persist in faint rippling motion while walls, floor and ceiling gradually steadied to complete rest.

A distant swishing sound came and went. Having awoken in the sitting position, the first step in getting to his feet would be to lean forward. Something heavy but yielding ran down against his spine. It dragged at the scar tissue, stinging him into full consciousness. Swinging his body around so that his legs were across the bed he collapsed back against the heavy lump. It wasn't a bed after all: he was on the floor - and so was Charo - slumped behind him and still unconscious. So! They had been left propped against each other.

Taking a few deep breaths, he rolled over onto his knees and felt her pulse. Not strong, but regular - and a pulse. He took off his jacket, folded it, raised her head gently (and aren't heads heavy when they are inert!) and slid the makeshift pillow beneath. He then swung her round by the feet into a more comfortable position and re-positioned the pillow.

And there was the hold-all. He tested the weight. Promising. He loosened the clips. The demonstrator was still inside. Things were becoming less nightmare by the minute.

The next thing was to try was the door handle. A stainless-steel item - Swedish-style - which simply turned freely without opening anything.

Such light as there was filtered in through narrow, horizontal slits in the wall opposite the door. On closer inspection the slits were gaps between horizontal planks which might have been fixed in position to cover a broken window. Above the top-most plank there was evidently a more substantial gap, because that was where most of the light was entering. If he were able to stand a bit higher it might be possible to see downwards to the source. The room was bare of furniture, so it would have to wait.

How long had they been here? He looked at his watch. Gone! He felt in his pocket for the phone. Likewise: gone. The faint swishing

The Bridge - *a love affair*

sound persisted. What he was most reminded of was waves on a shingle beach.

Nothing to do but to wait. If Bruce had given Charo the same syringe-full as himself, her lesser weight would mean that she would be out for a while.

He sat down on the floor against the wall opposite her. They had first met decades previously when both had worked in London. The more outgoing of the two - by far - she had been his introduction to MacDonald's - the one in the Strand near Charing Cross station. At a whim she would drag him from his work to Dunkin' Donuts in Holborn.

His notion of dining in style at the time had been Topo Gigio in Brewer Street. He must have eaten there with every close friend and colleague since being introduced to the place at its earlier home in Great Windmill Street. Every close friend that was, except Charo. It had changed hands a few years before Melt-down. Now the cardinal omission could never be remedied.

Their working association had been intermittent: she had returned to Spain, married and had a family - two bright and delightful children. As the world-wide web had evolved and exchange of e-mails had become routine - especially when the size of attachments had become effectively un-limited - they had increasingly found themselves in close collaboration.

She was totally different from him - as different as her scientific specialization was from his: she excelled at implementing logic in ultra-efficient computer code. She had kept up with the rapid rate of development of processors, taking advantage of speed and power the instant it became available. He had stuck with his traditional engineering thermodynamics. As regards coding, he had experimented with the competing scientific programming languages as they had become the fashion - Basic, Algol (Kalgol, Walgol and Algol 68R), Pascal and so on, but had always fallen back on the IMB Fortran to which he had been introduced in the early 1960s. A working-man's language. It did everything he needed. Why change?

He glanced at the unconscious body. Interesting how some of the clearest memories were those which had taken root in the context of apprehension or embarrassment: They had been in the kitchen of Charo's rented flat in Marble Arch. Out of the blue she had announced 'I will dance for you'. There had been no recorded music - and none had been needed. A fine singing voice was powered by vocal cords capable of all the decibels required. Was this as spontaneous as it seemed, or had she scoured the capital for shoes of the hardest, most un-yielding leather that money could buy? The footwork had changed forever Sewell's perception of tap dancing, which he had since come to view as indecisive foot-shuffling by comparison. And if all Spanish dancers could snap their fingers as she did, castanet makers would be out of business.

Sewell had watched the performance with a mixture of admiration and apprehension. The latter turned out to have been a waste of perfectly good apprehension: mercifully, neighbours above, below and to the sides had chosen that particular afternoon to be out, and the feared posse from the residents' association did not materialize - at least, not before Sewell had made good his escape to his flat in Bloomsbury.

Charo stirred, and then appeared to recover much more rapidly than he had done. She swung herself round into the sitting position. 'Where have they brought us?' The question suggested she recalled seeing Bruce knock him out, and had already put two and two together.

'If I didn't know better I'd say to some tropical island.' He changed tack: 'You still have your watch. What time does it say?'

'Exactly three.'

'Afternoon or a.m.?'

'Doesn't say. It's a real watch with hands. By local time it's obviously night.'

'Do you feel up to getting us a look outside? I think those boards cover a window. And the light's coming over the top. If you feel you've recovered I'll lift you up.'

She was on her feet in an instant. 'Not high enough. You'll have to put me down again. If you hold me round the legs you should be able to get my head up against the ceiling.'

This time was evidently high enough. 'It's the sea alright. Dead calm. And tropical, I'd say. Palms everywhere. Stunning in the moonlight: bright as daylight.'

He lowered her gently to her feet. 'So, where are we? I knew that tropical light was different, but this is the first time I've seen a direct comparison,' admitted Charo. 'Mine was a night flight and the weather was fine. The airport was on minimal lighting - like Madrid itself - so there can't have been much light pollution. But the moonlight was nothing like as bright as here. Anyway, how could it have been bright? There is only - how do you call it? the old moon. We must have come a *very* long way - to a different climate - to the southern hemisphere, maybe.'

'It was clear in Bristol, too. And, as you say, the moon was past its last quarter. Charo, I'm going to lift you again. This time tell me whether you can see the moon itself.'

'I can't see the moon, but there is a perfect reflection and . . . *Sewell*! He felt the convulsion run through her thighs. *It's full moon*! Put me down!'

'Full moon! Unless the moon's changed the habits of a few billion years we've been here - or travelling - for . . . he hesitated . . . last quarter . . . eighteen days - or so! What's the date by your watch?'

'Doesn't show the date.'

'That may be why they didn't bother to take it.'

'What about your mobile. Check the shoulder bag - it's still here.'

'The phone's gone! But if it helps with your arithmetic, I should like to point out that we have neither eaten nor drunk since coffee with the Minister. OK: I am beginning to feel like a cup of tea and a Big Mac. But I don't feel as if I have gone without for three weeks. And tell me why am I not busting to use the loo?'

'Anaesthetics for surgery have been getting more sophisticated by the minute. We must have been in pharmaceutically-induced hibernation. It's the only explanation.'

Sewell looked apologetically at the floor. 'It's me who got you into this.' He looked up. 'And it's me who is going to get you out of it. We start with reality: We are on an island - or at least a peninsula, and we're not in hand-cuffs. How far does a small, gas-turbine engined helicopter travel in two and a half hours? 300 - 500 miles? One of the Scilly Isles, perhaps. Step one: get out of the building. Getting back to the mainland has to wait until we know what and where the mainland is.

'They want us for something - the engine technology most likely. If we're to stand any sort of chance don't let the enemy know what we know. Let's sit down and make out we're still groggy.'

They sat where they had awoken. Within minutes there was the sound of a lock mechanism operating. Nick entered with Bruce in tow.

'Good to see you. No ill effects, I trust. Allow me to re-introduce ourselves: I'm Nikolai - Nikolai Sefanovskyi, and this is Boris. We're all going to come through this just fine if you will bear in mind that both of us are armed, and that Boris is particularly trigger-happy.

'You have the privilege of being accommodated in one of the more exotic outposts of the FSB. We are here for a purpose, and I can see no reason for not explaining why you - why we - are here.'

'I can probably guess. For the moment I'd be more interested in knowing whether your anaesthetist here uses clean needles.'

'There's a good chance they do, Sewell.' It was Charo. 'After Boris jabbed you he pinned me with one arm and passed the syringe to Nick. Nick took his time over breaking open a new package and changing the needle. He seemed to get a kick out of jabbing me himself.'

'You had us fooled with the behavioural-psychologist line.'

'Not at all. That is precisely my profession - at least when I'm working in the UK.'

'Well, how about telling us where you've brought us?'

The Bridge - *a love affair*

'You've hit on the one question I'm not going to answer: we don't want the remnants of your Royal Navy steaming to the rescue. That's why we have borrowed your watch and phones and frisked you for tracking devices. You will get them back just as soon as this little matter is resolved in our favour. Needn't take more than a few hours.

'And if you are thinking that Mother Russia wants your brain-child you would be wrong. First of all, we would need the cooperation of you and your assistant, which might be a bit messy to acquire. Secondly, our scientists and analysts don't just throw everything at the computer as you and your American friends do. We use our heads and our mathematical skills. That way we are well on the way to leap-frogging your technology - software as well as hardware.'

'So what are you after that justifies kidnap, guns and helicopter rides?'

'Something of national importance to us: since Melt-down the number of Russians - former oligarchs - living in London has trebled. They are openly - and with the connivance of your government - living the life of Riley while honest Russians back home starve and freeze to death. Our president wants them back to face charges of embezzlement and treason. They are also invited to contribute their financial resources to the State.'

'So where do I and my colleague fit in?'

'While you were on your way here, contracts were being signed and exchanged between your country and Canada: grain shipments paid for with your technology. We happen to know that this has triggered dependent contracts between Canada and the USA. It will be embarrassing for your government to say the least if it is unable to deliver - having only just signed.

'We have already offered safe return of you, your colleague and your demonstration model in exchange for your government's cooperation in getting our traitors on a Russian air force flight back to Moscow. It may help you to know that there are no plans to harm you - physically or otherwise - or, indeed, to detain you for a moment longer

87

The Bridge - *a love affair*

than necessary. We are going to have to feed you - and ourselves - if things don't move soon.'

'Shall we be eating standing up?' enquired Charo.'

'Consider that the least of your problems: Boris' catering does not bear thinking about. Your role is simple: to sit it out here and not to attempt to escape.'

'That I might believe if we were alone with you. But don't tell me the lugubrious Boris here is just along for the ride.'

'The FSB is not what your popular press would have you believe: only a minority of Russian agents are thugs. Weapons training and un-armed combat were wasted on me, for example. I have a gun, but I have yet to shoot anyone. The most effective arm of the service is intelligence gathering and processing. That calls for statisticians, mathematicians psychologists and linguists - like me. Tell me something, Dr Sewell, do you believe in God?'

'Am I being softened up to meet my maker after all?'

'Not at all: it is in the interests of all concerned that you - both of you - should stay alive and well - well enough anyway to remain an effective part of the original barter contract. Your authorities are, at this moment, dragging their feet. (He took an unnecessary look at his wrist-watch.) So allow me to add some relevant background. It will help explain why you should not doubt my determination to see this matter through to successful conclusion: I am a family man. I have a son, Pyotr Ilyich . . .'

'Tchaikowsky' interrupted Sewell. 'You wanted him to become a musician.'

'The years have not blunted your mental acuity, Dr Sewell. I did - and indeed he became one, surpassing my wildest expectations. Even before he entered the Moscow Conservatory he was playing all four of Rachmaninov's piano concertos and the Paganini rhapsody - to the orchestra-minus-one CDs, of course: we couldn't afford a symphony orchestra! He even learned the controversial Number Five - the re-worked second symphony. Warrenberg was so impressed with his

88

playing that he wrote out an orchestral reduction for second piano so that Pyotr could practise with a colleague.'

'Where does this fit with our together-ness on a tropical island?'

'It fits when you understand how things work in Russia. This business does not function on trust: it's all about leverage. I am under no specific threat. If any light pressure is needed on me, however, I can expect to be reminded that Pyotr requires a valid passport to fulfill engagements outside Russia. If I need pushing somewhat harder I can expect a reminder that a pianist's hands are especially vulnerable. Aren't you glad you live in the UK?'

Charo joined the conversation: 'Since we're engaged in a time-killing exercise, how about telling us about the wonder drug you hit us with. It slows down the metabolism to a state of hibernation.'

'I wouldn't mind knowing myself: we are issued with the kit that does the job. It's sourced within the UK. That's one of the many things your people were blind to when investigating the Litvinenko hit: it made greater political sense to lay a false trail to Moscow than to put your very capable forensic experts on the scent to our UK sources. Anyway: to the point: your escaping would put the well-being of Pyotr at risk. So, if you force me . . . '

'And what about Boris. Is he a dedicated family man too?'

'He is in a different position. Boris stepped out of line once, and will not be seeing his elder brother again. A younger brother is being held as hostage to Boris' improved conduct. For the moment, that means obeying instructions from me. I can think of a happier basis for a working relationship, but that's how it is.

'So, in summary, Dr Sewell, you -' he turned to Charo, '- and your charming colleague may wish to take note - there are three things to consider before thinking of escaping: Firstly, one can shoot to maim as well as shoot to kill, and Boris is capable of distinguishing; secondly, the first target will be the lady and, finally, there is your moral position: your succeeding in getting away - unlikely as it may be - would be the end, quite possibly a painful end, to the musical career of Pyotr.'

'Given the barbaric threats hanging over your son I'm surprised you see a moral dimension to the oligarch witch-hunt.'

'No westerner has ever understood the bond between Mother Russia and her sons. And no amount of time would explain it now, so I'm not going to start.'

'Nikolai. It is clear that you have infiltrated MERGE, so you will know perfectly well that I am under a legal and moral obligation in respect of the contents of that hold-all, of the technology embodied in it, and of the know-how I carry around in my head. At face value, it's my duty to escape. On the other hand, I am not alone in this.' He addressed Charo. 'The obligations don't extend to you. It's up to you.'

'If the financial wide-boys Nikolai is after are part of the bunch that brought the global economy to its knees, then I could actually approve of the Russians' wanting to call them to account. In fact, if something similar had been done in 2008 we would probably not be here now.' She turned to Nikolai. 'However, I don't approve of kidnapping, blackmail and coercion. I am a mother. I've made a lot of sacrifices to launch two wonderful children on the world - both with highly-successful careers, so the possible consequences for your son are not lost on me. I've also faced worse than what you are threatening. My faith has seen me through and it's not going to desert me now. So you may wish to prepare yourself: at the very first opportunity, David and I will be making a run for it together.'

Boris had been keeping a mobile phone to his ear. Nikolai said something to him in Russian. The huge man responded with a nod, a question to the phone in Russian and a second nod. The wrist-watch was consulted again. 'Moscow says that your Sir David is still talking with Canada. We can stand around in silence - or we can pass the time in conversation. It appears your colleague puts her trust in God - one of many topics I find irresistible. So, back to my earlier question. How about you, Dr Sewell. Do you believe in God?'

'I have a good friend - a Reverend Professor, no less - who would call that *une question mal posée*. You speak French, of course?'

'Mais bien sûr! Do proceed.'

'The question is a dead-end: you are asking on the basis of some pre-conceived notion of God *you* have in mind - rather than any concept *I* might have. And, by the way, Charo said *faith* - not God.'

'Fair enough. Perhaps we should have started from the opposite pole: does Darwin - does natural selection - provide all the answers? And if not, who - or what - fills the gaps?'

Charo took up the theme: 'Nice to know you allow a distinction between Darwin and natural selection. If ever an author used writing to develop ideas on the hoof it was him: never read such long-winded self-hypnosis. Disciples of natural selection look at fossils and speciation - *largely non-human*, by the way! They then consider themselves equipped to infer the statistical origin of the entire human condition. No-one's questioning natural selection: it's a self-evident reality. But that it serves to account for every facet of human evolution is an *assumption*.'

Sewell chipped in: 'She's dead right: aspects of evolution are consistent with natural selection - consistent full-stop! I'm not claiming there's some underlying purpose or that there's a spiritual dimension to life. And I'm not claiming there isn't. But Darwin offers no proof either way.'

'Ah!' It was Nikolai: 'But now you are up against your very own Bertrand Russell - his *Tea-pot** metaphor to be precise. Russell . . .'

'Listen, Nick: as a behavioural psychologist you know all about our subconscious capacity to manipulate by irrelevant distraction**.

---

*If Russell asserts that a tea-pot orbits the Sun somewhere in space between the Earth and Mars, it would be irrational for him to expect others to believe him merely on the grounds that they cannot prove him wrong. The 'burden of proof', according to Russell, is upon himself.

**'Does one of the doctors have an appointment vacant this afternoon?'
'I'm sorry – all the doctors are fully-booked.'
'But I live only five minutes away.'

The Bridge - *a love affair*

Russell exploits it: he dangles the red herrings of psychosis (his 'irrational') and subjectivity (his 'expect') to convert a perfectly unloaded equation (. . . x does not exclude y . .) into a meal-ticket for woolly intellectualism. The question as to whose job it is to prove or disprove has nothing whatsoever to do with *the equation per se*.' Sewell pressed on: 'Natural selection reveals *nothing* about the survival advantage to Rachmaninov of his ability to speak directly to the souls of millions *via* a piano concerto conjured out of thin air. 'Time', 'purpose', 'spirit', 'soul' remain up-for-grabs. As far as I know, only humans worry about gods. And what's the survival advantage of worry, by the way?

'Most people would nowadays think in terms of two distinct events: creation of the universe (which is generally accepted to have taken place to the accompaniment of a rather loud bang) and, very much later, the creation of elementary organic life.'

'You used the word *creation* - twice!'

'Of course: created by an interaction between all the laws of physics - all the laws of nature - those we already know, those we may know one day, and some which are perhaps un-knowable to a brain which, after all, has limits: it's just a product of those interactions. The notion that the brain could be an objective analyst of the chance dimensions of its own origins is no more than a reflection of its unique vanity - as supported by the fact that it would be unable to design itself. It knows next-to-nothing, and it understands even less.'

'Anyway, created by some agency other than a super-mind or super-being?'

'Yes - and that's straight Darwin by the way: he makes no apologies for deifying natural selection as an active power: his 'Nature' is the *aggregate action and product of many natural laws*. So at last you're homing in on the relevant question. Personally I would be unable to distinguish between, on the one hand, a supermind capable of understanding and applying all these natural laws and, on the other hand, the sum total of those laws themselves - a Life Force, evidently.'

'Why evidently?'

'Because the net result has been life on earth!'

'So that's your god? An abstraction? A Life Force. Can one *worship* an abstraction?'

'Well, does anybody of sound mind these days suggest worshipping a physical being - made of bone, muscle and sinew? Just think of the adjectives the Anglican liturgy uses for the Almighty: immutable, everlasting, omnipotent, omniscient, transcendent, unforgiving of abuse - it takes *every single adjective and more* to describe the Ultimate Truth.'

'So you are with your Don Cupitt on this?'

'As I interpret Cupitt not at all! He internalizes his god. Nothing could be more external or objective than the sum total of all the laws of nature.'

Charo. 'Now isn't that just like men. Take a simple question and give a complicated answer. What Nikolai was originally asking boils down to a straightforward matter: do you pray, and, if so, to whom or to what? David, answer him, please, then perhaps we can move on to matters of the moment.'

'You know, Dr Sewell, your colleague impresses me more and more.'

'Listen, Nikolai. If we are to continue talking you can stop addressing Dr Jiménez *via* me: she is a very much a person in her own right - and at least as much of a thinker as you or me. Speak to her direct or not at all.'

'My apologies. Well, Dr Sewell, are your prayers directed to your Ultimate Truth?'

'Sure I pray. But not to the vengeful god of the Old Testament - the god who created the world in six days and who needed to be appeased with blood sacrifices and burnt offerings. I would not expect him to get me out of this scrape. And, if he did, where am I going to get an offering to burn at this time of night?

'A child always appealing to a parent for help is never going to become self-sufficient. Prayer can be a focusing of the strengths and realities of one's own resources. Dealing with situations in that way is empowering. Believe me, Nikolai, with the aid of prayer - my sort of prayer - Charo and I shall be getting ourselves out of this one. You can rely on it - and I shall not be looking for miracles.'

'Oliver Cromwell - your God's Englishman - was half-way to that point of view in the 1640s with his *Pray to God - but keep your powder dry* - unless, of course, he was just hedging his bets.'

'I don't have the impression of Cromwell as one who hedged bets.'

'Well, you two boys appear to be reaching some kind of consensus.' It was Charo. 'And, typically, you have overlooked fifty-percent of the matter. Traditional prayer contains a substantial element of giving thanks - where I come from it's about half. And I'm not thinking about Cromwell and his perverse thanks for victory in battle. No, for a lot of people there are moments - lengthy intervals maybe - of feeling rewarded far beyond what it takes to exist in this life. And our response is nothing to do with parents, nor school teaching, nor that it's virtuous to express gratitude. Nor is it because we do a deal with life whereby gratitude qualifies us for further favours. It is simply that there are times when it is instinctively right to focus thanks outside one's self.'

'Charo, I have a suggestion: The instant we are out of here we shall have something to be immensely thankful for. Let's deal with it when the time comes.'

Boris had been on his phone and chose that moment to catch Nikolai's eye with one of his minimalist gestures. After a couple of words in Russian, Boris turned in the direction of the door. Sewell tensed: would this be the moment? Boris reached for the handle. It was now or never. 'I need the toilet. If Boris is going out, can he show me where it is?'

Nikolai affected a gracious gesture. He tossed a small object which flickered in the dim light and which Boris snatched out of the air with a deft gesture inconsistent with his enormous bulk.

'What was that? Another syringe?'

'Just a little LED torch - it's night-time, remember.'

The Bridge - *a love affair*

'Show.' demanded Sewell. Boris demonstrated without hesitation. So, the man understands English after all. Useful to know.

The latter gave another energy-saving gesture and moved towards the door. Sewell must not mess up this chance.

Boris led the way. After a couple of paces they were descending steps. 'Steady on! How about a bit of light: I need to see the steps.' With the torch pointing down between them the circle of light was just large enough to include both pairs of feet - but did not extend far enough to confirm an impression that the flight of stairs was slightly curved - a spiral staircase of huge diameter.

As an opening appeared to the right the sound of waves grew noticeably louder. The tropical scents were suddenly overpowering. A narrow outline of pale, hesitant light suggested a heavy curtain. The beach - or shore - must be only yards away. The escape route! And only a curtain to break through: how typically tropical: the most popular restaurant in São José dos Campos where he had worked in Brazil had been *O Fino*. It had no doors at all: a bit chilly in winter, but luxuriously airy in the summer.

The staircase continued downwards in the gentle spiral, so they were evidently on the way to some sort of basement. Finally they were in an open area dimly lit by illuminated emergency exit signs. Then it was through an archway to two cubicles, both unoccupied. Excellent.

And then he could hardly believe his luck: Boris was clearly as much in need of the facilities as Sewell was affecting to be: the big man forged ahead, entered the far cubicle, slammed the door and slid the catch. Sewell swiftly occupied the first, pushed the door to - but then re-opened it slightly before noisily sliding the catch. As he let the seat drop he un-buckled the titanium clasp of belt, made sound-effects of metal-on-metal and removed the belt completely. The tailored trousers stayed put. Sewell half-unzipped - and re-zipped. A similar sequence of sounds was reaching his ears as he wound several turns of the strap tightly around his right hand, leaving the buckle on the end of a foot or so of leather. Encouraged by a 'plop' from next door, he silently opened the

The Bridge - *a love affair*

door, moved across, stepped back a pace and threw his weight against the closed door. The latch offered no resistance.

He brought the buckle down on the shaven pate with all the force he could muster. With no attempt to rise Boris clasped both hands to his head. Sewell raised the belt again, grimacing in anticipation of the sound of cracking finger bones. However, the hands fell limply to Boris' side just as the blow descended. Sewell watched horrified for perhaps five seconds as a thin, crimson cut slowly opened into a huge elliptical wound. The blood had barely started to flow, and a huge area of bare, white skull was framed in a crimson outline which was slowly expanding from a straight line to an oval.

For no particular reason Sewell expected the man to slump forwards. Instead he fell back, slipping off the seat towards him, jamming Sewell between his enormous legs against the half-open door. It took a while to lever himself free, but the process confirmed that Boris was out for the count.

Holding the belt aloft as a precaution Sewell fished in the jacket pocket for the pistol and transferred it to his own pocket. No sign of a mobile phone. He stepped outside, groped for wash-basin and taps, rinsed the titanium buckle and washed his hands.

It had all taken less than a minute. Nikolai would not come looking - yet, but what if anyone else came in? Half of Boris remained clearly visible. Sewell lifted the left foot high enough to pass behind the door to join the right - and let the considerable weight of the legs close the door. The gap under the door revealed no sign of Boris. Perfect.

As far as it went, that was. He had divided - at least for the time being - but not conquered. The next phase desperately needed some kind of plan. He had a pistol, but had not fired one for years. He retrieved it from his pocket. A Browning! How quaint! Hardly the most probable FSB issue. Stolen - or a dummy replica from e-Bay, perhaps. Was Boris self-employed? Maybe the Russians had started sub-contracting their dirty-work.

But at least he knew the Browning. The safety-catch was on, but the weapon was not cocked. Strange. He would have judged Boris a 'locked-and-cocked' man. He pulled the clip part-way out. Heavy enough to be live rounds.

He put the weapon back in the pocket of his suit-coat and made towards the archway. Stopping abruptly, he turned around. It required all his strength to re-open the door against the weight of the massive limbs. Using one hand to prevent it closing again, he fished through the rest of the pockets and pulled out the 'lighter'. A quick shake suggested that a small amount of 'fuel' remained - enough to make for interesting analysis when - or, rather, if - they got back to the UK.

Releasing the velcro on Boris' shoes he pulled them off. Might as well minimize the chances of his coming in hot pursuit: the trousers were already around the ankles. Yanking them off with one hand was tricky, but getting out if the door slammed behind him would be trickier. The trousers eventually released their hold and he let go the door. Under the weight of Boris' limbs it shut with an impact which shook both cubicles.

He took the opportunity to relieve himself in the nearer cubicle, washed his hands again, checked that the torch has survived the violence, and started back towards the stairs.

Suppose the pistol were a replica. Manufacturers had been pandering to the perfection demanded by weapons fans. Nikolai would know, and Sewell might well be better-off threatening him with a banana. If it were real, and if Nikolai were as out-of-practice as his gratuitous autobiographical account had suggested, there could be a messy shoot out.

Not with Charo there. The pistol was not an asset - at least, not for the moment.

He passed the opening, still curtained off, much too concerned about the next phase to explore.

Even if the door were un-latched he could not just walk in: too much time for Nikolai to grab Charo. Nikolai had to be brought to the door. He gave a confident knock. The muffled response must have been in Russian. What now? Was Boris expected back? He had never felt under such pressure to think fast. 'Come on! My colleague will be busting for the loo by now.'

To his relief the handle moved. The instant the door cracked open he hurled his full weight against it. Carried into the room by his own momentum he hurtled right past Nikolai, who kept his balance by holding on to the door handle. But at least Sewell was between him and Charo. Nikolai did not even reach for a weapon. The room was bare: there were no candle-sticks to grab, no bottles. This was going to be a punch-up pure and simple. Nikolai was younger, but Sewell had lost little muscle-mass since his ballast-shovelling days - and nothing whatsoever of his determination. Taking a step forward he aimed a punch at the Russian's head. The blow threw the recipient against the wall behind the door, but had not connected where it had been aimed. Nikolai bounced back off the wall while Sewell lurched forward and to one side.

The position was now reversed, Nikolai with his nose pouring blood but still on his feet, and between himself and Charo. He must get no chance to turn to Charo. Sewell took a step forward and, in a move that would have taken an ocelot by surprise, Charo dropped to her knees behind Nikolai. *What a girl.* Sewell's second punch landed right on target. For an instant there was flailing of arms, then a sharp crack of skull against hard floor. Charo was already pushing Nikolai's legs out of the way, and Sewell helped her to her feet.

'I'd say we make quite a team: Darwinism one moment; guerrilla warfare the next.'

Sewell loosened Nikolai's belt and together they rolled him onto his stomach. A couple of turns of belt around the arms at elbow level, pass the free end through the buckle, pull tight and - bingo. 'Sorry about this Nikolai. But look on the bright side: I've got a brand new licence-to-kill. Ink's hardly dry. It's a big temptation to test it.'

The jacket pockets yielded Sewell's wrist watch and no fewer than three mobile phones. Charo selected hers. Nikolai's phone joined the syringe for later analysis. The other pocket yielded a pistol. It felt a bit light, and Sewell did not recognize the make. Stage prop, possibly. Would explain why Nikolai had not even attempted to draw it.

The man was wearing polished, slip-on shoes - or had been until Sewell slipped them off. Without even exchanging glances, they each picked up a handle of the hold-all and made for the door. 'Wait. Assuming we find a way out of this building, we've still got to vanish into the local scenery, find out what the language is, what are possible routes home - and all the time hobbled by this bag. We need all the head-start we can get. Minutes will be crucial.'

'So what are we waiting for? Let's go!'

'Give a hand with Nikolai. Roll him onto his back. We're going to take his trousers.'

With the belt already tied up elsewhere the trousers were rapidly removed.

'And the under-pants.'

'Do we have to?'

'If the chances of getting a head start increase by one percent, then yes, we do: for all we know tomorrow could be Sunday and the locals might take their Sundays rather seriously. If so, lack of trousers *and* underwear could keep Nick off the streets until the shops open on Monday morning.'

'Best leave the door closed.' suggested Sewell. 'Put the bag down a moment.' With the door still open he could try the inside handle with one hand and the outside with the other. It was soon obvious how it locked from the outside. 'You take the torch. I can cope with the shoes and clothes with my free hand. We're off - but don't rush it: I think the steps are on a slight spiral. Makes it easy to mis-judge - and we don't want to trip.'

They were soon at the heavy curtain. 'This has to be the exit. Hold on here while I check the coast's clear.' He pulled the curtain slowly to one side. 'Still can't see much: it's a kind of short tunnel.' He let go the curtain, advanced a few paces - and was back in an instant. You're not going to believe this!'

'Well?

'The bag'll be fine for a second. Come in here.'
They returned through the curtain together. '*Madre mia! No es possible!*'
'Oh yes it is. Ever felt you have been taken for a ride?'

6
Less steam, more traction

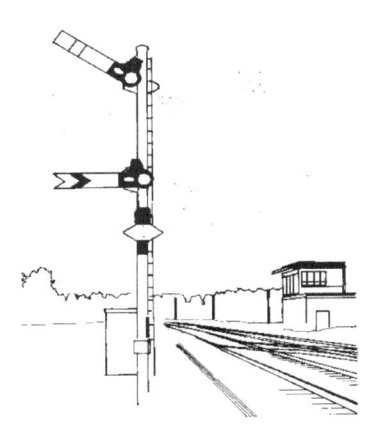

'No me lo creo! Un I-Max!'

The cunning old Nikolai! Of course! Municipal authorities had been commandeering cinemas as night shelters. Some - this one, evidently - ran soporific digital beamer images continuously over-night. Some UK cinemas did a turn as soup kitchens during the day. This one was a soup kitchen without the soup - or maybe the soup was a subtle blend of jacarandá and maracujá. 'Let's find the real exit. Suddenly I've had enough of tropics from a spray can.

'The only way from here is down. Come on.'

Picking up the hold-all they were soon passing the area where the toilets were situated. Someone was hammering on a cubicle door, encouraging the occupant in a limited vocabulary of four-letter words to complete his business and to vacate. English four-letter words! An I-Max in some UK town then!

A large area of pale natural light suggested an exit, and they were soon on the street. It was night, and a silver moon hung in a clear sky - a moon in its last quarter!

They set the bag down yet again. In the earlier haste Sewell had put his wrist-watch into a jacket pocket. He returned it to its rightful place: 'Five past four - and it's Wednesday 28th. No wonder we're not starving: not all that long since we were in Whitehall. Means we're probably not far from London either.'

'Don't you English usually ask a policeman?'

'Invariably - when there's one to ask.'

'So what are we going to do? Call a cab? Call the Ministry on that special number?'

'We'll get more thanks for waking somebody at four a.m. if we can tell them where we are. Assuming we're still in the UK there can't be all that many I-Max. Just for the moment I'm not sure where we start. The only certainty is that we've got to get moving. Nikolai and Boris are not in this alone. Sooner or later someone's going to check up on them.'

As if to confirm the prediction a ring-tone sounded. 'Not me.' It was Charo.

'Not mine either - unless Security changed the ring-tone in London.' He pulled two phones from the jacket pocket. 'It's Nikiolai's - it's them. Decision - quick.'

'If you take the call can they get a position fix on it?'

'Charo. However much they're paying you, it's not enough. Good girl.' He returned the phone, still ringing, to his pocket. 'Let's walk.'

'Where are we going?'

'Let's stay in the moonlight. Across this pedestrian area - see where it leads.'

After a dozen paces or so, Sewell looked around. *The Aquarium*! 'Charo. You are never going to believe this! It can only be the old Bristol I-Max. We must have been in the projection room. We're in Bristol!'

'How far's your place. You design engines which are way too heavy. I'm getting tired. Let's just bed down there. And I need the loo.'

'They know where I live for sure.'

'OK, then. Forget it's past somebody's bed-time. Ring that Ministry number.'

Once more the hold-all was set down. Looking around and thinking for several seconds Sewell scrolled through the directory for *Andorinha* and pressed. The response was instantaneous. Not in bed, anyway. 'I've been given this number because . . . '

'Where are you?'

'Got any transport in Bristol?'

'Just say where you want to be picked up.'

Sewell looked around again. 'How about Prince Street bridge? Give us twenty minutes - we got ourselves a bit lost in the dark.' Without a further word the other party rang off.

'Where's the bridge.'

'You're looking at it.'

'That's not twenty minutes' walk away.'

'No. And the chap who took the call may not be the Ministry. They think Nikolai is on our side - and he had his hands on our phones, remember? I find it hard to believe that Whitehall have got anything operating from Bristol at twenty minutes' notice. We stay here and keep eyes and ears open. If the transport looks friendly we can ring again and tell them we're still a few steps away.'

Either twenty minutes passed in record time, or things started happening more quickly than expected: the stillness of the small hours was cut by the characteristic sizzling of bicycle free-wheel mechanisms as two helmeted riders on mountain bikes sped down Prince Street, stopping just short of the bridge. The machines were wheeled out of sight and the riders melted into the shadows. Two more could be seen arriving - and taking cover - at the south end of the bridge. With fifteen minutes still to go, all fell silent again.'

'Now what?'

'Well, that's one route we don't take.'

'Route to where? Where are we heading anyway?'

'To Didcot. We're due at a conference, remember? That means train, and train means Temple Meads station.'

'And where's that?'
'Ten minutes' walk away.'
'When's the train?'
'Six-thirty.'
'So we hide in someone's garden till six, nip to the station and mingle with the crowd?'
'Won't work.'
'Why not?'
'They don't even need to be able to recognize us: How many couples will be carrying an over-size hold-all between them? They've got the advantage: we don't know them from Adam. I can't believe Boris is the only one who's been issued with a magic cigarette lighter. Someone in the crowd on the platform jostles us and jabs us. We keel over, they announce themselves to be para-medics and help us with our bag back to face the music - music played by Nikolai and Boris. Not for me, thanks.'
'What then, Mr Bond?'
'We get ourselves to the station right now. Grab the bag.'
'Haven't you just contradicted yourself, James?'
'They don't need to look for us before six.' He dropped the bundle of trousers and footwear in the water as they crossed Pero's bridge. 'The carriage doors are locked until the locomotive is coupled up - and she's in the shed being fired up for the run. They will probably place a watch on my place in Leigh Woods. We know they're based locally: so they'll go back to bed. I'd say we've got the streets to ourselves 'til six. But for one thing we could stroll to the station in the middle of the road singing your signature tune.'
'What's that one thing?'
'Life has been trying to tell me that I shall run into fewer problems if I learn to expect the unexpected. We'll take advantage of what cover we can find, keep our ears open - and leave the singing until we're out of the wood.'

'To the station it is, then, conceded Charo wearily. She reached down for the handle of the hold-all. It's your Bristol. Let's go. And what's my signature tune by the way?'

'Could be either of those you used to sing non-stop in London: *You fill up my senses* - John Denver, wasn't it? - or the Spanish one: *Yo recuerdo aquel día que nos fuimos a bañar.*'

'Memory for trivia: excellent. Pronunciation: lamentable - but yes. Both mean a great deal to me still.'

For a while they walked in silence. Then: 'Your family isn't from Bristol, is it? I know - because you took me to meet your mother once - train from Paddington to Moreton-in-something-or-other where you kept your car, then on to a small village.'

'Moreton-in-Marsh. Someone else has a memory too! You're quite right: moved to Bristol on retiring from retirement. I'd been living in the previous house for thirty-four years. After that length of time you're functioning on auto-pilot. Only a comprehensive shake-up would do. I considered returning to the town where I had been born and spent my teens, but everybody warned that would be turning the clock back too far - that the comparisons would always be un-settling. I had never lived - or even stayed overnight - in Bristol, so that qualified it as a shake-up. But also it held an air of mystery for me - a fascination not far short of magic - possibly because I encountered it in a magical context - can try to explain if you want.'

'You may explain if we can just put the bag down for a moment and swap arms.'

They stopped, taking the opportunity to look around and listen. Sewell pressed on: 'My childhood was spent during post-war austerity. The family got a holiday by the sea each year thanks to distant relatives who ran a bed-and-breakfast in Weston Super Mare. If there was a room spare, we got it for a week for next-to-nothing - cost of the breakfasts, maybe. We had no car. However, a coach company - Black and White Motorways - ran a service from Cheltenham *via* Bristol. All we had to do was get to Cheltenham - which we did *via* Stratford.'

105

The Bridge - *a love affair*

They picked up the hold-all again and set off. 'I always aimed for a window seat on the right of the bus because the Bomford and Evershed yard was on that side: the bridge over the railway at Salford Priors gave a view of a whole Industrial Revolution's-worth of steam-powered machinery: traction engines, steam rollers, ploughing engines and iron-wheeled road-man's wagons. If this sounds like a digression I suppose it is, but half-a-century later I got to know a Norris Bomford. Turned out he is the great-grandson of one of the two men who had founded the company in 1904. Norris' Stirling-powered skiff may have been a UK first - but what you need to know right now is that he is due at ERU - like us. You'll really enjoy meeting him.'

'Yes! And the first thing I shall ask him is whether his Stirling engines are as heavy as yours.'

'He'll have an answer for you: he's great value-for-money. So's the entire family. Business acumen runs in the veins: the two daughters started their own business from scratch. It took less than two years to achieve fame and fortune. Did a UK TV programme *The Apprentice* make it as far as Spain?'

'I've heard of it.'

'Well, those two make an *Apprentice* win look like a failed attempt to give away Smarties at school play-time. And, by the way, you are carrying the lightest Stirling engine that ever turned out five kilowatts.'

'That must be why we've got to put it down again right now so that I can change hands.' Sewell obliged. 'You might as well carry on reminiscing: I'm physically and mentally numb.'

'The change at Cheltenham was to something more like a twentieth-century vehicle - a coach with diesel engine, no less, and boasting a 'Royal Tiger' chassis according to lettering on the side. Coaches didn't have audio systems back then, but a running commentary from my father compensated: from Stroud southwards we would be subjected to an oral build-up to the suspension bridge - *the* suspension bridge. He had worked as a plant layout draughtsman in Coventry's

The Bridge - *a love affair*

thriving automobile industry - structural design - but that alone could hardly have accounted for the passion he obviously felt for the bridge.

'The road into Bristol passed beneath the bridge, and as we left it behind there was an anti-climax you could have photographed - but always the chance of a counter-attraction on the opposite side of gorge: the explosion of steam and smoke from the rail tunnel exit as a tank locomotive popped out.

'In those days there was no soul-less, concrete, efficient Brunel Way: the coach had to thread its way around the floating harbour. Those gigantic metal lock gates looked - and were - capable of holding back a whole tide. The biggest building I had ever seen towered over everything - the W.D. & H.O. Wills tobacco building.'

They had reached the point where Temple Gate merges with Bath Road. 'That's the station. We've made it. One last change-over and we're home and dry.'

'I thought you English had an expression *don't holler until you're out of the wood*. Seems to me there's more wood ahead than behind.'

'We have - and there is. But trust me. Come on.'

The last fifty yards would give time to finish the account of his childhood introduction to Bristol - but was this the moment? From the security of the coach he had found it possible to contemplate the lock with its hints at other-worldly mystery - inky-black, bottomless, brooding, quasi-stagnant, sullen. On foot he would have been unable to approach it, and doing so would cause him difficulties to this very day. Locks - and one canal lock in particular on the Wey Navigation - had provided the experience which had convinced him of the reality of epi-genetics. Thinking about it sent shivers down the spine. Save it for later, maybe.

They reached the short, paved area leading into the old Passenger Shed. On the far side of the approach road Sewell fancied he could see the outline of his bike. 'Still there. Good omen. Feels like a month since I was tethering it to the hawser. Let's go.'

The ticket barrier would be manned twenty-four hours a day, but at this hour those doing the manning might be awake - or they might not. Either way, Sewell anticipated no problem: was he not back in possession of his hologram warrant card? - and, in any case, the two Army Reserve volunteers on duty would be junior to him.

In the event, they were sound asleep (why not take it as another good omen?), remaining in that blissful state while the barrier was raised and lowered. Sewell and Charo turned left onto the first platform and walked towards the roller-shutter door.

The next move would require thinking through. He had no idea whether tonight's duty engineer would be from the Reserve and - expect the unexpected - Nikolai's lot may have second-guessed and headed for the engine shed. Well, the only way now was forward and - yet another good omen: the wicket gate was wide open! 'Charo. The gods are on our side. See that bottom rail? Just don't trip over it - or even kick it. You'll wake the dead.'

Token illumination from the two light bulbs suspended from the high ceiling cast more shadow than light, but there was sufficient of the latter to confirm that the locomotive quietly simmering and making occasional ticking noises was Tornado.

They were beside the tender with a hold-all which now felt at least twice as heavy as when they had started out from the I-Max. Sewell indicated downwards and it was lowered gently to the floor.

Thoughtful drivers would use the last gasp of the coal fire to deliver the locomotive to the shed at the end of the evening run. This eased the overnight maintenance task of clearing the smoke box of ash, raking clinker out of the grate and either keeping a small fire going or re-lighting. It was then only necessary to keep an eye on boiler pressure and water level and to stoke as necessary. But for an occasional whiff of steam up the blast pipe to draw the fire, rate of water consumption would be low. An engineer bent on getting away with a perfunctory job could get the oiling done and then make a brief visit to the cab once in fifteen or twenty minutes. Much now depended upon whether the engineer was dozing on one of the seats in the cab, or whether he (or she) was

The Bridge - *a love affair*

occupied in the PortaKabin set against the far wall - and, indeed, whether he (or she) was being restrained by Nikolai's lot.

He trod silently along the right-hand side of the tender as far as the cab steps. The cab door on his side was open. A gently pulsating glow from the partially open fire-doors illuminated the roof and far side of the cab.

The steps to the cab were high anyway, and the extra height of the rails above the floor put them effectively out of reach. He might haul himself up to the first step, but then what about the hold-all - and Charo?

Clearly, the engineer and crew did not have to face this problem, so there must be a platform or a ladder or something the other side. He walked back towards Charo. 'Don't follow me - in fact, don't move: there may be a pit between the rails. I'll be back.'

He walked to the rear of the tender and explored between the rails with his foot. The pit - if there were one - evidently did not extend that far. He crossed cautiously - this was not the moment to trip. And there it was, a set of steps sitting next to the cab. Perfect! Steps can be moved - borrowed, you might say.

Everything now hung on getting those steps around behind the tender without being detected. A minute or so watching for some sign of life would be a good investment. To the left of the PortaKabin a solid-fuel fire glowed, and sitting on top of it a small machine was making a high-speed ticking noise. The source of electricity: with petroleum fuels virtually unobtainable, engineers both amateur and professional had lost no time in re-realizing the nineteenth-century 'hot-air' engine using commonly-available twenty-first century materials. A couple of stainless-steel vacuum flasks of slightly different diameters and you were half-way to an engine. Two hundred and fifty watts from the engine he was looking at would power the light in the PortaKabin and the two bulbs overhead which swayed gently in the air currents convected from the hot boiler. The moving shadows could not have offered better cover. He walked crouching as far as the steps, kneeled and looked around. The steps were light-weight - domestic variety.

Picking them up easily he walked towards the rear of the tender with an eye on the PortaKabin door.

There were a few paces to go when the level of hissing from the boiler increased slightly. He hesitated. There followed an ear-splitting screech. He froze. Obvious: safety-valve blowing - but would it be the cue for someone to come and make an adjustment? As suddenly as it had begun the hissing stopped, giving way to deafening silence. Still nothing from the PortaKabin. Grasping the steps he walked smartly behind the tender and set his trophy down beside Charo.

'We're in business.' Sewell carried the steps in one hand and shared the weight of the hold-all in the other. He was soon holding on to the handrails with his eyes level with the cab floor. Empty! His heart now pumping with a mixture of apprehension and excitement, he climbed into the cab, and looked down at Charo. For there to be any chance of passing the hold-all up hand-to-hand, Charo would have to lift it above her head. Not possible! It would be one thing to steal a locomotive with a view to returning Government property - but another thing entirely to abandon the goods and make a personal get-away.

Whoever was tending the locomotive took little pride in doing so. Lumps of coal littered the floor, a broom lolled against the tender on the fireman's side, and the handle of the stoking shovel protruded into the cab from the floor of the coal hopper. Propped in a corner was a long metal rod, more than a centimeter in diameter, with a loop at one end and formed into an L-shape at the other. The tool for raking the clinker from between the fire bars! Any self-respecting fireman would have returned it after use to its stowage in the tender - but if he had, Sewell would not have known where to look for it!

He grasped the rod, lowering the cranked end towards the hold-all. Words were not needed: Charo slipped the two carrying loops into position. As he hauled on the rod she took part of the weight until the hold-all was above her head. With the cargo safely on board Sewell reached down and helped her up the steps.

Nothing to be gained by looking at the boiler pressure: the safety valve had just said it all: if she didn't move off it would not be for

110

The Bridge - *a love affair*

lack of a head of steam. He looked for the mechanical parking brake in the customary place - on the tender bulk-head. An initial tug and the handle un-wound easily and quietly. The valve gear had been left in neutral and would need cranking into the full-ahead position. Sewell tried the gear handle. Like the tender brake, it moved readily and smoothly - surprising considering the weight of the linkage to which it connected ahead of the cab.

It was now or never: The levers which actuated the cylinder drains were in the open position. The technique on his driver experience courses had been to crack the regulator open - but then to shut it again immediately. This let a limited amount of steam - or steam and water - into the superheater and from there into the cylinders to get the locomotive rolling. If it worked for a Standard Five locomotive it should work for Tornado.

In the confines of the engine shed the hiss from the cylinder drains numbed the senses. But then - nothing? Sewell looked at Charo, then to his left, where a rectangular area of yellow light showed that the PortaKabin door had opened.

After all that! He looked back at the expressionless face of Charo. As he searched for something to say he was aware of the light overhead becoming brighter. No - it wasn't getting brighter! Tornado had made the gentlest of starts and they were passing beneath one of the shed lights.

Could this hundred-and-twenty-ton machine really ease off so smoothly? Suddenly the locomotive emitted a crisp exhaust 'chuff' which had to be the most beautiful music Sewell had ever heard. Successive chuffs became rapidly weaker. Good news: no water had passed into the superheater and flashed into steam. Sewell carried out another open-and-shut on the regulator.

They were still not aware of acceleration, but they were certainly moving. Someone was running by the side of the cab, arm outstretched towards the hand-rail. The cab door would not hold back a determined boarding party, but Sewell slammed it shut anyway. He reached for the shovel and waited for hands or a head to appear. He need

The Bridge - *a love affair*

not have bothered: at that moment the locomotive burst out of the shed. The heavy, vertical plastic strips which served for doors had taken care of the prospective boarding party.

He cracked the regulator open, and this time left it open. The exhaust beats were now crisp barks and speed was building alarmingly. 'Hey - I think that was the coaling hopper we just passed under.'

'So?'

'If that's where she's coaled up for the trip then we might be low on coal.'

'So let's back up and do it!'

'Good grief, no: they will be on us before we've worked out how to use the hopper. I'll have a look how much we've got, and carry on until we run out. We seem to have a tender full of water - that's the most important thing.'

He had no idea where the siding curved to join the main line, but it would be unsafe to rely on its being a high-speed radius. He wound back the gear handle to the 35 percent mark. The exhaust softened, but speed continued to build. He pushed the regulator fully closed. The sound of the exhaust disappeared, but there was no sense of deceleration: a steam locomotive can be impressively free-running. There were two levers on the driver's side which resembled the brakes on the standard five. If that's what they were, one would be the locomotive brake, the other could be a vacuum brake for the coach set. He couldn't be sure, and had no idea of the consequences of actuating the wrong one. They were still rolling at 35 miles per hour. Sewell pulled Charo unceremoniously aside and spun the handle of the mechanical tender brake as fast as he could. It took several turns for the brake to start to bite, but when it did it was reassuringly effective. They were not being followed, so they could trickle onto the main line at five miles per hour - vastly preferable to coming off the track.

They felt a slight lurch first to the right, then to the left. They were on the main track and on their way to Didcot - and in the most handsome locomotive that ever ran on rails!

On an ordinary day the crew would stop, the points would be switched and the locomotive run back to pick up the carriages. This, however, was no ordinary day. He closed the cylinder drains and the hissing stopped. 'Charo. You've seen how that tender brake works: get it un-wound.'

He pulled the steam whistle handle three times. 'Charo: one for you, one for me, and one for luck'.

The Bridge - *a love affair*

7

Bolero

'Provided we don't let the fire go out - and don't forget to check the water level - it's Didcot next stop.' pronounced Sewell. 'Without carriages we're carrying more than enough coal and water - but a steam locomotive needs the right amount of both.'

A pair of water-level gauges was rapidly located in the usual place. 'These indicate accurately provided we're not braking, accelerating, or going up- or down-hill. We're doing none of these things at the moment.' He opened and closed the blow-down cock of the nearer of the two gauges. 'This is the water level - about two-thirds up the sight-glass right now. Safest thing is for both of us to take a look at regular intervals. When it drops we operate the steam injector. I'd better remind myself how to do that straight away. You keep looking out of the driver's window. Shout if you see a red light: we're not stopping for anything other than a solid object - but we should at least slow down.'

There would be two injectors, one actuated by steam at boiler pressure, the other by exhaust steam, so: look for two, similar valve housings, both with two connections, one for steam, the other for water. The wheel of the unit on the left opened to a gratifying increase in the background simmering sounds from the boiler. The pressure gauge indicated a slight fall. Both signs of cold water entering the boiler. Good.

'Better check the fire.' He opened the fire door. 'There was talk of Tornado having - or getting - an automatic stoker. Either way, I wouldn't know what to do with it. Here's the fire and there's the shovel, so nothing lost. When I was on the shovel at Nene Valley Railway the aim was to keep the depth of the fire uniform over the entire grate. Tornado's got a huge grate area. If we need you to shovel, don't just throw it all to the middle. Maybe concentrate on one quarter of the grate at any one time - and don't neglect the part nearest the fire-door: try to fling it around the corner - left and right.'

Another tug on the regulator. The effect of the exhaust beat on the fire was hypnotic: Each beat drew a gulp of fire into the boiler tubes.

'We're free!' said Charo. 'But with all those cross-over things how do we know we're going towards London and not Blackpool?'

'We don't. But this is the only service, at least as far as Swindon. I don't see any reason for re-setting the points between runs. There are catch-points to divert run-away wagons - but it wouldn't make sense to risk de-railing three-million pounds-worth of locomotive.'

'In that case I *must* have a go on the whistle.'

'It's open countryside out there: there's no-one to object.'

She experimented with several blasts, long and short. 'It's no good. I've got to dance.'

Of course, Charo's passion for Flamenco. 'What? Here? Now?'

'Have you forgotten London? Can't you feel that three-four rhythm? Well, it's too fast. You're just not paying attention. Slow it down - right down. Do you know Bolero?'

It took a hefty shove to close the regulator. 'Ravel: I should hope so.'

'Could you knock out the rhythm on something if I sing the top line? It's a two-bar pattern in three/four: dumdiddly, dumdiddly dum-dum; dumdiddly, dumdiddly diddly-diddly.'

'So it is - and guess what! Tornado is a three-cylinder locomotive, which means six beats per revolution of the main wheels - or two bars of three/four!

'Ravel's tempo marking was crotchet 72. How many of your English miles per hour is that?'

'No idea - but it's only arithmetic to find out: the driving wheels are six feet eight inches in diameter, so one revolution takes us six-and-two-thirds times pi - times three-and-a-bit. Say, 21 feet - roughly: I forgot to pack my calculator.'

'OK - so how fast?'

'You get six 'chuffs' every 21 feet. You want 72 'chuffs' each minute, so that's 72/6 revolutions - exactly 12 revolutions per minute.'

'Come on, before I get too old for this dancing business.'

'Patience, woman! 12 revolutions takes us 12 times 21 feet - a bit more than 240 - say 250 feet.'

'Well, professor?'

'Easier than it might have been: there are 5280 feet in a mile, so we want to go 240/5280 feet in one minute - or that amount multiplied 60 miles in an hour: a bit less than three miles per hour. Tornado is a race-horse. Who knows whether she likes walking to heel.'

'So is it going to be arithmetic all day - or do we find out! It's getting light, and I want to dance.'

The only way to keep life bearable on the footplate would be to do as the woman said. With the regulator closed, and thanks to a slight upwards gradient, Tornado had coasted to what seemed like walking pace. The needle of the speedometer was sitting off the bottom of the scale, so it was going to be a case of playing by ear.

The steam regulator has a long handle partly because no-one has ever managed to design an admission valve which is not stiff. The eventual setting - if there was to be one - had to be found by successive tugs and pushes on the handle. Sewell gave a tentative tug. Nothing. A second. Tornado obliged with a succession of restrained, clipped 'chuffs'. Not uniform, because the valve gear had remained at maximum

The Bridge - *a love affair*

cut-off, where slight mis-adjustments and wear have the most noticeable effect.

But then the 'chuffs' petered out - with no reduction in speed.

'No good. She's not pulling a load, and she's so free-running it takes only the slightest whiff of steam to keep her going.'

'If what this 'she' of yours needs is something to pull, then she's about to get it.' Charo turned around and began winding the handle of the tender brake.

'That's just a park-brake: we don't want to overheat the shoes.'

'I don't know what's happened to you since we lived in London - but it's not an improvement. Do I get my 72 'chuffs' per minute at 3 miles per hour or do I drive while you shovel?'

Sewell kept silent - but Tornado obliged. Charo uttered a squeal of delight: 'Perfect, Sewell, perfect. I always knew you had genius waiting for the moment to shine.' She looked round, located the hand-bag, blew off a layer of coal-dust and reached inside.

'That bag's for carrying *castanets*!?

'What would you rather it be used for - rolling tobacco? syringe - needles? Now, just sing dumdiddly, dumdiddly dum-dum *etc.* and hit that tea kettle thing - preferably in time with the singing. Quietly to start with: Bolero starts *pp* - double-piano.'

Sewell waited for the strongest 'chuff', held off for another two 'bars' and launched into what was to be his first ever foot-plate accompaniment - and last, probably, if he didn't get it right.

Charo was instantaneously transformed - no longer the boffin. One arm reached upwards with wrist and elbow at the jagged angle connoting one thing only - Flamenco. The other arm mirrored the gesture downwards. With head angled sideways and downwards she was a tightly-coiled spring waiting to explode.

But an explosion was evidently not the plan: joining in after Sewell's improvized four-bar introduction, she began a slow, sinuous writhing while humming Ravel's introductory statement of the haunting flute melody. Under the effect of the hypnotic combination of pent-up energy and restraint Sewell found himself tapping out the two-bar riff without even concentrating. How many times had he been told that music 'played the musician' rather than vice-versa? Suddenly, and in a somewhat improbable location, he was experiencing that reality.

On retiring from retirement (a purely nominal gesture as things had worked out) Sewell had committed an average of an hour a week to attempts to adapt a basic proficiency in classical piano into a facility in jazz. The experience had left him with the conviction that the only hope was to be born again with the innate ability for independent control of left and right hands. Not that a jazz performance should sound like two, one-armed musicians at different pianos. Just the reverse: the elusive effect to which he aspired was the apparently effortless integration of left- and right-hand elements into a tasteful rhythmic whole.

Something of the sort was now unfolding before his eyes - and ears. Tornado was obliging with metronomic adherence to tempo, and Charo's movements were gaining emphasis. Humming had given way to wordless song. As the swings of the torso reversed direction, the hem of her mid-length skirt swept first the tender and then the fire doors. It did not remain stationary long enough for Sewell to see whether it was black with coal dust - although it seemed safe to assume it would be.

How, he wondered, was it possible for human movement to be supremely sensuous and yet free from all hint of cheap eroticism? The question might, perhaps, be discussed in terms of aesthetics. After all, at one level Tornado was so much iron, steel and phosphor-bronze harmonized by a layer of coach-paint. But the whole was possessed of an aesthetic which spoke to the emotions as directly as any work of art.

The orchestration was augmented at last by the foot-tapping and stamping - as Sewell well knew it would be. At least this time there would be no neighbours registering complaints - although he was suddenly less certain: the regular check through the driver's window confirmed that they were entering a built-up area - the outskirts of Bath, possibly. How Charo's footwork could cut through the background noise of a hundred-and-twenty ton steam locomotive - admittedly doing a

The Bridge - *a love affair*

crawling pace - was something of a wonder. Presumably, like many of her generation, she had fallen back on stocks of obsolete leather shoes when the modern, un-repairable variety had worn out. At any rate, the clatter, as it had been on the kitchen floor of the flat in Marble Arch, could well have been audible to early risers in Bath - of which there would be many aiming to be out with the first of the scavengers.

Bolero is famous for building to its climax by adding instruments of the orchestra to an essentially un-developed motif. The modest four-piece orchestra (Sewell, Charo and Tornado as percussion section, Charo on flute, deputizing on clarinet, oboe, bassoon *etc.*) had little scope to follow Ravel's performance instructions, but with jaw-dropping initiative - and possibly some prior practice - Charo had both defied and accommodated the master: she had been slowly incrementing body movements, voice, castanets and percussive footwork until, finally, all synchronized into explicit statement of the rhythmic theme.

Sewell had retreated into his hypnotic state: with apologies to the good citizens of Bath, and to the rationing and despair they faced that morning, he was transported to an alternative reality. Even Tornado was an animate part of the shared consciousness.

A partial return to earth was called for in order to anticipate the ending of the piece. There could be no trombone glissando *via* a discord to the home key. How would Charo manage this one?

The blinding flash was accompanied by a stunning explosion. Sewell felt himself thrown against the driver's side of the cab. Attempts at taking a breath were gagged as his throat snapped shut like a non-return valve. The tissues of his nose, tongue, mouth and throat instantly gained a thin film of brittle rice-paper laced with phosphoric acid.

He fought for air and managed to propel a shallow cough. Drawing a tentative half-breath, he coughed more productively. The procedure was repeated several times accompanied by shameless spitting onto the cab floor. Eventually, by blinking non-stop, he was able to see Charo going through a similar procedure. A further minute or so later he was able to croak: 'What the hell was that?

8

Energy Research Unit

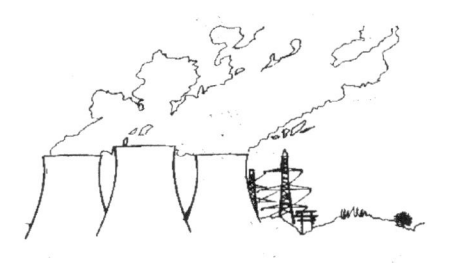

The locomotive had continued at the earlier, steady pace. Charo was leaning out of the cab on the fireman's side - convulsions suggesting that she was vomiting. The swirling dust was clearing - but there was neither sight nor sound of escaping steam. He looked at the pressure gauge. Unchanged. He operated the cocks on the water sight-glasses. Water level a bit low, but still between the marks. They had not, after all, let the water level drop and fused a plug in the fire-box.

'Sewell - look!'

Charo had stepped back into the cab. On the parallel track was a tank locomotive running next to them in reverse. Someone was on the coal hopper taking aim with a hand-held object. A stun grenade! That's what it had been: Must have landed at the bottom of Tornado's coal hopper, sending the blast into the cab through the door in the tender.

'Go Sewell, go!' She was already unwinding the brake. 'Go! What are you waiting for?'

He tugged the regulator to something like half-way. 'We can't turn this into a race: We'd win hands down if we knew what we were doing, but that would mean knowing the road. There are cross-overs every so often: If we hit them too fast we could come off the rails - depends how they're set. If we hit one neck-and-neck we could both be de-railed. We'll just have to keep accelerating and braking so that they can't get another direct shot.'

The brakes of a steam locomotive can operate unexpectedly smoothly - and firmly. Shoving the regulator closed with one hand, he operated the brake lever. The tank locomotive fairly shot ahead, the would-be bomber still sitting on the coal hopper poised to throw.

'Rather an extreme reaction to our recital, don't you think.'

'Nothing wrong with the performance itself. They must be from the Performing Rights Society: you need a licence to do what we've been doing.'

Sewell released the brake, tugged the regulator half open and Tornado overtook again. They could keep this up to Didcot if necessary - but Charo was going to have to do all the shovelling.

'They are taking one hell of a chance: if anything is coming on the down line they will hit it head on. We've got to stay ahead or run the risk of hitting wreckage.'

A red light flashed past on the driver's side as Chippenham station was passed at seventy-five miles per hour. Two offences for the price of one! Fifteen miles to Swindon: twelve minutes or so at this speed. The tank locomotive was falling noticeably behind. Sewell shut the regulator.

'Why are we slowing? Fast is fun.'

'We're not stopping. We are just not pushing our luck by going faster than necessary. Have you thought how lucky we have been to get this far? If we can stay on the rails as far as Swindon I think we'll see something interesting.'

Charo shovelled: she was getting good. Sewell operated the injector a couple of times to top up the water level. Both of them kept an eye on the pursuing locomotive. To Sewell's un-trained eye it was making disproportionate amounts of smoke and steam. Perhaps their footplate was manned by amateurs as well!

Another red light. Sewell touched the brake. 'You haven't suddenly gone soft, have you?'

'Swindon coming up. We need to see what happens.'

The Bridge - *a love affair*

Progress during Bolero had been slow, meaning they were entering Swindon only a short time before Tornado would normally have been due with its customary rake of coaches. The platform ahead was already quite full. 'Keep an eye on that tank engine. Tell me what happens. We can't hurtle past this crowd: they are expecting a normal arrival - not a fly-past.'

Another application of the brake and: 'The tank engine's disappeared - behind the far platform.'

'They will reappear at the other end of the station - or they won't.' There was not long to wait. Sewell opened up again before the end of the platform and they were soon gathering speed. Tracks converged from left and right to disappear beneath Tornado's wheels. Of the tank engine there was no sign. 'They are in a siding somewhere. So much for their navigation. Hope they managed to stop - for the sake of the siding - not theirs.'

'Maybe thirty miles now to Didcot.'

'Seeing all those passengers changes things. Shouldn't we have stopped? They'd have been only too glad to offer us road transport to Rutherford in exchange for getting their locomotive back - in a chauffeur-driven Rolls Royce in all probability.'

'Have you thought how long it would take to explain? At Didcot the locomotive is theirs. You can bet someone will be there to pick us up: they must have put two and two together by now.'

'Sewell, you were going to tell me about your epi-genetic experience. Does it fit the timetable to Didcot?'

'Why not? My mother had been one of seven siblings - who threw her out of the family home at a young age. Fortunately she had somewhere to go - to Byfleet rectory, where a live-in servant, a dear lady called Dorothy, became her *de facto* mother and eventually my 'auntie'.

'Dorothy married Bert, and they moved into their own house in West Byfleet. My mother married, moved away and I was born - but, at every excuse mother could contrive, she took me by train - steam train, of course - to visit my 'aunt' and 'uncle'.

123

The Bridge - *a love affair*

'Dorothy had a dog - a Sealyham - called Sarah. I must have been eight or nine at the time - anyway, old enough to be trusted to take Sarah for walks. A walk she particularly liked was along the towpath of a canal - the Basingstoke - from Scotland Bridge east. That day we must have gone further than usual: just before where the M25 crosses today there is a lock. We got within sight of the lock gates and I froze - nightmare feeling in the spine. Fear - fear of nothing in particular - just pure, unadulterated, disembodied fear. My feet had turned to lead. Turning around was a real effort of will, but I got moving again back the way we had come. Sarah had still been pulling, so this was the reverse of the usual show of canine sixth sense.

'Back at Dorothy's house I told my mother. I can remember the feeling of betrayal when she made no comment: mothers are supposed to reassure about anything and everything. She left it until we had got back to our own home.

'She had already told me many times about one of her brothers having been something of a cricketer. Apparently it had been routine for him to be carried shoulder-high from the cricket field having won the match pretty-well single-handed. However, being a local hero had not saved him from call-up to the First World War.

'But she had never before told me what had followed. Presumably painful memories are bottled-up until some purpose is served by letting them out. Anyway, the brother had been one of the lucky ones who not only survived, but had done so un-injured, and had come home and received a gratuity. He had taken it - or some of it - to a local pub, and had made the mistake of talking about it. He had been found - eventually - minus gratuity in a canal lock. Guess which one: the one which had stopped me in my tracks - and this was something which had happened fifteen years before I was born! Just telling you about it now makes the flesh of my back creep through the scar tissue.

'With hindsight I had already had a watered-down version of the experience before - on those Black and White coach trips. Remember I told you about the alien feelings I got whenever we passed the entrance to the floating harbour? I have never been back to test my adult reaction

The Bridge - *a love affair*

to the Basingstoke lock, but to this very day, locks in general are approached with a great deal of caution.'

Charo was silent. Either she had switched off out of lack of interest - or was dealing with troubled thoughts. But then 'Hey! Station coming up. Is this your Didcot?' A red light showed ahead, and for the first time Sewell was glad to see it.

They brought the locomotive to a halt. Charo wound on the tender brake like a professional. A sea of surprised faces watched as a hold-all was lowered on the end of the clinker rake. Surprise turned to gasps as the driver, attired in pin-stripes, tie and what had been a white shirt followed and reached back to steady Charo down the steps.

Two men manoeuvred their way through the crowd - the two from the Diplomatic Protection Service who had met them just 24 hours previously. Preliminaries were unnecessary. 'We're the transport. You look as if you could do with a shower. The station master has laid one on.'

'Pretty good of him, considering what we've done to his timetable.'

'Just his way of saying thank you: it's a cold shower!'

'Thanks. I feel like something more drastic anyway - decontamination, perhaps. Harwell has the best facilities in the world. Should we skip the cold shower and go straight there?'

The little cortège threaded its way through a sea of curious faces towards the exit, the security men parting the way like the Red Sea so that Sewell and Charo could carry the hold-all side-by-side. The Recently Humanized One appeared to have reverted to type. At any rate, providing transport was evidently not going to extend to giving a hand with the luggage this time. As they passed, would-be passengers offered helpful suggestions: 'Hey, driver. How about bringing a few carriages next time. Not suggesting you have to bring the lot.'

Eventually they were outside the station. 'Is that the navy-blue suit you were wearing yesterday?'

125

'The suit? Sure. Aquascutum, Regent Street. Recommend them - especially after the past 24 hours. Turned out to be quite hard-wearing.'

They reached the vehicle and set the hold-all down next to the luggage compartment. Sewell left it there and got into the back seat. If the DPS man didn't get the hint he would answer to Sir David.

To the reassuring sound of the baggage locker opening and closing Sewell felt a profound wave of fatigue come over him. He was aware of nothing until he felt a hand on his shoulder: 'Come on, sir. The Minister will see you straight away.'

'What? Looking like this?' He sleep-walked into the entrance lobby holding on to Charo. When they stopped he could still feel the motion of the footplate beneath his feet.

'Where is Sewell? Time's getting on.'

'This is Dr Sewell right here, Minister.'

'Not him, McIntyre. The star of the show, the keynote speaker - the professor with the burn-anything engine.'

'Minister, this is Dr Sewell.'

'Help me with this one, McIntyre, if you will. How come he looks like a coal miner?'

'He has spent a lot of time since about five o'clock this morning shovelling coal, Minister.'

'Don't fool with me, McIntyre. Ah, but of course. Didn't we read about his school holiday exploits shovelling for the GWR?' Sir David turned to Sewell. 'But could you not have abstained from the habit for just long enough to get this conference under way?'

Sewell was beyond weariness, and not inclined to justify his physical appearance - or, indeed, his shovelling. 'That's why they are called habits, Minister. Because they are compulsive.'

'I see. Well, then, while we are indulging your pet subject, do I understand that your quiet engine can run on coal?'

'Yes, sir. But the coal has to be pulverized first - turned into a fine dust.'

The Bridge - *a love affair*

'Ah. The dust. Of course. Everything falls into place. He turned back to the under-secretary. McIntyre!'

'Yes, Minister.'

'See if you can persuade the professor to take a shower before we go onto the podium. I'm going to call Canada and put minds at rest. He's about my size. How many changes of clothing did you pack?'

'Two suits, Minister. Five shirts.

'He's about my size. Use one of the suits, for pity's sake.'

'Right away, Minister.'

****

Charo and Sewell were ushered to seats at one end of the podium by a man who would subsequently turn out to be the projectionist. At the opposite end of the row of empty chairs a smartly-dressed woman was getting to her feet. 'I'm the Radiation Protection and Safety Officer. There has been a late start and you have important business to get on with, so I shall make this as short as my statutory brief allows.

'Our safety team works three, eight-hour shifts, seven days a week, ensuring that every last thing we do, right down to brewing tea in the canteen, complies with relevant codes of safety practice. We are even fully compliant with counterpart US and European codes, despite not being legally bound to be so. Every bench-top experiment, every fume-cupboard, every waste-skip is monitored, and if some of my team had their way, every tea-pot would be monitored too.

'Why am I telling you this? Because we function within the economic constraints of post-Melt-down reality - of an ageing infra-structure - all our alarms are connected to the original fire-alarm circuit: if they sound, they don't distinguish between a mini-reactor over-heating or someone burning the toast in the canteen.'

Sewell fought a temptation to drift off. Sitting on a podium awaiting your turn to speak is a unique challenge. If you haven't tried it you will never know: a mixture of excitement, stage-fright, of 'why did I ever agree to this' to 'let's get on with it', 'why don't they just read the damned paper?' He chided himself: he had been in Cheltenham High Street years ago - in the nineteen-seventies - when fire had ripped through Woolworths. He recalled an elegant, if not one-hundred-percent-practical, black-and-white, half-timbered building. One instant the sight of pedestrians gazing upwards had drawn his attention to smoke from a dormer window on the top floor. Within less than a minute the roof had been ablaze. He ought to be focusing on some way of supporting the safety officer grinding through her thankless routine.

'If the alarm sounds, you drop everything and make like a herd of turtles for one of the illuminated exits - one in each corner of the lecture hall. There are strip lights to an external assembly point for each. Just to reassure you, all three evacuations this month have been due to false alarms. But don't be complacent: if the alarm sounds just DO IT!

'Finally, (there was a feeling of relief you could have photographed) in the unlikely event of landing in water, there is a life-jacket under each seat. Please don't inflate until you are out of the building - and then attend to your own jacket before that of your children.'

A few polite laughs from first-time hearers of the laboured humour covered arrival on the platform of Sir David, of John McIntyre and the Director. The former two took centre seats, while the Director remained standing: 'Minister, Deputy Minister, ladies and gentlemen. As Director of the Micro-Generation Unit it is my pleasure to welcome you, on behalf of the Energy Research Unit and of our sponsor, HM's Provisional Government, to this important conference. Minister, you have kindly agreed to declare the conference open.'

Sir David stood up. He spoke without notes. 'Everyone has accepted, since the day my Department was established, that there is no point in convening a conference of bankers. On the other hand, it has taken the best part of a year for the truth to dawn that our economic future - if we have one - lies not with the City, but in the hands of technology - the technology of engineering, of physics, of chemistry, of farming and the technology of health-care.

The Bridge - *a love affair*

'Technology is powered by energy. Increasingly, energy is coming to be equated with wealth: the more energy we can harness and convert, the faster will be our return to material well-being and economic prosperity.

'The Prime Minister sends his best wishes. It is my pleasure to introduce your keynote speaker: A number of factors combined to make Professor David Sewell the obvious choice for the rôle. He has long enjoyed an international reputation as analyst and academic researcher, but it has taken his attendance at this conference to reveal the full spectrum of his personal strengths. Being here today has required him to be escapologist, hijacker, steam locomotive driver and quick-change artist: he will be addressing you attired in the very shirt, tie and suit that the Secretary of State for Economic Regeneration had ear-marked for wear on this occasion. He is evidently a man of taste as well.'

The Minister took the statutory token sip of water and resumed his seat. The floor exchanged puzzled glances. The platform showed their amusement and approval.

Sewell: 'Thank you, Minister.

'Minister, Deputy Minister, Director, ladies and gentlemen. If this were a sermon, it would start with a text. A sermon it is not (the Lord be praised) - but it does start with a text.' He actuated the first slide:

> Technology has put more shirts on more backs than the charity of all the monarchs in history.
>
> LeMoyne?

'Of course, you don't have to look far to find a dozen glib aphorisms offering the opposite point of view - denying the benefits. Aldous Huxley in particular mis-uses his literary skills in his *Ends and Means*: *Technological progress has merely provided us with more efficient means for going backwards*. This perverse contrary view is from people who benefit from technology every minute of their lives.

'The next slide has something to say about what the detractors would have us do without:

129

The Bridge - *a love affair*

oil-well drill (steered through rock a <u>mile</u> below the surface)	dentist's high-speed drill
bag of cement	Ibuprofen capsule
Boeing 747	Airfix plastic model B-747
Buck-eye locomotive coupling	zip fastener
articulated lorry	bicycle (hydraulic disc brakes and full suspension)
washing machine	pop-up toaster
combine-harvester with satnav air-conditioned cab and on-board radio-isotope monitoring	nail clippers
printing press	ball-point pen
milk tanker	soft-drinks can
MRI scanner	mobile phone
escalator, 50-storey elevator	kitchen steps

NB: The technology of each item includes the specialist machinery designed and developed for its mass-manufacture!

As author of *Literature and Science* Huxley would have been well-placed to know that mechanization - in other words, technology - eventually played a rôle in getting rid of slavery from the plantations of the Americas. Admittedly it was by making the perceived 'necessity' redundant - but hardly a contribution to going backwards whichever way you look at it.'

Another slide. 'An engineering lecture would not be an engineering lecture without an equation:'

$$1 \text{ gall. hex} \cong 30 \text{ man-days' work}$$

The Bridge - *a love affair*

For good measure he paraphrased: 'A gallon of hydro-carbon fuel - petrol or diesel, say - does the day's work of thirty fit labourers. Obviously, the equation doesn't claim numerical precision. But it has more to say in our current predicament than does Einstein's $E = mc^2$.

'It means that one man can plough, harrow, drill and harvest while twenty-nine others get on with designing, ministering to the sick, baking bread, inventing, prospecting for further petroleum supplies, teaching or, if they insist, becoming celebrities, or estate agents: One of the . . . '

There was an interruption from the floor: 'Hey. Steady on! What's wrong with estate agents?'

'Nothing - as long as an economy can afford them. When an estate agent sells you a house for £300,000 and 'makes' 1% on the deal - that's three thousand English pounds, by the way - no wealth has been created. In fact, wealth has been dissipated and overall house-purchasing power reduced.

'One consequence of Melt-down has been the interruption to supplies of conventional raw fuels - to our access to energy. So at face value the equation leads directly to our remit - to identify means of converting alternative raw energies.'

The account was cut short by the piercing sound of the fire alarm. Before Sewell had a chance to look in Charo's direction, McIntyre had grabbed him, the Minister and the Director and was hustling them towards the appropriate exit.

In what turned out to be a quick and efficient exodus, Sewell ended up, together with about forty others, on a grassy area about half the size of a football pitch. The assembly rapidly broke up and re-coalesced into small groups eagerly chatting with no evident concern that they might shortly be witnessing the Energy Research Unit burning to the ground.

A sense of relief took over. Suddenly he could give in to the exhaustion now threatening to overwhelm him. He had got his keynote address under way. It might not go down on record as a great piece of oratory - and he hadn't got as far as his recipe for getting the economy moving again - but he had survived the ordeal. Time to check on Charo.

Looking back at the building he tried to work out where the assembly points would be for the other exits. He had left *via* the south-east. Charo would have taken the north-east door. His feet simply could not be persuaded to hurry. Charo would be fine: the building was showing no sign of smouldering. As he rounded a corner, one of two fire appliances was drawing slowly out of its garage. He dismissed the matter - even when the vehicle drew to a halt obstructing his progress. He could rely on its all being part of a well-rehearsed routine.

He emerged from his musings to see a face looking down at him from the cab through the driver's side window. The owner of the face wore a woolly hat. Showing below the hat were several turns of white gauze bandage.

Boris.

9

Fire escapade

Boris gestured towards the passenger seat. It was Charo. That brute was a survivor alright. His left arm jerked something, producing a grimace. Pointing his right index finger downwards he traced a path around the front of the vehicle and indicated behind him.

Sewell did as directed, giving the vehicle a wide berth just in case the idea was to run over him. It was Charo in the left-hand seat, sure enough, and looking down-in-the mouth, but not in distress. She nodded - an un-smiling, resigned nod. Unusual for her. Perhaps she felt guilty about having fallen hostage again - and about being used as bait. No wave of the hand, either. It was a good bet that Boris had tied them.

He mounted the rear crew compartment *via* the single step, groping behind him for the door handle. Before he could locate it, the vehicle lurched ahead, throwing him off balance and against the backrest of the forward-facing bench seat. No sooner had he steadied himself than Boris braked violently - and immediately accelerated again. Either Boris was using the opportunity to learn to drive, or the plan was to break a few bones. With the door flapping, a sharp right turn would throw Sewell out onto the road, giving Boris the opportunity to reverse over him.

The door flailed, and Sewell made desperate grasps for the various seat belts as they swung into and out of reach. At last he got hold of a pair of straps belonging to the rear-facing bench seat. He hauled himself into the sitting position and, after several false starts, finally prevailed upon two halves of the buckle to unite.

He was now securely attached to the sort of utilitarian wooden-slatted furniture of the whining, petrol-engined, Midland Red buses which, for the princely sum of a penny-half-penny return fare, had carried him between home and primary school. With or without Boris' notion of driving, the seats were as uncomfortable now as he remembered them from seven decades ago.

The vehicle made two violent leaps in succession, causing both arms to fly upwards and yanking the harness painfully tight across his thighs. Speed bumps, possibly. Red and white fragments of a wooden barrier flew past the open door corroborating the diagnosis.

The ninety-degree left-turn out of the facility was taken on two wheels, and served to close the flailing door. Boris shifted up a gear, and they accelerated through a speed at which the appliance rode sickeningly up and down through the full travel of its suspension - which evidently lacked the benefit of customary hydraulic damping. Dampers of large vehicles had become a source of scarce hydrocarbon fluid which could be re-cycled, burned or - well - simply stolen and traded.

Each upward surge was now accompanied by a deafening crash overhead. The encounter with the speed bumps had probably caused the ladder to break free from its forward attachment. In any event, having identified the natural frequency of the vehicle, Boris stuck to it. Again the ladder struck the roof with an ear-splitting impact, to be flung back into the air by the next prance of the vehicle.

The experience was so exhausting that Sewell had no idea how far they had travelled when a sudden deceleration pinned him to the seat-back, throwing his head back against something rock-hard. The front of the vehicle reared up, came to a halt and slid slowly backwards, returning to the level with a spine-jarring jolt.

A blue water-colour wash descended over his field of vision, slowly dissolving into a pixellated panorama through which he was conscious of a torrent of verbal abuse from somewhere behind him. Russian. Dreamily he mused that it must be worth mastering the language simply for the benefit of being able to vent steam like that.

The vehicle rocked slightly, as if in response to the removal of a load. The verbal abuse was now at least ten decibels louder, apparently coming from road level and now on the move - like a demonstration of SenSurround™ at the cinema. Charo! Galvanized, he undid the belt. As he slid painfully along the slatted seat, a sickening thud from above flattened the suspension of the vehicle, bursting open the near-side door and leaving it hanging limp on a single hinge.

'Sewell - are you alright?'

Good. Charo had survived the impact. He climbed painfully down from the rear cab.'

'Don't go under the bridge - just don't!'

He stopped and looked up: The end of the ladder was embedded in the masonry, a huge chunk of which had detached and fallen onto the front cab - and evidently onto Boris: the extra slight movement of the ladder as the man had got out had been his undoing.

The door on Charo's side yielded to a succession of tugs. She was strapped with hold-all lengthwise upwards between her knees. The seat belt had been threaded through the handles and around her wrists. 'Almost pulled my arms off when we hit the bridge.'

Sewell wrestled with the belt for a good half-minute before teasing out sufficient slack to get the catch to release. Freeing the hold-all, he checked overhead, backed out of the cab and placed the bag on the grass verge. He steadied Charo as she climbed down, and they walked over to the hold-all in an awkward bear hug - nothing romantic - sheer relief. When they finally let go there were tears in Charo's eyes. 'Sewell, do you think we have seen the last of these people, and that we can go home soon? - Oh! your neck is bleeding - or the back of your head - look at my hands! And the shirt - the Minister's shirt!'

'Ministerial shirts are on expenses, you can bet on it. Suits as well, I should think. We had better sort out the chauffeur.'

'Leave him. He was coming round to my side to get me - I know he was. Anyway, you're not going under that bridge. It's not safe.'

Sewell looked up. 'That chunk of masonry has been waiting to fall for years: the cavity is green with moss. Look, there's lots of kit in the rear cab - rope for example. I'll have a quick try at pulling Boris clear by myself. If he's too heavy I'll lassoo his feet and we can both stand clear and pull.'

He couldn't - but together they did.

'Now what?' asked Charo.

'We make him as comfortable as we can and start walking.'

He felt the jugular again. 'He's alive, alright.' He took off the ministerial jacket, folded it and handed it to Charo. Unable to raise the huge head from beside the body, he stood astride it to use both arms. Charo eased the makeshift pillow into position and stood well back.

'That's the last thing I'm ever doing for him! If . . . Listen! Something coming!'

The field ambulance came to a halt a few yards behind the fire truck. Two men in uniform got out - the same two security men again! Neither spoke, their silence telling all. It was left to Sewell: 'Where have you been? Thought you'd never come. And how did you know we needed an ambulance?'

'Didn't. It was the only vehicle with fuel. All the others had been drained some time since the last daily check.' Boris again, thought Sewell.

'Are shirt, tie and cuff-links the latest in fire-fighting gear?'

'Blame the casualty here. Didn't give me time to slip into something more comfortable. Watch him, by the way. He's out now - but lethal when awake. Does your stretcher come with restraints?'

'They all do: got just the job. What's the damage?'

'Mainly head injuries. Just watch it: he's a no-account assassin. Don't expect Charo and me to hang around while you stabilize him.'

'Fair enough.' The stretcher was placed beside Boris, and with one to each limb he was lifted on. The restraints were secured, it took all four to lift him again and slide him into the back of the ambulance. Sewell loaded up the hold-all. The driver flung in the blood-stained jacket and closed the door: 'You two travel in the cab. One of us will stay in the back and fix up a drip.'

Squeezed between Sewell and the driver, the warmth of Charo's body was welcome and comforting. She might have felt the same: 'I haven't seen you in anything less formal than a jacket since we played squash at the central YMCA on Tottenham Court Road. Want to know why it registered with me? Because every lamp-post and litter-bin in the city had a poster advertizing Arnold Schwartzenegger in *Pumping Iron*, and I remember thinking how much more attractive your naturally muscular physique was than the corrugated iron look. Arnie might look impressive without clothes - but completely out-of-place in any kind of jacket. You look great with or without.'

How to defuse a situation like this? 'Even in a suit borrowed from the Secretary of State for Economic Regeneration?'

'In that suit particularly. Given the condition it's in, Sir David might not want it back. How about making him an offer for it. It might even be washable.'

They stopped at the security check-point. Work to repair the damage inflicted by Boris on the exit barrier was already in progress. The ambulance was evidently expected and the driver well-known, so they were waved through - but not without a bit of banter about the occupant of the stretcher.

'If you're worrying about the care your assassin is going to get - don't: the entire medical establishment is on duty for the conference. In a way it's a pity he's not a radiation casualty: no place in the land is better equipped. Do I drop you off at the conference centre - or somewhere to clean up first?'

'Nothing to change into. Conference centre, please.'

Several people were waiting as they drew up, driver's side to the entrance. Heading the reception committee was the Minister with

The Bridge - *a love affair*

John McIntyre a step behind. Relief registered on Sir David's face as Sewell stepped from the far side of the cab, his head showing over the cab roof. 'The demonstrator? Is it safe?'

On the basis that actions speak louder than words Sewell carried on to the back door of the vehicle, withdrawing hold-all and jacket while nodding acknowledgement to the officer holding the drip. Straightening up, he walked round the open rear door into the view of the Minister, for whose facial expression this writer has no adjective. 'And the clothes, Sewell? The jacket? Where's the jacket? What happened this time?'

Sewell opened his mouth to speak 'Minister . . . ' But it was Charo. 'Minister. Ever since I first met my colleague in London, he has hankered after a suit like that - and that means since the nineteen-seventies. But he's never been able to afford one. To you it's just another perk. If you don't mind me saying so, it's an even better fit on him than on you. We've already agreed that we would like to make you an offer for it.'

The side to Sir David which was his ministerial office was evidently doing battle with his deep Methodist humanity - and losing. 'Just what do I get in exchange for my piece of Saville Row?'

'Well, Minister, the contents of this hold-all we're carrying are potentially worth decades' production of hand-tailored suits.'

There was the briefest pause. The Minister stepped forward, took Charo's hand and put an arm round her shoulder. 'Maybe you two should think about becoming more than colleagues: you make quite a team.' He turned to his aide: 'McIntyre! The reserve change of clothing from the car, if you please. While I phone Canada yet again get Dr. Sewell cleaned up and back to the conference room.'

'Yes, Minister.'

Half-an-hour later, with the platform re-assembled, the Minister stood up. 'Three items of good news, ladies and gentlemen. The first is that we have tracked down our keynote speaker - again. The second is that the Director has arranged for the reception and dinner to be put back by half-an-hour. If we cut thirty minutes from mingling time

The Bridge - *a love affair*

that allows us to pick up where we left off without cutting the programme. The third is that I have come to appreciate that my original introduction of Dr Sewell failed to do him justice, and I should like to go some way to putting that right: you should know that he agreed to waive the fee that most keynote speakers would expect, and to demonstrate his technology - all in return for expenses only. So in the . . .'

The Minister raising his hand, stemming a ripple of applause. 'Hold your fire - I'm almost done. In the current climate of openness you are entitled to hear what those expenses are: well, if we include provision for the loss of today's London-Bristol rail service, for the replacement cost of a fire appliance and for his liability in respect of structural damage to a road-bridge, then that leaves only one other item of significance - a Saville Row suit, blackmailed out of my possession only an hour ago. And I should point out that the inventory does not account for the suit he is modelling at this very moment, since in this case I see some chance of getting it back. Dr Sewell, the platform is yours. Pray let us hear the rest of your half-of-a-million pounds-worth.'

Clapping was visible - although drowned by the laughter.

Charo was sitting in the second row. Sewell had been watching her face during the build-up. Years before in London they had confided about his uphill struggle with public-speaking. At the Minister's suggestion that he should justify this arbitrary sum, her face spoke disbelief and indignation. Sewell read it. Suddenly an audience could include someone who cared - someone about whom he himself cared a great deal - whose support outweighed any degree of antipathy or indifference the other one hundred-and-sixty souls could marshal.

'Thank you, Minister. I have, in fact, grown so attached to the suit - not only on account of the quality, but of the fit as well - that I have decided to waive the other half-million and hang on to the suit - both suits, in fact - on the basis that they are only spares anyway.'

Charo joined in with the applause, bouncing up and down in her seat.

'Before the fire alarm I got as far as suggesting that the challenge is to motivate volume manufacture of new technologies - to shift the emphasis from financial services back towards wealth creation - towards value-adding.

    'Implementing it is an entirely different challenge. Let's say that we have got as far as the prototype on an engine that will convert whatever source of raw energy is to hand - discarded Christmas trees, old thermodynamics lecture notes, worn-out suits - you name it. Until the converter's in volume production - and on the market at a viable price - economic impact is zero. It's where the real soul-searching has to start - where the only way forward is a radical re-think of priorities.

    'That's not going to happen of its own accord, if only because of the scale of the counter-attractions.

    'Suppose supplies of raw energy have been restored (that's a bit outside our remit anyway). But assume we've got a brand new technology for generating electric power by converting that energy - call it an engine.' He actuated another slide.

Manufacturer of new energy converter.	*vs*	Currency speculator
Acquire multi-million funding		Acquire desk, PC, phone, supply of coffee
Acquire or design/build factory		
Transfer relevant technology		
Re-design prototype for volume production		
Acquire production machinery		
Design/set up production lines		
Establish quality control		

Recruit/train work-force
        - shop-floor
        - admin.
        - sales

If the money has not already run out:
        advertising
        distribution
        labour relations
        health-and-safety-at-work
        after-sales service
        product liability
        pensions

(Cadbury and Lever Bros. built village
to accommodate work-force)

    The time before a return on investment in the manufacturing enterprise could be anything from two to five years. From currency speculation a matter of days - maybe hours.

    'How on earth do we balance the motivation? Well, there's obviously nothing doing until the economy starts moving and the social dust settles. But when it does, one measure would be to **invert** the VAT system. VAT's a misnomer anyway: what needs to be done is to set a rate of zero on profits from wealth creation - *i.e.* for value-adding, but tax the living daylights out of revenue from speculation on currency, commodities and so on.

    'The idea's already been floated: while Melt-down was becoming increasingly inevitable I wrote to two successive Chancellors - and got courteous acknowledgements. It seemed I might do better with Boris Johnson, and put the idea to him by letter - early 2013 I think. I got a reply from the Office of the Mayor but, obviously, no action. I continue to believe in it as one of the measures which we are going to be forced into if we are ever to balance the books sustainably.

'I leave it to the next slide to underline the case for giving it a try:'

Banking per se has never directly generated a penny of wealth.

'Just to elaborate: for a million pounds to be pocketed by a banker, somebody else has to shell out *at least* a million. Wealth has been dissipated. Overall it has *decreased*.

'I'll finish with personal hope: that when we come through this, it will be with a different perspective - with a heightened appreciation of technology, with fiscal policies which distinguish currency from wealth, and which encourage creation of the latter. One last slide:

'A litre of diesel fuel is worth something like 35 MegaJoules, of which the engine might convert up to forty percent to mechanical work or electrical energy - or could take your car about ten miles - or do the work of an able-bodied labourer for six days: - 14 MegaJoules of wealth per litre! Take a look at a price comparison:'

Diesel fuel   **Cola drink**

Surveying/prospecting
        seismography
        drilling
Rig construction
        transport for crew
            helicopter operation
        offshore
        more drilling
        instrumentation
        safety
Transport ashore
        pipeline
        tanker ship
Refining
Distribution - road tanker

Research/investment/training
De-commissioning exhausted wells/rigs

     £0.55p/litre   **£1.125p/litre**

Fuel tax   £0.57

VAT @ 20% on total of £1.12

      £1.35/litre   £1.35/litre

'Petro-chemical technology has given us wealth, health and mobility. Soft drinks have given dental cavities and excess weight. Under rampant capitalism pre-Melt-down we've lived with distorted values - at all levels.

'Melt-down offers us the nearest possible thing to a clean sheet. Let's put the opportunity to good use.'

As he sat down the Minister leaned across and, under cover of the statutory applause, confided 'I set you up - and you rode it. Good man. It's mingling time - but see you at dinner. You and your charming colleague are seated with me at the top table. If you can keep that suit in wearable condition for just half-an-hour longer we'll get on just fine. McIntyre has your travel itinerary and documents. You are off this Friday - *via* Canada - so there won't be another chance to discuss arrangements in London. Better sort it all out tonight.' He stood up. 'Can't deny it's an uncommon stylish fit. It's yours with the compliments of my department.'

'Oh, Minister. Thank you so much.' It was Charo. 'I promise you'll never regret that generous decision. Come on, David.' She tugged at the sleeve now under new ownership. 'Now you can relax. Let's mingle.'

'I'm so exhausted I'd prefer to mingle with a purpose and then snatch ten minutes' zuzz before dinner: we've got the Minister for company. Let's look for Norris.'

A quick tour of the poster displays soon located Sewell's friend from Salford Priors. 'Norris, I'd like you to meet my best friend and colleague, Charo Jiménez. Charo, this is Norris: I told you a bit about the family businesses when you were getting my life-story.'

'I'm surrounded by beautiful women at home.' confessed Norris. 'Came to the conference just to escape them. Seems I can't win.' With Charo instantly at ease and soon deep in conversation, Sewell homed-in on a waiter distributing glasses from a tray. 'Elderberry?'

'Not at all, sir. The real thing - Tempranillo - and a rather juicy one. The Director's an MA of one of the Cambridge colleges. Their wine cellar's got stocks for the next five years, apparently. He did a deal.'

'Good move! Look, I'm going to take a seat in one of those comfortable-looking chairs in the foyer: can't keep my eyes open. Would you wake me with a glass when it's time to go in for dinner - very last minute if you can.'

'Leave it to me, sir.'

10
Lígia

Under the barter arrangements Sewell was to travel to North America, spending up to a year ensuring that transfer of the technology was based on a full understanding of operating principles rather than on mere reverse-engineering of the demonstrator.

McIntyre had returned to London taking the demonstrator, dropping Sewell and Charo at Didcot Parkway where they said farewell. Sewell had travelled back to Bristol behind Tornado - keeping a low profile - retrieved the bicycle and packed a suitcase.

The outward journey took him first to Ottawa and to an appointment with Sir David's counterpart at the Canadian Ministry of Defence, Jan Sernas. According to name-plates on the door, the personal assistant who greeted him was a Ms Z Whalon. Fifty, maybe, and prepossessing to the extent that the first time she invited Sewell to call her by her first name - Zoë - the invitation failed to register.

Sernas disarmingly blended casual personal style with immaculate attire. He operated from an office noticeably less ponderous than that of Sir David, and rye whisky substituted for coffee. In Canadian fashion his professional qualifications were framed on the wall behind the un-cluttered desk: the statutory certificate of incorporation as Professional Engineer (in his case of the Province of Ontario) and two degree certificates - Master of Applied Science and Doctor of Philosophy - hung below the Companion of the Order of Canada.

The man was evidently well qualified to talk technology, but showed no inclination to do so. Indeed, it was soon apparent that the purpose of the encounter was little more than to let Sewell in on a reality: that the ultimate destination for his technology was the United States - and had been so all along. Enjoying the trust of both bartering parties, Canada had acted as broker. Perhaps when such disclosures arrived from on-high, and over a fine rye whiskey, any possible misunderstandings would be de-fused. Had this indeed been the ploy, it had worked: the most memorable feature of the encounter remained Zoë: even without the help of the make-up department she could have passed for Miss Moneypenny of the early Bond films - those featuring Sean Connery - the soft Canadian accent completing the picture.

She walked with him to a hotel close to the parliament buildings, outlining arrangements on the way: the entire schedule on North American soil had been pre-planned in detail with the US military to avoid his having to obtain tickets or visas or to pay for living accommodation. He would be collected at seven o'clock the next morning and taken to the airport where the driver would put him on a flight to Buffalo.

At the hotel she gave the receptionist instructions for dealing with the account for the night's stay. The immediate task done, she relaxed noticeably. 'There's something in this for Canada, and those of us in the know are grateful.' She took his hand in a protracted handshake which was something more than a polite formality. 'You come back next year *via* the same route with a stop in Ottawa. I shall look forward to welcoming you to a more optimistic economic climate. Perhaps we could celebrate it over a lunch.' She left with a smile and a wave.

If that warm glow was what you felt as holder of a licence to kill, then he had just been given his first insight into the perks of being a secret agent. He picked up the suitcase, hesitated, sighed, collected the plastic key from the reception desk and walked up two flights of stairs to the all too familiar solitude of the hotel room.

Breakfast at six o'clock the next morning included griddle cakes and maple syrup. The contrast with breakfast fare back home

The Bridge - *a love affair*

provoked a pang of guilt. On the other hand, had not Zoë said that there was something in it for Canada? On that basis, guilt and coffee were swallowed together. He thanked the receptionist and went outside to wait for the transport.

The ride was uneventful, and after a brief exchange with an official at a barricade, the vehicle was waved onto the apron. No customs formalities then! It came to a stop beneath the wing-tip of a Hercules aircraft bearing the maple leaf emblem. Wasn't this the most peaceable of all military insignia? So - he was evidently travelling with the Royal Canadian Air Force. Climbing the folding steps he looked to the right into a cavernous fuselage. A few packing cases were strapped to the floor. Cabin and flight-deck were one, and to his left, pilot and co-pilot were working through checklists in the vast greenhouse which is the cockpit of the Hercules.

Someone boosted him by the arm to a skeletal metal seat directly behind the captain. To his right, behind the co-pilot, a man with steel-grey hair in an impossibly smart olive-green uniform was flipping through a sheaf of buff-colored papers.

With urgency not inconsistent with a military operation, number-one engine was started immediately the hatch was secured and checked, and they were taxiing as engines three and four were winding up.

The impressively short take-off run suggested that the machine was not carrying its rated load of military vehicles. The flying was noticeably more sporty than the civilian counterpart. Immediately on levelling off, the two outboard engines were shut down. If this was a fuel-saving measure, then it was the first concession to shortages he had seen since arrival. A straight-in approach at Toronto amounted to re-starting the outboard engines and dropping out of the sky onto the runway. The instant the wheels touched the runway there was the roar of reverse pitch, and they took the first turnoff at a speed at which Sewell felt the aircraft was still capable flying. The only concession to the clock was to shut down the engines on the apron. No sooner had the smart uniform exited and been replaced by an equally smart woman in civilian

147

clothes than the engines were re-started for a brisk taxy to the holding point - except that there was no holding! The Hercules entered the runway accelerating under what might have been full power - and strode into the air.

A second re-start of the outboard engines signalled another rapid descent, this time into Buffalo. Immediately the machine came to rest Sewell was ushered to the hatch with a warning about the steepness of the steps. Reaching the tarmac he looked up - directly into the face of a sartorially-dressed civilian of his own height and build. 'Erwin! Don't tell me this is coincidence.'

'Hardly! Let's get us a coffee and a seat inside and I'll tell you about it.'

Clearing security amounted to smiles and waves: Sewell was not even asked to produce papers. Dr Erwin Corey had evidently advanced in the world since their first face-to-face meeting at a conference in Groningen five years or so before Melt-down. 'This is beginning to look like special treatment, Erwin. What have I done to deserve it?'

'It may be a case of what you are going to do - but, by the way, the demonstrator's already arrived: it's at Los Alamos. The alternative to my grabbing you on the tarmac was half-a-day minimum in customs and immigration. A man doesn't need that when he's come here to work on economic regeneration for a modest daily allowance.'

The lounge was populated by personnel in military attire. Sewell and Erwin watched the Hercules re-start and depart, and turned to commercial-strength coffees and field-kitchen do-nuts, the latter having sufficient calories to sustain a non-stop march from Land's End to John O'Groats carrying an eighty-five pound back-pack.

Erwin explained that he now stalked the corridors of the Pentagon - a mere one notch below secretary of state: technology relating to power production from renewable or unconventional energy sources - particularly where it had a bearing on propulsion - had taken over funding priorities previously enjoyed by space exploration. And Erwin was in charge of assessing and administering those priorities!

'We've had your project under surveillance since before Melt-down - just performance figures rather than intimate details of design. I'm telling you as a friend before somebody uses the word spying because I'd like to keep things this way.' Erwin had been at the helm of a program years previously when the conventional Stirling engine had been under consideration for road vehicle propulsion. This left him uniquely qualified to evaluate Sewell's derivative design. It was now clear why 'selling' the deal on to the Americans had not required Jan Sernas to rehearse technical aspects.

Erwin reminded Sewell of his pathological inability to remain awake on aircraft, and suggested they had better not rely on the flight for comparing notes. The purpose of the stop at Buffalo, he explained, was to connect with a US Army flight to Albuquerque, New Mexico. There, at the Los Alamos laboratory, the reality of the technology transfer would begin - a technology which had made the trip to North America on just four 8 GB flash drives. With the exception of anything disclosing the workings of the micro-processor controller, Sewell's leather passport wallet contained all the information required to duplicate the prototype demonstrated at Harwell. Making a mock formality of handing the tiny package to Erwin, he emphasized that this was not quite the world-saving Bond-like gesture it might appear: there were back-up copies with Jan Sernas, with Sir David's department and, indeed, with Charo.

All drawing files were to be converted to an American system. It had been agreed that this would mean generating machining files afresh, and that this, in turn, was going to require comprehensive re-test of the resulting hardware. Easily-machined materials would serve to achieve the necessary checks of dimensions and tolerances. Then would come trial assembly. Corrections and modifications would inevitably follow, to be followed in turn by machining and fabrication in locally-sourced materials - largely proprietary metal alloys. These would need to be selected on the basis of properties as close as possible to those of prototypes on endurance test in the UK - a task scheduled to take place at NIST in Denver.

The Bridge - *a love affair*

If the near-empty flight from Ottawa had seemed an extravagance, this one, by contrast, was already earning its keep, with turn-around at Cleveland, Columbus and Indianapolis. Each stop involved much disembarking, freight-handling, and boarding - with St Louis and Oklahoma still to come. Erwin had fallen asleep shortly after fastening his seat belt, and had thus remained for the duration, evidently immune to the powerful stimulus of military coffee. Sewell had accepted the offer of head-phones and was following the invitation to listen to the exchanges between the crew and air traffic control on the channel carrying the R/T.

As the sky began to brighten behind the port wing there was a frequency change to St Louis approach. Sewell held an R/T licence from gliding days, and had a sneaking admiration for the pragmatic attitude taken by Americans to radio communication. After checking whether the flight had visual contact with a Boeing 707 ahead, the approach controller instructed 'Indicate one five zero knots and follow him!'

R/T exchanges on the next leg of the flight were along similar lines: only the numbers were different. He abandoned the head-phones. A mere few days previously he had been on a train leaving Temple Meads. His friend Michael had enquired how he proposed to pass the time travelling. Michael, he knew, could occupy himself for hours mentally designing mediaeval castles - or was it re-designing? Hadn't he been going to think through his career, his marriage and how each had shaped the other? The current re-run of the mental routine had got under way in the grounds of Bristol Cathedral, but had seen some interruptions. Erwin remained sound asleep, so he would pick up where he had left off, reminiscing in peace at least as far as Oklahoma.

Sewell had never doubted that life held a spiritual dimension - his own life in particular - although he would not for a moment call himself religious. He liked music, and wasn't there some magnificent music for church organ? - not just the old war-horses like Bach, but contemporary compositions by British composers - Percy Whitlock's *Fanfare*, for example. Or *Elegy* by George Thalben-Ball. Boy! Had that man combined the regal with the poignant - and on the hoof, too: the

The Bridge - a love affair

piece had been composed in two minutes as an improvisation to fill an unscheduled gap of precisely that duration in a live broadcast! Genius.

St Mary's had a fine pipe organ and choir to match. The organist was dynamite, clearly able to play anything that had ever been written for the instrument - and plenty that hadn't. He was a fluent and iconoclastic improviser. So it should be clear that Sewell's church attendance in the 1960s owed more to the prospect of hearing the organist do just that than to any religious fervour.

Unusually for parish churches at the time, post-devotional refreshments were routinely available at a family-run tea-shop a quarter of a mile from the church. Sunday trading was unheard of in that era. However, the proprietor was a church warden, and as no money changed hands on the Sabbath, no objections were raised.

Sewell joined two others at a table for four: Stephen was a graduate in English from Oxford who made a living out of private tuition. Ian was a junior with a firm of accountants. Sewell and they had shared a lively conversation the previous Sunday. 'David! What kept you?'

'Got talking. Every time I hear an organist improvise I try out the same question: *can you teach me?*'

'And . . . .'

'Stock reply: *It's one of those things you can do - or you can't*. They must be taught that line at music school.'

'But can it possibly be right?' It was Stephen the private tutor, as indignant as Sewell was resigned. 'That would make it unique: anything which can be learned can be taught.'

Sewell was about to reply when a woman approached the table. 'David. You probably don't know Lígia. She's giving St Mary's a try.'

Sewell stood up and held out his hand. 'Pleased to meet you. I'm David.' They both sat down. 'Lígia's a name I've never heard before.'

'Brazilian.' was the reply. 'My father's from Belo Horizonte. Came here in the nineteen thirties. I was a war baby.'

151

'Can't have been much to attract South Americans at that time. What brought him here?'

'He was in aviation - aircraft design. He reckoned Britain was where it was all happening: Mitchell and the Schneider Trophy races - and more companies developing aircraft and engines than you could shake a stick at: deHavilland, Avro, Shorts, Hawker, Bristol, Handley-Page - you name it.'

'OK then: Sopwith, Gloster, Vickers, Supermarine, Blackburn, Napier . . . And Brazil had an aviation industry before the war?'

'Where on this planet were you educated - if at all? Haven't you heard of Santos Dumont?'

'The municipal airport in Rio.'

'*No!* - *yes* but only because it's named for the Brazilian pioneer: Santos Dumont was designing and building heavier-than-air machines at the same time as the Wright Brothers. His first machine flew in France - a matter of months after Kitty-Hawk.'

'Best not to argue with Lígia about aviation, David.' It was Stephen. 'Her hobby is gliding - when she's not skiing, that is.'

'Or rock-climbing', added Ian

Sewell had been in the university air squadron which flew Chipmunks out of RAF Shawbury. No point in wasting ammunition on a non-battle. Could come in handy later, maybe.

'I don't want to be a bore.' It was Stephen again 'But any chance of steering the conversation back to this morning's service. How about an expert opinion on the visiting preacher.' And then, for Sewell's benefit: 'Lígia studied theology for a year before switching to medicine. Gives the address at family service sometimes. Worth hearing: knows all there is to know about Saint Paul.'

Lígia required no further prompting: 'Good job the vicar is only away for the weekend - otherwise you wouldn't see me here next Sunday. Ninety-nine percent of parish-level theology is tired metaphor - shepherds, sheep and so on. Trouble is, reality has been forgotten, and

152

metaphor has taken over. So we get sermons using metaphor to explain metaphor.'

Sewell looked cautiously around to see whether the visiting preacher had dropped in for coffee. Mercifully not, because Lígia pressed on with her critique in a slightly-raised voice. 'Sometimes it takes a satirist to cut straight to the point: I've got a cartoon somewhere - could be from Punch magazine - pen-and-ink sketch of a preacher in the pulpit in clerical garb with a hand in the air as if holding a small object - egg-cup size, say. The caption reads: *"Then you carefully clean each spark-plug with fine sand-paper - but I digress."* Says it all.'

She forged ahead and Sewell took a more careful look. At first impression she had been un-remarkable, not helped by dull, somewhat shapeless outer clothing. A face that had originally registered as somewhat plain was now animated and undeniably attractive. Here, without doubt, was some unusual woman.

Sewell was happy to leave the conversation to the other three while he attempted to make sense of Lígia. Once or twice she smiled - a stunningly beautiful smile, but one which seemed to represent a not-too-successful attempt to suppress inner pain or uncertainty.

Some money was put together for Ian to pass on to the proprietor during the week, and it was agreed that they would pick up discussion the following Sunday.

Sewell could not recall a week passing more slowly. The pace quickened somewhat for a couple of days following an announcement that the Labour government had cancelled an order for American aircraft intended to replace an earlier cancellation - that of the TSR-2, thereby forfeiting a multi-million pound deposit. What ignited discussion around the engineering department was that, with performance targets in sight and, in some cases, already demonstrated, the TSR-2 project itself had been summarily scrapped and aircraft already built or under construction destroyed, together with all manufacturing jigs and drawings. World-leadership had been thrown away and the UK aviation industry emasculated. The RAF had no replacement aircraft in prospect, and the

The Bridge - *a love affair*

Americans had pocketed millions without having been called upon to deliver a single machine.

Sunday arrived - eventually. The vicar elaborated on the second letter of Paul to the Corinthians, the organist dismissed them with *Nun danket alle Gott*, by Karg Elert (a pot-boiler not calling for comment) and the coffee-drinkers headed for the cafe.

If Sewell had wondered how to sound out Lígia for her view on the cancellation, he need not have bothered. Even as she sat down she was reaching in her bag for a pen and a piece of paper. Within seconds the three males were getting a running commentary as the arithmetic of development costs, cost per aircraft had it entered production, social cost of the cancellation and forfeit cancellation fee built up into a neatly-written balance sheet. 'And you know the supreme irony of this madness, of course?'

Sewell was confident he knew what was coming, but held back. 'This is a carbon-copy re-run of the Avro Canada *Arrow* project of a few years previously: an aircraft of world-beating specification already flying with six built. Not just cancelled, but destroyed - manufacturing jigs, drawings - economic and technological vandalism! About fifteen thousand out of work directly. The only material difference was that the 'replacement' that Diefenbaker ordered from the Americans was a job-lot of Bomark missiles - *but minus the warheads they were designed to deliver*!' By this stage her eyes were flashing. 'Can you even start to believe it?'

Harold Wilson and John Diefenbaker might have been thankful not to have been at coffee that morning: she would have wiped the floor with them.

If anyone could believe it Sewell could. His engineering master's studies had been in Canada. In 1962 Toronto had still been reeling from the unemployment wrought by the Arrow debacle. One of the thousands made redundant who had since found re-employment was Charlie Mellor, now assistant professor in Sewell's department, researching and teaching magneto-hydrodynamics. Graduate students shared the common room with faculty members, so it was not long

The Bridge - *a love affair*

before morning coffee found Sewell and Charlie seated together. Conversation would not quite serve as *le mot juste* for what ensued. If Charlie's passionate monologue had merely elaborated on the short-sightedness and sheer incomprehensibility of the cancellation it would have added little to what Sewell already knew. But the unprecedented specification of the Arrow had called for a jet engine of equally unprecedented performance. The engine project had become known as the Iroquois, and Charlie's work in the Orenda Engines division had contributed directly to successful ground tests of this revolutionary, twin-spool unit with its pioneering use of titanium in the compressor stages.

Having sensed Sewell's interest, Charlie let up only when the morning's supply of coffee ran out. Every subsequent break, however - morning coffee or afternoon tea - found Charlie poised to pick up where he had left off. By the time Sewell submitted his dissertation he felt qualified to justify every single design priority which had gone into the Arrow - and comprehensively to demolish any related political decision.

Over coffee a couple of years on, this particular post-devotional get-together was not the moment to air the privileged insight. Strongly as he felt about both Arrow and TSR-2, the matter of the moment was the woman herself - this Lígia. Both Ian and Stephen were unattached: he knew that already. He watched both for the tell-tale signs: attempts to impress. He detected none. Was it even possible to be so indifferent?

After a few perfunctory exchanges about an un-remarkable morning service, the meeting broke up. Sewell timed his exit to that of Lígia and put his prepared question: 'So, what is it you do in real life?'

He was rewarded with that disarming smile. 'I'm doing a post-graduate medical degree - immunology.'

'Does that give time for a coffee during the week?'

'It might - it's a whole lot more flexible than the MB ChB - but if there's spare time I spend it with Pam Rhodes. She's terminally ill with cancer. Doesn't have long.'

On the basis of Sewell's previous observation of high-flying professionals - and this woman was undoubtedly in the category - they tended to focus on their own ambitions and to leave those less fortunate to fend for themselves. How many more admirable qualities lurked beneath that unprepossessing attire?

So, it would have to be Sunday morning coffee meetings. Could be worse: the door had not been slammed in his face. But this business of wishing time away during the week must stop. *If you want to kill time, try working it to death.* Perhaps he would give that a try.

It took a few days to re-adjust, but there were soon dividends beyond expectation: His interest at the time had been in a recently-identified phenomenon in unsteady heat transfer. He was confident that he had set up the relevant differential equation, and now needed the solution. He had already focused two months' research time on this, and it was now a week into the students' Christmas vacation with no solution in sight. He was eating, drinking and breathing the problem. The amount of time he allowed himself for thoughts about Lígia had - mercifully - become more of a conscious choice.

Then, shortly after Christmas, he had awoken one night with a vivid mental picture - not of the algebraic symbols with which he had been wrestling for months, but of a graph, and not any old graph, but one in three dimensions - a sort of landscape relief. He got out of bed, turned on the light, sketched the image on the desk-top blotting-pad and went back to sleep.

On inspecting the sketch in the morning it was evidently the solution - the very picture which would have resulted had he obtained the elusive symbolic answer, fed it with numerical values and plotted the result. From this it was a simple matter to work backwards to the formal solution. His conclusion, which was to serve him well during the rest of his career, was that if you drive the conscious mind hard enough, the sub-conscious eventually lends a hand - and does so in a way the logical mind would have no way of predicting. There would be further evidence of this phenomenon at work as he delved ever deeper into the intricacies of his chosen line of research.

The Bridge - *a love affair*

A morning service in early spring had started with an announcement: following a long illness, a member of the congregation had passed away during the week: Pam Rhodes. The funeral would take place at St Mary's on Monday week. Well, Lígia would have to accept a coffee invitation now - or find an alternative excuse.

It had become routine for them to walk part-way home together. He waited until they had crossed the market place. 'How about putting that new-found free time to use? Lunch on Tuesday?'

'I'm not free until evening on Tuesday.'

'Better still! If you are still interested in the Avro Arrow I've got a bit of background to the entire programme - not exactly first-hand, but not far off, either. And the RCAF flew a group of us engineering research students to their base in Cold Lake, Alberta, so I've got lots of 35-millimetre colour slides - close-ups of the Arrow's predecessor, the CF-104.'

'You make it impossible to refuse. Where's this intimate little restaurant that offers 35 millimetre projection facilities?'

'My place or yours? The projector can travel.'

'I'm re-decorating: place is in chaos. How about yours? Just tell me where. I could make seven-thirty.'

'Please just bear in mind that cooking's not my forté. Nibbles and wine?'

'Perfect. Nothing too serious.'

He gave the directions in a heady daze. Home was not the place right now - insufficient to occupy his spinning mind. He turned back and walked to the laboratory - on air.

That afternoon passed in a frenzy of writing - as did the Monday and the Tuesday. The rather satisfying result by mid-afternoon was a paper on the solution of his heat transfer problem. The timing could hardly have been better. Leaving work early he returned home *via* the off-licence to pick up a bottle of *Egri Bikavér* - nothing too serious!

Some months previously, a machinist friend who kept goats had become disillusioned with what he saw as the ambivalent stance of the UK government towards technology, and had re-located to the

The Bridge - *a love affair*

Basque region of Spain in search of subsistence living. Shortly after Christmas Sewell had received a parcel franked *Vizcaya - Ermula*. The contents included a selection of cheeses which, according to hand-written labels, were a Roncal, an Ossau-Iraty and an Idiazabel. All he had been able to find out was that they were made from sheep's milk. Exotic: what better to impress. As a precaution he bought back-up supplies of brie, camembert, Danish blue and cheddar from the corner shop, where he stocked up with biscuits and Ryvita.

At seven thirty there was a knock at the door. Seven-thirty precisely. Good sign as far as Sewell was concerned. Without the need to enquire, she located exactly the right place to park top-coat and boots - instantly at ease. In jeans and a nondescript navy-blue sweater she had hardly dressed to kill. Maybe she had even dressed down. On the other hand, without the trademark, drab outdoor clothing she was transformed. And that *smile*!

To have worried that they would not hit it off would have been a waste of perfectly good worry. She did not merely approve of the *Egri Bikavér* and the cheeses - she articulated exactly why. And far from being a struggle, conversation was more of a competition. Everything interested her - and in turn she interested - fascinated. During a rare break in the exchanges he reflected that these were possibly two sides of the same thing.

The slide-show provoked so much animated discussion that he got through less than a quarter of the planned programme. Great! Material for another get-together. The evening flew, and when eleven o'clock came there seemed little doubt that this thing had potential to blossom. 'Can I walk you home?'

'Thanks. Another time, definitely - but tonight I need to be alone with my thoughts.'

Opting for the positive interpretation, Sewell decided to test the water and complimented her on her looks. 'Blow-dried my hair. Coffee after church on Sunday?'

'Count on it.'

The Bridge - *a love affair*

So! Fashion definitely not a priority. On the other hand, there had been a token gesture to impress. Promising.

Re-living the events of the evening kept him awake until two o'clock. The only negative thought: was this too good to be true? What a beautiful personality! If she was as independent as he judged, nothing would be gained - and all might be lost - by rushing things. On this basis he was able to deal with the otherwise irrepressible urge to contact her before Sunday.

Time dragged, but eventually Sunday came. He became aware that his contribution to conversation over post-mattins coffee was stilted. Was the anxiety showing? Everything now depended on what would happen when the meeting broke up.

Again, he need not have worried. As they left they fell into step as if by years of habit. The previous day he had checked the dinner menu of a pub-cum-restaurant thirty minutes' drive away, the Saracen's Head. They were barely half-way across the market square when he suggested dinner - and she had accepted. 'Is it formal? My wardrobe doesn't include a little black number.'

Not exactly a shock revelation. He was getting to know a person rather than a wardrobe, and would have welcomed the privilege of dining with that person clad in a mud-stained tarpaulin.

In the event he was pretty sure that dinner had gone well - an impression reinforced on the way home by an offer to cook for him that coming Saturday evening, when, over a mouth-watering pork casserole, he was to discover two further skills she took in her stride - cooking and photography. He had set up a darkroom for developing film taken with a Konica FP single-lens reflex camera and for making black-and-white prints. Discussion led to the suggestion that she should take-black-and-white photos of him. Possibly the most promising sign so far.

On the walk home he thought back to that Sunday and to the first introduction to the woman in the drab overcoat. Never again would he allow the adjective 'plain' to form in his mind.

They settled into a routine of seeing each other three evenings a week, Wednesday, Saturday and Sunday - and on other occasions as

The Bridge - *a love affair*

they arose. Attendance at St Mary's had given way to a drive to choral evensong at the cathedral followed by an evening in - his place or hers. If the former there was frequently music: she played violin and recorder, and he would play the piano accompaniment from her books of Handel sonatas.

Then another suggestion: could he make use of a muse? It could only have come from Lígia - and the imagination could only boggle. He was not involved in creating anything artistic - music, poetry, literature - but had recently embarked on another sort of writing - printed handouts to complement lectures. Eliminating the need for chalking up equations and tedious derivations had not only eased the sheer physical work of writing on the blackboard, but had freed up lecture time to elaborate, for illustrating applications to engineering practice and, above all, for inviting questions and stimulating discussion.

Possibly because he felt he was now justifying his 50 minutes in front of the class, sweaty moments were becoming less frequent. Progress had not come without price, however. Preparation time had more than doubled: handouts needed to be prepared on Gestetner stencils and, with no secretarial help available for this unorthodox activity, one did one's own typing - time-consuming at the best of times even without the messy business of using correcting fluid and a brush for mis-typings.

He had moved up in the scale of lecturing slots - to Tuesdays, but still 09.00. Printing invariably turned into a last-minute affair, with Monday nights spent hand-cranking a mechanically-operated Gestetner duplicator and collating quarto-size pages.

It would be decades before he met a student who had attended his classes and gone on to lecture at Cambridge. The first topic of conversation on being recognized was that of printed lecture notes! Sewell's had been the first encountered by the former student, and had become the model for the latter's own lectures.

Not quite Lotte Lenya's muse to Kurt Weill, then, but Sewell was in no doubt as to Lígia's indirect influence on his progress towards coming to terms with his professional *bête noire*.

One Sunday she decided to talk about her choice of career, the resulting choice of 'A'-level subjects, biology, chemistry and physics - not a choice, really - and the regrets at not having included mathematics. The rest of the evening was spent at the kitchen table as Sewell improvised an explanation of differentiation. As he recalled his own introduction to differential calculus, it had involved several lectures together with assistance from a flat-mate a year ahead of him for the principles to begin to make sense. Lígia picked up first time: it was never necessary to repeat. He restored some self-esteem with the conclusion that his explanations must have been at least adequate. But what a woman!

And wasn't that a feature of their communication? - she *picked up*. Even if not there-and-then, *everything* registered: she would come back on something said - maybe a week previously - but she would come back to it and pursue it. And more often than not with her trademark twist of originality. Here was a woman one could marry. Much too soon to sound her out now, but this one was not getting away before she had been made aware of how much he thought of her.

Putting on her coat half-an-hour later she reached into a pocket, pulling out a folded sheet of flimsy paper. Over a hug she slipped it into his hand. 'Here, treat us to this' - and slipped away without waiting for a reply.

A minute or two was spent - invested, perhaps - in savouring the recollection of the hug. With rationality seeping back he unfolded a page cut from the *Gloucestershire Echo*. An item circled under *Cheltenham Music Festival* was Beethoven' symphony number five. Had it been Rachmaninov . . . . But steady on! No point in ending up helplessly in love with orchestra, conductor and everybody else as well as with Lígia. Safer with a composer he could enjoy objectively. Beethoven was the choice. Had she known that too?

Attending would mean an over-night stay. Half-a-dozen telephone calls the following Monday morning revealed the obvious: the festival had accounted for all the hotel accommodation. Eventually a bed-and-breakfast in Prestbury had a double room still free - which, however, the proprietor was not prepared to hold while Sewell checked with Lígia. It had been less routine then than now for couples to rush to bed before discussing prospects. However, the 'option' was to book now, check later.

He had expected her to take the news in her stride - as, indeed, she did, and the evening of the concert duly arrived without the matter arising again. They drove *via* Prestbury to collect a key to avoid hurrying to the bed-and-breakfast after the performance - a concession which called for payment in advance.

The programme started with a spirited rendering of Ravel's *La Valse* sufficient to convince that this had been the correct choice to open the concert - as it would be to open *any* concert - *all* concerts.

In the applause which accompanied the violin soloist onto the stage, Ligia indicated a man on her right as the maker of the soloist's instrument.

'I didn't know you moved in those circles?'

'I don't. I heard him talking about it as we sat down. That's why he's come - to hear how his craftsmanship responds to a master's touch.'

Whether the violin-maker heard what he was hoping for, Sewell was doubtful. As the disjointed outpourings of an evidently tortured soul, the piece was a triumph of dazzling technique over conventional harmonic and melodic development. Only in the closing bars did Sewell identify a theme of sorts - a succession of jagged intervals. The concerto was clearly not in the programme as a crowd-pleaser, and the prolonged applause could only have been for the skill and stamina of the violinist. The Beethoven which followed the interval was, well, Beethoven.

As they left the town hall she enquired 'Did you notice that the soloist had joined the violin section for the Beethoven? I wonder whose instrument he borrowed.'

'I thought it was him, but wasn't sure. Why would he need a different instrument?

'Let's talk over a glass of wine.'

The Bridge - *a love affair*

They walked through a rotating door of a likely-looking hotel, sat and ordered. The concert seats had been two rows back, directly opposite the leader - hardly the ideal location from the point of view of acoustic balance, but one which insisted on comparisons between soloist and leader. Sewell had found the soloist's tone thin and hard by comparison with the leader's richer sound - rather as Miles Davies' trumpet tone with, say, the nut-brown sound achieved by Maurice André. But he wasn't going to attempt to distinguish musicality from technique. Lígia the violinist saw things differently - as a conscious choice of instrument, bow and technique - essential complements to the piece.

They talked on, and years later - as, indeed, right now - he would wonder why he had not been distracted by nervous anticipation of the prospect of a night of passion. Well, with Lígia everything was different: things would happen as they happened, and could be relied upon to defy expectation. It would merely be a variation on the sheer fun she brought to everything. And thus they chatted for half an hour before walking to the car and making the short drive to Prestbury.

Happily exhausted, they tumbled into bed as though into a familiar nightly routine. She started - and kept up - a running commentary on the 'little helpless noises' of arousal. Writhing to change sleeping position, she would enquire 'whose legs are these?' And as for the increasingly drowsy one-sided observations to which she fell asleep, it would not be possible to improve on her choice of word - 'burbling'.

Now seemed as good a time as any. 'Will you marry me?'
'When?'
'Early September? - time for a honeymoon before term starts'
'Better start planning tomorrow.'

Straightforward as that! As, indeed, were the ensuing preparations. The magic formula, he concluded, was this *communication* - direct soul-to-soul: something absent from the relationships with Jean, with his parents - or with anyone else - a level of intimacy in its own right.

Arrangements for the September wedding fell into place almost automatically: she was a no-nonsense organiser and they functioned effortlessly as a team. The guest list for the reception at the Abbey Hotel stretched to a modest fifty-two: Lígia was the only child of a small family. Sewell had been born to parents in their forties, an elder brother having died young. There were no surviving relatives on his father's side. His mother had been brought up from early childhood by a self-appointed foster-mother, Dorothy. The dear lady had made it to ninety-two - but not to the wedding. None of the siblings had kept in contact, so it was just parents and friends.

On the recommendation of a colleague from Eire, Sewell had been reading Maurice O'Sullivan's lyrical *Twenty Years A-Growing* about childhood on the Blasket Islands. Lígia had never visited the Republic, and took little persuading that the honeymoon should be spent in the Dingle peninsula. They spent the night of the reception at the Abbey hotel, and early the next day drove to Preston, putting Sewell's high-mileage Mercedes 190 on the ferry to Larne, from where the roads south were well-made and traffic-free but for the occasional tractor towing a miniature haystack. As a local observed at a stop for refreshment: 'If the Irish can't build roads, who can?'

They agreed that neither of them had seen green before - not that sort of green, anyway. And the rural landscape was dotted with brilliant, pastel-coloured dwellings - about one per square mile - pink, primrose, blue. Almost every grass verge was grazed by a hobbled donkey.

Looking back (as he was now doing at about six thousand feet over the United States) he was glad they had seen Ireland when they did - while it remained the western-most limit of European civilization - before the era of the motorized caravan, and before the traditional houses had been razed to make way for the uniform bungaloid replacements. Vastly better, of course, for the inhabitants, but soul-less: magical would no longer be the first word to spring to mind.

The Mercedes 190 negotiated the stunning Connor Pass without incident, getting them to Dingle on what turned out to be market

The Bridge - *a love affair*

day. There was nothing for it but to park and wait for donkeys, flocks of sheep and goats to clear from the streets. Then it was on *via* Dunquin and past Mount Brandon to Ballyferriter, where they had reserved a room at Gaeltacht House run by Mrs O'Shea. From the outside it could have been any pub-cum-hotel, but turned out to be petrol-station, bicycle shop, tobacconist, fishing-tackle shop, general store and restaurant. The wonderful Mrs O'Shea looked after them as family, and dealt with the inconvenience of Sunday trading legislation by locking the front door and un-locking the back.

Daylight hours were spent exploring locations featured in *Twenty Years A'Growing* - and invariably encountering somebody eager to recommend further places of interest - the Gallarus Oratory, for example - and, for after-hours culture, Seamus Begley's quayside pub in Ballydavid. When the latter had accumulated three such recommendations, nothing remained but to give it a try.

It was over a glass each of unrecognizably well-kept Guinness that a man in fisherman's roll-neck sweater and wellington boots introduced himself as Kevin Kennedy. The local school had two teachers, he told them, and he was fifty-percent of the establishment. Having a professional salary meant that he was able to run a small fishing boat with outboard motor. This he lent out to local fishermen who would otherwise have to go about their business in a currach.

Kevin was a teacher of Irish and English, and wrote poetry in both languages. He was an inexhaustible supply of lyrical commentary on the human condition. Some time after midnight they parted on an invitation: 'This rain will have cleared by tomorrow morning. If you'd like to meet me at the jetty after lunch, we'll go mackerel fishing.'

They drove back to Ballyferriter in a torrential downpour, water from roadside ditches washing over the road. They parked, scooted to the entrance, threaded their way through Mrs O'Shea's customers and upstairs to the room.

Much, much later there was a knock at the bedroom door. Mrs O'Shea peered in: 'You're safe, thank God.' - and quietly closed the door.

The Bridge - *a love affair*

Over breakfast she apologized for the intrusion: neither she nor Mr O'Shea had noticed their return. The customers had been talking about the storm, and the wonderful lady had waited up until three-thirty, increasing concerned that they had ended up in a water-filled ditch.

They met Kevin as arranged. He helped them down into the rocking boat, suggesting they might like to travel facing him in the stern. The seat was the transom - a wooden plank set transverse to the keel. Embedded therein was a horse-shoe-shaped pattern of deep impressions which several layers of paint had failed to fill. 'Conger eel', explained Kevin. 'Cut the head from the body and it will still bite your arm off.'

'Can we stick to fishing for mackerel?' suggested Lígia.

The boat rode the light swell for about half-an-hour, Kevin at the helm expounding on a favourite topic - man in harmony with his environment. They did a circuit of a small island teeming with bird-life. As they headed back, Kevin let the boat steer itself and broke out a bucket and a couple of lines, the latter with ten hooks each baited with silver foil. These they paid out over the side, hauling them back in immediately, each with ten wriggling mackerel. These were detached effortlessly by Kevin, and in minutes there was a bucket full of fish.

The expedition concluded with photographs on the jetty and an exchange of contact details over Guinness at Seamus Begley's ever-open pub (Ballydavid 4 was Kevin's intriguing telephone number!). Seamus provided newspaper for wrapping four mackerel ('must be eaten fresh!'), and exacted a promise that, on their next visit, Sewell and Lígia would not pay for accommodation, but would be his guests.

It was the final evening of the stay. For dinner, Mrs O'Shea recommended mackerel baked in oatmeal. Salmon, it was later agreed - smoked or otherwise - would never taste the same again. A good enough reason, Lígia suggested, for extending by another week. However, before setting off for Ireland, Sewell had signed up with his TA unit for an exercise on the weekend immediately following their return. It just wasn't the sort of thing you telephoned and cancelled.

Mr O'Shea cranked the manually-operated petrol pump, they packed the car for an early departure and headed upstairs for an early night.

Morning dawned clear and bright. Rounding Slea head they stopped to wave goodbye to the Great Blasket. After a stop at Dingle for a proper look around, the Mercedes made it over Connor pass - not without effort, but again without incident. Less than twenty-four hours later they were home - a married couple!

There was just time to settle in and for Sewell to attend the briefings for his TA exercise.

At 02.30 on the Sunday morning Lígia was awoken by the telephone ringing. 'Mrs Sewell? I'm the CO of your husband's unit. There's been an accident. Not fatal - but serious. I've got transport standing by to pick you up. We'll be going to Birmingham. You may want to pack an overnight bag. Do you think you could be ready in twenty minutes?'

The Bridge - *a love affair*

11

Musical interlude

There was a snort beside him followed by indulgent stretching. As Sewell mused idly that the crew might like to check their navigation against Erwin's waking schedule, a reduction in engine gearbox noise accompanied by a gentle nose-down pitch suggested the start of the descent to their destination.

They disembarked into a waiting mini-bus driven by a giant of an army private, who whisked them without a word to an hotel - evidently pre-booked. Sewell was asleep on his feet, but somehow found his way to a room bearing the number on the plastic room key. He fell asleep fully-dressed.

What happened over the next eighteen hours he would possibly never know - except that suddenly it was daylight, that he was fully-dressed, and that the rasping of the stubble on the side of his throat against his collar suggested a healthy two days' growth. To save weight he had not packed a razor, but the compact bathroom provided a disposable item boasting more plastic in the packaging than in the razor itself. He dealt with the stubble first, pausing for a moment in front of the mirror to recall his shaving companion on the Homeric. The welcome shower was reserved to last as the best way of avoiding meeting the outside world with remnants of shaving soap in ears and nostrils.

He ventured downstairs to the welcome, spicy smell of cooked breakfast. Male waiters crisply-attired in white were taking orders at tables, which he diagnosed as meaning that he had landed in a military environment. On its arrival - which was prompt - the strength of the coffee supported the diagnosis.

If he carried on eating in this style he would be returning to the real world looking like the roly-poly Michelin man and, like as not, would be resented for it. As he pondered the options, Erwin entered, making a bee-line for his table. 'Car's waiting. Let's eat up and go.'

Unless Erwin was carrying some hidden radio device, his face served as an *open sesame*. Soon they were walking through the famous Los Alamos National Laboratory, greeting staff as though Erwin owned and ran the place. 'I'll introduce you to your project leader and then I'm off to Washington. Back again in thirty days for a progress meeting. Assuming all has gone to schedule, we then move on to Denver - to the National Institute of Standards and Technology, NIST.'

Erwin made the relevant introduction and handed over the flash drives. These hand-overs were beginning to trigger an eerie experience - as if the career-lifetime's accumulation of neuro-connections in his brain had been packaged and passed from hand to hand independently of the owner.

Sewell was taken on a whistle-stop tour of facilities and personnel. Despite Melt-down, the famous laboratory had held on to a strong core of specialists in the technology of regenerative coolers, together with crucial support staff. The latter included their top 'CAD-jockey', Ozzie Watt, fluent in the use of every solid-modelling package that had ever been marketed - Pro-Engineer, SolidWorks, AutoCad, UniGraphics, AutoDesk - the lot.

Numerically-controlled machines ('NC' machines) had eliminated the need for the skills for which Sewell had served his engineering apprenticeship: drawings were now generated with the aid of solid-modelling software and could be displayed not as cryptic orthographic views in first- or third-angle projection requiring interpretation by an experienced machinist, but in photo-realistic quality as perspective images of the finished component. If required, the corresponding file could be exported to a rapid-prototyping machine to create the component in plastic - faithful in every geometric detail to the eventual counterpart in metal.

He was never told the detail of the target schedule - possibly a critical path analysis - but it was evident as work proceeded that it never deviated from plan by more than a day or so. Someone, probably under Erwin's supervision, had carried out meticulous preparation.

The net outcome, on day twenty-nine, was a piece of hardware, indistinguishable visually from the demonstrator that had accompanied Sewell to the Rutherford laboratory. That it did not function as an engine was due to the fact that components intended for eventual fabrication were not compatible with electron-beam welding, and that some bolted joints designed to seal against high pressure at high temperature would not withstand rated tightening torque.

At any event, the progress meeting on day thirty was a formality. Erwin, Sewell and the project leader enjoyed another global-economy-defying dinner on somebody's account, and Sewell slept rather well.

Predictably, Erwin spent the flight to Denver asleep, while Sewell listened in on the R/T exchanges. Arrival and introductions at NIST followed a pattern which was becoming familiar.

On the afternoon of arrival, Sewell and his American counterpart began the task of converting specifications - principally those of metal alloys - from UK to US standards. A contributory factor to Melt-down in the UK had been the decline in industrial output, not only of finished goods, but of the raw materials required to manufacture them - steel, sheet metal, light alloys *etc*. The decline had been self-fuelling, and an early casualty had been choice: when a component was to be in aluminium alloy you could get HE-30 in the WP condition - or you could get HE-30 in the WP condition - not ideal when the application called for 2014A in the TF condition. Steels which had continued to be available had increasingly been specified in terms of the traditional - but obsolete - British 'En' code. 'En' stood for 'emergency number' which, as a colleague had never tired of observing, had been obsolescent when granny was a lad.

The situation gave rise to a bizarre side to the task at NIST: For a source of En specifications Sewell had been forced to fall back on a booklet he had been given by the then thriving United Steel Companies of Sheffield under the title *Steel Specifications*. It was dated 1964. As luck would have it, it was a diminutive, imitation-leather volume, and had travelled in his pocket. A typical day would see Sewell at a desk with the little book, his counterpart at a separate desk with a computer calling up American specifications - SAE, AISI and ASTM. Between them was a small table with today's hard-copy print of one of Ozzie's CAD drawings. First they would document the reasons for the original choice of material to the En specification - fatigue characteristics, thermal conductivity, high-temperature creep resistance and so on. Candidates from the closest chemical matches would be checked on the internet for availability against suppliers' stock-holdings. The eventual short-list showing required sizes and quantities was e-mailed to the purchasing department at the end of each working day.

Despite the fact that the enforced *modus operandi* must have been beyond anyone's power of prediction (except, possibly, that of Erwin Corey) work again proceeded with never more than twenty-four hours' departure from schedule.

The return to Albuquerque was a bit like going home. Materials had been purchased as fast as NIST had been approving them. With the code for the NC machines already tested and stored, half-a-dozen identical copies of each component were being turned out in a fraction of the original set-up time. Motivation was at fever pitch, and by pre-Melt-down standards, progress was spectacular, provoking comparison with a war-time achievement of Marshall of Cambridge: That company could take delivery of a battle-damaged DC-3 aircraft one evening, repair it overnight - sometimes inter-changing a wing with another damaged machine - and had a serviceable aircraft ready for the ferry pilot the next morning.

Within a month, six engines had been assembled. Unlike conventional reciprocating engines they could not be motored for initial test. However, the six micro-processors duly arrived from Cambridge UK. With the necessary connections made to transducers embedded in engine and combustion system, start-up was trouble-free. Work paused for celebrations after the first engine delivered design output at rated frequency. Thereafter, progress was routine. Sewell moved on as all six were being installed on dynamometers for preliminary endurance testing.

In Ohio a firm of specialist consultants was to take the project a further step towards volume production. Since its origins in the mass-manufacture of the Springfield rifle, mass-production had evolved into a technology remote from prototype manufacture. Every single component would now be re-examined for the most economical way of producing one thousand, then ten thousand and then one hundred thousand - each identical to the extent of being interchangeable. In most cases, this meant that NC machining - if required at all - would be reduced to a finishing process applied to a 'piece-part' which was itself the result of a process of pre-forming - casting, extrusion, hot-forging, cold-forging, warm-forging or, indeed, powder-compaction and sintering.

Work got under way at eight o'clock in the morning of day one. In a gruelling meeting lasting all day, each component was discussed by reference to its respective CAD rendering by Ozzie, and then assigned to one of the specialist consultants, who thus became section leader. That consultant then chose his or her team of two, three or four from the establishment of seven partners.

It was soon apparent that few of the skills acquired by Sewell in the course of his engineering apprenticeship and subsequent industrial experience would be directly relevant - turning, milling, hand-welding and so on. On the other hand, a component produced by cold extrusion to given dimensions from a given material ends up with different properties from a component machined 'from-the-solid' to identical dimensions and tolerances from the same material. Sewell would be in constant demand for his view as to the possible implications of such changes. Together with Ozzie he was accordingly an honorary member of every team.

The result of many hours' intensive work on a component would be a comprehensive specification and one or more CAD renderings modified by Ozzie from his original files. These would be put out to quotation by e-mail to US manufacturers having appropriate credentials - the most crucial being that they had survived Melt-down! Only if the trawl of the US drew a blank, would the net be extended 'off-shore'. Quotations came in almost instantaneously, triggering e-mail contact with a woman from outside the consultancy. Sewell would come to know her simply as Jas. Jas would respond by calling a meeting of the team, and if it was set for six o'clock in the morning, then that was the hour at which the meeting would start. Likewise if she called it for ten o'clock at night.

He did not have to wait long for his first encounter. She spoke with a soft, Boston accent - soft because all present were on tenterhooks, making a raised voice unnecessary. She would grill each member of the team as to his or her contribution to paring costs to the absolute minimum. There would be a pause during which all present held their breath. Then: 'I think we can shave off another x percent' - where x would be five, ten, fifteen or, on occasion, twenty - but never zero. She would then invite Sewell's view as to the impact on performance. A further pause, and then: 'Thank you for your time and expertise. E-mail me as soon as you are down to target cost. Then we will meet again and get this one signed off.'

The uncanny thing was that her target percentage was achieved on each component without exception. What a woman, that Jas! In all probability Erwin Corey's appointment. Sewell made a mental note to check.

There would be no clear-cut end to this aspect of the project. If, in a few months' time, it resulted in a pre-production prototype whose performance and reliability justified volume manufacture, the process of cost reduction would continue for as long as the design remained in production.

The Bridge - *a love affair*

Finally there was a week of intensive discussions at the Los Alamos Lab. Erwin arrived to take part in the final day, which concluded with a dinner memorable for a string of spontaneous speeches. Next morning a five o'clock alarm call got Sewell and Erwin aboard the city-hopping flight back to Buffalo. He had always found a return journey - long or short - to pass more quickly than the out-bound leg: the memorable high-calorie donuts and strong coffee helped occupy the wait for the Hercules. The landing at Ottawa got them to the hotel by early evening.

Agreeing to go their separate ways until breakfast the next morning gave Sewell a leisurely evening to himself. He had visited this handsome and welcoming city once before with Cécile, a great friend from days as a graduate student in Toronto. They had taken a tour of the parliament buildings and followed it with a visit to a nearby hotel for coffee - memorable for the fact that it had boasted a fine grand piano - and a pianist with an impressive repertoire.

Sewell had always been in awe of the cocktail-bar piano style - the ease and fluency with which the 'standards' were interpreted and suggested - often without being explicitly stated. That one-and-only visit to Ottawa had been at least thirty years previously, and in economic times which could not have been more different. But, who knows? The place might still be there.

All he could recall was that it had been within walking distance of the parliament building. It was coming back to him: they had left her car in the parking area which evidently served the parliament building - and next to a street sign in French. Sewell was far from fluent, but something had jarred. He queried it with his Cécile - a native speaker - who confirmed. No wonder French Canadians felt the English-speakers treated their culture and language with less respect than it deserved. Their beef was justified on the strength of that particular street sign alone.

He would look for the car-parking area and branch out from there. It was easily-enough located, and within a short walk he was passing frontages of premises which, if not flourishing, at least gave the appearance of functioning. A hotel entrance beckoned. The decor looked promisingly familiar - 1970s English spa - Cheltenham or Leamington, say. There were several diners - but no piano. He searched until street lighting started to come on. About one lamp in ten was functioning, so he headed back to the hotel while street names and other aids to navigation remained legible.

A chalk-board above the bar offered a glass of un-specified house red for double figures in US dollars, and twice that amount in Canadian. This could well be his last night in Ottawa - the last in North America, possibly. That decided it: he would live dangerously. Indicating his choice to the barman he reached towards his back pocket. 'Can't accept that, sir: your account has to go to the Ministry. Ms Whalon's instructions.'

'In that case, hold it a moment, please.' What was Zoë going to think of this indulgence? But, of course! She was not just Zoë - was she not also Moneypenny? He took another look at the chalk-board. There were cocktails - and at prices actually less stratospheric than for wine. 'How about a vodka-Martini: shaken, not stirred.'

'The barman grinned broadly, apparently delighted to oblige.' I'll put that one down to MI6, Mr Bond.'

Taking care not to spill a drop of its high-value contents, Sewell picked up the glass and walked to a low table in the corner. This was a moment to be savoured. How would Bond deal with it? He was still deciding, when an immaculately-dressed, middle-aged woman set her own glass on the table, confessing that she had been left with no option but to join him because he so put her in mind of her former husband: *so* distinguished. A perfectly adequate pick-up line hardly in need of elaboration, but: 'Surely you must be in the military, no?'

A brief account of the difference between the UK regular army and the Reserve got conversation irreversibly under way. Up to Melt-down, she had made a living as a writer. Circumstances since had imposed more reading than writing, and the life and work of Canadian newspaper-man, novelist and academic, Robertson Davies had become a preoccupation. Sewell had read *Leaven of Malice* and *Murther and*

Walking Spirits, and might well have got to bed a whole lot earlier that night had he not admitted to having heard Robertson Davies read one of his Christmas ghost stories to students at Massey College. Still, a couple of hours had passed in pleasant company, the Ministry would be picking up the tab for two more vodka-Martinis and, after all, there was no nine-o'clock lecture to face the next morning.

Indeed, the meeting in Sernas' office would not be until eleven. The hotel staff had embraced the notion that the Ministry had an account, and nine-thirty found Mr Bond being served griddle cakes and maple syrup - together with anything else he might care to put on the open-ended bill. At precisely ten, Erwin Corey walked in, fresh as a daisy, evidently having slept soundly through his overnight flight. 'Ever wondered why I volunteered to coordinate this barter? Griddle cakes and maple syrup!'

Discussion in which one eats and the other does not can become lop-sided, so by ten thirty the Ministry had picked up the tab for two further breakfasts. Sewell collected his anorak and suitcase from reception, and on a beautiful fall day they walked to their destination.

They were met by Zoë, who confirmed that they were expected, and showed them in to Sernas' office. The nearest discussion came to technicalities was that the grain shipments due under the barter were being delivered to schedule and without a hitch - a success story due partly to the deterrent effect of the submarine escorts.

Erwin outlined the progress of the engine towards volume production, an achievement which he generously attributed to having received a comprehensively-tested design. Forty minutes passed quickly, and the Minister stood up. Sewell guessed he should do likewise. 'In the old days I've no doubt we would have given you one hell of a farewell party - rye-and-ginger without limit. Partying's not back in fashion yet. But maybe people of our age are not in fashion either. So what we have laid on instead might well appeal more: Erwin and I are going to carry on talking, while Zoë takes you to lunch. I know it's a bit early, but at two-thirty you will be on your way, and we don't want to rush you: no point leaving Canada with indigestion. So, any stuff that's going with you on the trip - take it to the restaurant with you now.'

Sewell exchanged a wordless bear-hug with Erwin. There was a prolonged hand-shake with the Minister who walked with him through the door where Zoë was getting up from her desk. 'He's all yours!'

They walked out to the street. 'Whose idea was the lunch?'

'Mine. Do you mind?'

'Do I mind! If it's got to be goodbye I couldn't imagine a nicer send-off. Where are we going?'

'You'll see. I'm really looking forward to talking to somebody on the wavelength.'

'There's something different from last time. Your walk. Have you shaken off some chronic millstone while I've been gone?'

'I have and I haven't. Walter - my husband - died six months ago. You don't want them to die, you don't want them to live to suffer more. When it finally happens you are in physical and emotional shreds. If Jan hadn't been so understanding and supportive I couldn't have kept the job going. Then we wouldn't have been here right now.'

'You will have heard all the clichés of sympathy, so I won't add to them - except to say that I have some experience of how you must have felt.'

'Such a pity you did not meet: so much in common. He was a sculptor - but not one of those who bolt a rusty old car brake disc to a piece of drift-wood and call it art. He got a commission once to carve a relief in Ketton stone. Expensive stuff - imported from England. Anyway, the design involved a horse's head - huge - larger than life. He prepared by getting a head from the knacker's yard and buying a huge cauldron. He boiled the skin and flesh off the skeleton in the yard outside his studio. We were living in a suburb, but it had a sort of town centre, and his studio was right in the middle. He stank the centre out for two days. Apparently shoppers defected to the next suburb. He was unrepentant: he saw his work as a never-ending search for ways of expressing some underlying truth.'

'Sounds a lot like engineering already. If it helps to talk you could tell me what happened. Was it an accident?'

'Not at all. One day he told me he was having difficulty coordinating. A few weeks later he couldn't walk or do anything for himself. Some rare neurological problem - rare enough that they couldn't agree on a diagnosis. And no diagnosis means no treatment. He hung on deteriorating for over three months.'

'Was Walter a native of Montreal?'

'Yes. Why?'

'But did he travel abroad?'

'Not after we married. Before that he had spent some time studying with a stone-mason in Paris - a chap who restored carvings in cathedrals and churches.'

'I shared a cabin on the Homeric with three others - one a war historian, one a sculptor from Ottawa. The third was a nobody. I don't recall that surnames ever arose, but now that you remind me, Walter rings a bell. Slim but not thin, not quite as tall as me. Short, dark, wavy hair - possibly thinning even then: made it difficult to judge his age - a bit older than me, possibly - twenty-five, maybe? Nineteen sixty-two it was.'

'Can you believe it!? It *was* the Homeric he had come home on, sure enough - best week's holiday of his life is how he spoke about the trip. So you *did* know him! What an incredible coincidence.'

'Don't start me on coincidences. In my experience they're more normal than normality.'

'I'm so glad we have Walter in common: makes it easier to tell you something important.'

'Go on.'

'That I'm not "available". Much too soon. There: I've told you!'

'Please don't worry. I've been there. Half-a-century on and I still haven't fully recovered. I'm no longer expecting to.'

They paused in front of a magnificent building - Château Laurier.

'We're here. I've been looking forward to this lunch for weeks. Now we shall be able to talk without any misunderstandings or false expectations. This is shaping up to be the most enjoyable lunch in ages.'

They entered a lobby where she handed over her coat. There was a smile of recognition for Zoë. The receptionist held out a hand for Sewell's suitcase. 'Your private room's ready for you, Ms Whalon.'

Zoë paused: 'You have imagination - it stands out a mile. How about just for two hours I am your Moneypenny and you my James Bond? This could be the lunch date that poor old Moneypenny so much wanted - but never got.'

He followed her into a dining-room in Melt-down-defying décor. 'What do you think?'

'Well, I suppose . . .' And there it was – a grand piano. *The* grand piano? 'Does your dossier on me say I've been here before?'

'Canada House in London traced your immigrant visa application from nineteen sixty-two, and we know you came and went through customs twice before the turn of the century. But no - not in that detail.'

'Well, it would have been impossible to choose a better place.'

'You can say that again: It's the only one still functioning at this sort of level! And boy! Do they make the most of it. Wait until you see.'

A waiter approached and steered them to a table near the piano - a Steinway model B, no less. Silverware glinted and crystal sparkled against a brilliant white table-cloth. 'Can you make do with this, James?'

He sat down, pulled a cotton napkin from a silver ring, pausing as if in difficulty over the reply. 'I'll do my best to suppress any dissatisfaction. Plenty of tables are occupied: how does that square with this being your private room?'

'An in-joke: it's actually called Zoë's Lounge. Just a coincidence - no family connection. Before Melt-down it served light refreshments - afternoon teas and so on - but *what* teas! Full meals were served in the main dining rooms. By focusing everything on Zoë's Lounge they've kept standards up.'

'Has a grand piano always been a feature?'

'For as long as I've been coming it has. Why?'

'I could swear I've been here before - in the seventies. Even tried to find the place last evening - not that I could have missed if I'd remembered it by the outside. What was memorable for me was the piano-playing. Would the décor have been ultra-conservative then - barely-adequate lighting - a bit like an English spa-town hotel of the era?'

'Almost certainly - like everything else. The piano's come into its own over the past eighteen months because it means there can be music independent of electricity supply. When power's off it's dining by candlelight - plus the music! The place is packed for dinner. No chance of eating without booking.'

'Does it get played at lunchtime?'

'We're early. The pianist usually arrives a bit before one o'clock. He speaks French and some other language, but struggles in English - communicates through his playing instead. I've heard him compared to Oscar Peterson.

'By the way, there's no printed menu: supplies are still unpredictable. The day's menu is stored in the waiters' heads. The chef cooks like the pianist plays - with that elusive ingredient - magic. So if the waiter says that soup of the day is sawdust and iron filings, take it: you'll never crave caviar again.'

'Sounds as if I shall be trying the soup. What about you?'

'If he's got an avocado pear *au point*, it'll be that with vinaigrette. Otherwise the soup. And for the main course, chef's got a way with lake trout. Can't go wrong.'

Having read their gestures from a distance, the waiter returned, explained the menu, and retreated to the kitchen with an order for two lake trout.

'Now all we need now is the wine list.'

'There isn't one. But presumably we are both on the white. The only thing they bring to the table by the bottle is German Riesling. We shalln't know which until it arrives: they don't tell us, and the price is never spoken. But chef doesn't allow anything less than a Trockenbeerenlese or Eislese onto the premises, so it won't disappoint. Goodness knows how he gets his hands on supplies.'

The waiter was placing the starters in front of them as the pianist arrived, swarthy, dark-skinned and dressed in tuxedo. Sewell watched and as he moved the stool out and raised the piano lid - not fully: just as far as the lowest prop. Huge hands - not so much in terms of span as in thickness of the fingers. How many times had he noticed pianists so incongruously equipped, only to marvel at the delicacy of touch and sheer rapidity of movement.

As if in response to his own tastes, the opening medley consisted of Gershwin standards - *Can't help lovin' dat man*, *Summertime* and *I got rhythm*. If the artist felt a temptation to exploit the rhythmic opportunities in this last number, he resisted it in favour of a restrained, intricate filigree of legato semi-quavers. Transitions of key and rhythm from one piece and the next were achieved through a succession of tastefully-conceived allusions to *Rhapsody in Blue*.

Sewell applauded without waiting to test the etiquette of the environment. A few other diners looked up and joined in hesitantly. To make a point that clearly needed making, Sewell out-clapped them. The pianist turned towards them with an appreciative smile and a slightly raised left hand. 'I'll bet he wouldn't mind getting a request. This audience probably never bothers. Let's hear him in bossa rhythm. Moneypenny, when he stops after the next set, you ask him for a medley of Latin standards - ask for *Girl from Ipanema*.'

At the next break, Zoë walked the few steps to the piano. A few words were exchanged, and another smile signified that the request had been welcome.

The lake trout arrived just as she was sitting down again. They toasted each other, the meal and the music in a dreamily-smooth Trockenbeerenlese as the pianist improvised an eight-bar introduction to

The Bridge - *a love affair*

A garota de Ipanema. There followed two further standards by Antonio Carlos Jobim - *Samba de uma nota so*, and *Desafinado*, dazzling for the skill by which the piano was persuaded to take on the personality of the guitar.

Sewell applauded while the rest of the diners impassively pursued their eating. 'Only a Brazilian has that rhythm in the blood. That's where he's from - Brazil - for certain. When he's played his next medley, he's going to get another request - for Jobim's *Lígia* - that was my wife's name - Lígia. With or without the association, it is the most soul-wrenching song ever written.'

'You're on file as married, but living alone. And there's no record of divorce or bereavement. Do we know each other well enough for you to tell me what the situation is?'

'Estranged. She doesn't live in Bristol. Things went wrong years before I re-located there. She knows where I am, but hasn't asked for a divorce - so far, and I haven't considered asking for one: I was too fond of her. She was the love of my life - still is. She doesn't communicate, but neither that nor anything she could do would make me ever dislike her - or get me to accept that she is not the 'other-half' of Greek mythology: there's only ever the one.'

'I'm so sorry. And you've soldiered on alone for a half-century. I must say that it hasn't aged you externally. There's something about you creative people - engineers and sculptors - and the challenges you rise to: a career-lifetime's search for the truth can't happen without an exceptional sort of commitment. Imagine commitment like that channelled into a relationship - into a marriage. It's the diametric opposite of the James Bond approach.'

'Maybe - but with this lake trout and Riesling there's no substitute for a bit of Bond-style hedonism. From what you said earlier we may have less than an hour left. Should we get back to our rôles?'

She raised her glass in an un-spoken 'Yes, James'.

The pianist was rounding off a medley in another genre - Rachmaninov's *Vocalise*, the fifth and best-known of Villa-Lobos'

The Bridge - *a love affair*

Bachianas Brasileiros and *Baïlèro* from Canteloube's *Chants d'Auvergne*. Sewell rose and walked to the Steinway.

'Será que o Sr. é do Brasil?'

'Sou, sim. E o Sr.?'

(Told you so!). 'Sou inglês - mas inglês da Inglaterra. Porém conheço mais ou menos o Brasil: passei uns dois anos aí - mas faz muito tempo, sabe.'

'São raros as pessoas que falam Português aqui em Ottawa. Como é que se chamam, o Sr. e a Sra? Gostaria de dedicá-lhes uma música. Chamo-me Claudio.'

'Prazer em conheçê-lo, Claudio.' They shook hands. Sewell turned to Zoë: 'Claudio has offered to let us choose a piece.' And back to Claudio: 'Minha amiga se chama Zoë, e eu sou David - mas hoje a gente se chama Moneypenny e James - somente para hoje, entende?'

Claudio had, indeed, understood - and more than there was to understand, judging by the broad smile.

'E quanto a uma dedicação, isso é justamente o que ia lhe pedir! Conheçe *Lígia*?

'Claro que conheço. Inclusive vou cantar. Letra original, naturalmente.'

Sewell returned to his seat. 'He'll play it - *Lígia*. He sings it too. These will be the Tom Jobim lyrics in Portuguese.'

Claudio turned to the piano and appeared to study the keyboard.

'The lyrics are enigmatic - a friend of Jobim, Fernando Sabino, was married to one Lygia. The lyrics are unusual in being largely in the negative: *I've never dreamed about you; never been to a movie; when I phoned I hung up - sorry: my mistake, I don't know your name; never wanted you at my side on a weekend.* Sung by Jobim himself, and against the background (tell you later) . . Whew! just got to hope I don't crack up.'

And then: Debussy? Sewell looked in the direction of the Steinway. Surely there can't have been a misunderstanding.

The Bridge - *a love affair*

Eu nunca sonhei com voce,
Nunca foi ao cinema . . .

Of course! Brilliant intro! This wasn't your usual bossa nova - more of a ballad - except not like any old ballad. And Jobim had been influenced by the French impressionist style. So - this is what was meant by a performer getting under the skin of a composer!

Sewell became aware that he was chewing on the cotton serviette. And now his breathing was becoming jerky and - Damn! Zoë had noticed. 'David, don't worry: I much prefer my James Bonds human. Real people just have to let go sometimes.' She reached across the table and put a hand on his wrist: 'I don't understand the words, but there's something hauntingly beautiful about the overall effect.'

She held his hand until Claudio had finished, paused and looked around. The artist had spoken through his music - and a restrained hint of a smile said that he knew it.

Taking a few slow, deep breaths, Sewell sat back in his chair. 'How are we doing for time?'

Zoë consulted her watch. 'Your transport goes in about twenty minutes. Why don't I go and thank chef. You've got time to take in the next medley. If you are going to say goodbye to Claudio, please tell him that, if he doesn't see me here again, it's only because I would get too emotional. Otherwise I could listen all day.'

They thanked the receptionist as she handed Sewell the suitcase, and walked out into the September sunshine. 'You are no longer on the way to Montreal. Originally we thought it would be great if you could sail with the final grain shipment. I haven't exactly pulled strings, but I kept my ear to the ground: the grain boat goes at the speed which minimizes overall fuel consumption - takes more than a fortnight. I've since fixed something which will get you there in a fraction of that time. Should be more interesting, too!'

'The same resourceful Moneypenny! What would I do without you?'

'The same as you've been doing for the past half-century, I guess: I can't stop thinking about your song, *Lígia*. You said there was more background to the lyrics.'

'There is. Jobim originally denied that he had a crush on his friend's wife. Years after the song became famous in Brazil and the United States, he admitted that it reflected *something you deny so much that it turns into an affirmation - a supreme affirmation of love*. Does that shed any light?

'Does it ever! I was just thinking back to what I told you on the way to lunch - about not being available.'

'Well, I'd say we've cut it a bit fine this time, Moneypenny.'

'Come back one day, James. Please. Jan will let me fix you a flight with the RCAF any time. Have you got all your stuff?'

'All my worldly goods fit this suitcase now.'

'You'll be going to Halifax by road, driving day and night. The convoy stops to change drivers but for little else. Soon after you are home and settled there will be an invitation to Canada House in London for formal thanks and a bit of a knees-up. It's just possible I might get there.' She looked at her watch again. 'Transport in a couple of minutes. That just leaves time for a hug and . . .'

He dropped the suitcase and they wrapped arms around each other. How natural - and how flattering - that she evidently did not care who might be looking. 'Moneypenny, you are the ideal height for a stand-up hug. It should happen more often. And thanks: the lunch date has been the highlight of the entire twelve months. Up to today I'd forgotten I had emotions. I'm going away with a lot to think about.'

A drab-looking vehicle slowed to a halt - as did the line of drab-looking vehicles in its wake. 'This is it, James. Goodbye, good luck and, James . . .'

'Moneypenny?'

'James, *do* be careful.'

12

Hitchhiker's guide to the Atlantic

Moneypenny had implied that it would be an arduous drive - and thus it turned out.

Sewell was in the somewhat spartan rear cab with a woman in uniform who would turn out to be one of the drivers. She was polite (and if there were a defining characteristic of Canadians in Sewell's experience, it was politeness) although evidently not anxious to chat. A pity: there were accents and accents, and French Canadian was one of the more attractive. After precisely four hours of monotonous motorway cruising the convoy stopped and his travelling companion got out. She was replaced by a male in uniform who had presumably driven the initial leg. He greeted Sewell courteously, settled himself and almost instantly fell asleep.

The third changeover involved a break for refreshment and took considerably longer as the vehicles had to remain under guard during visits to the 'rest-room' - a quaint euphemism, Sewell thought. By the time the cycle had been repeated five times he had come to accept that sleeping by numbers was part of military training - and that Canadians excelled at it. At any event, the routine got them to the intermediate destination without incident - the ferry terminal in Halifax.

Somewhat saddle-sore he stepped from the vehicle to be intercepted by a man in uniform who led him briskly into the ferry terminal. We're dead on schedule, sir. You will be boarding the launch in an hour.

A slight sinking feeling took over. Shortage of sleep invariably meant two things: first of all, time slowed down. And secondly it did so to the accompaniment of an unpleasant taste in the mouth. He chose the least uncomfortable seat and prepared for the worst - which, as it happened, he did not have to face. Within less than five minutes an immaculately-dressed mountie entered and held out his hand. Dr Sewell? If you would like to show me your passport, sir, we can start getting you through security.

Returning the passport to its rightful pocket, he was ushered into the next room. The familiar airport system - but with a queue of one: this should be quick and painless. By the time he was declared not to be a security risk he had worked out how they operated: if there were thirty travellers and there were thirty minutes to boarding, then the ration was one minute per traveller. If there was one traveller, then the inspection was pro-rated to thirty minutes per traveller. The belt with titanium buckle attracted meticulous scrutiny, enjoying two passes through the X-ray machine. The suitcase had to be content with one pass, but was subsequently emptied - and, he had to admit, meticulously re-packed.

Suddenly the pace increased. He was led along a jetty and down steps and relieved of the suitcase while being assisted into the launch. The latter set off with a surge of power - evidently a military craft not restricted by fuel allocation. Fifteen minutes later they rounded a headland - or it might have been an island - and there she was!

She towered over the launch as it drew alongside. For a vessel which was supposed to do its business below the surface there was a heck of a lot above. Sewell was to recall little of the frantic minutes which ensued: a couple of impressively agile men dropped into the launch from nowhere in particular. 'You are about to set foot on Swedish territory, sir. You have your papers, of course. Show me, please.'

The Bridge - *a love affair*

It seemed a reasonable request: the submarine which loomed over him looked bigger than Stockholm - perhaps bigger even than Södermanland - and that didn't include the bit below the waterline. So, his problem aboard was not going to be claustrophobia after all - agoraphobia, more like. A metal detector appeared out of thin air. The frisking would have been a tedious repeat but for the fact that, the previous time around, the floor beneath his feet had been boringly stationary. The suitcase was emptied, examined yet again - and repacked as painstakingly as before, his watch being added to the contents. The sailor kept hold of his mobile phone and held up the belt. 'Is this a fashion accessory, sir - or are you likely to lose an essential item of clothing if we ask you to go aboard without it.'

'Can't guarantee remaining respectable.'

'Put it back on, then - but I'll have to ask for it again the moment you are aboard.'

He had been anticipating the formality of requesting permission to come aboard, and was geared up for something like the entry to the footplate of Tornado. It turned out to be nothing of the sort: the athletic ones evidently did not trust a septuagenarian's command of his limbs, and he found himself bundled aboard with very little control - or recollection - as to how he arrived there.

He handed over the belt, took a hold on his trouser-band and looked around. Any possibility of claustrophobia was swept away by the spellbinding reassurance of the high-tech. equipment. A hospital operating theatre looked like a shoddily-run re-cycle centre by comparison - and he had seen both.

'This way, sir.' An immaculately-dressed officer (they were all immaculately dressed) led him through an opening which might have been a watertight bulkhead, and opened the door to a compact but attractive cabin. 'You passengers have both had long journeys. I'll have sandwiches and coffee sent along and then you can catch up on sleep. By the time you wake up we shall be under way.'

The Bridge - *a love affair*

'Excuse me, sir.' It was the man who had taken charge of his shoulder-bag. 'Here's your stuff - all except the mobile phone. You'll get that back when you disembark. But I need to ask your blood group.'

'My blood group? Sure. Same as everybody else: O-positive.'

'Not quite everyone's, sir. There are microscopic traces of blood on the belt buckle. If you are O-positive they're not yours. I shall have to log it, sir. Any suggestions?'

'The only blood donor who comes to mind was a Russian thug - KGB or ex-KGB. Answers to Boris. Last I saw of him he was being loaded into an ambulance on the way to UKAEA Harwell.'

'Some of us earn our living - and other people's security - by being suspicious, sir. Anything more on his identity?'

'Only that his minder calls himself Nikolai. Oh - Nikolai might very well be traceable. Has a son Pyotr who's an up-and-coming concert pianist. Early twenties I would guess. Already established as an interpreter of Rachmaninov.'

'We'll leave it at that for the moment, sir. You are under orders not to wander around the ship. If you want to leave the cabin, open the door and wait just inside. Someone is bound to be passing within minutes. Laundry, fitness facilities and so on are things you will pick up as we get under way.'

The man left, closing the cabin door as he did so. Sewell sat on the side of the bunk and removed his shoes. The submarine was in slight motion, and there were various background noises - not disconcerting, but decidedly alien and paradoxically familiar at the same time. That was it! Charles Chilton's science fiction serial for the BBC in the 1950s, *Journey into space.* It had held half the nation rivetted to the Light Programme each week between 7.00 and 7.30. An essential part of the formula had been the eerie sound effects produced by the BBC Radiophonic Workshop. Today they were real.

There was a knock at the cabin door. A man entered in a spotless white tunic and chequered trousers. Reaching over he folded down a panel opposite the bed to form a table. Cheese sandwiches and coffee! This trip was shaping up nicely.

Sewell stretched out on the bunk - and evidently slept. A further knock at the cabin door brought him back to reality. 'Some of the crew will be eating lunch shortly, sir. Care to join us?' The officer held out his hand. 'I'm Henrik when the captain's not around. Lieutenant when he is. Fish on the menu today: chef had quite a catch while we were on top at Halifax. Call back for you in five minutes.'

Henrik duly returned and led Sewell to a table. 'I'll give you an outline of the trip before the others get here so that we don't bore them: We are juggling three priorities: we've got some manoeuvres, a rendezvous and an escort sector. After that we have to make the UK in the shortest possible time, to arrive during dark and at high tide. It's not that straightforward because main propulsion is by air-breathing diesel engine or battery. The batteries are charged either by the diesels or by auxiliary air-independent engines - Stirling engines - or by both. Battery amp-hours are limited, as you will know. The ship goes about twice as fast submerged as on the surface - so you will be seeing nothing of the Atlantic until we are within a few miles of the UK mainland - and then it will be dark. Ah. Here comes one of our propulsion specialists. Stig - meet Dr David Sewell - knows all about Stirling engines.'

'Well, that means he knows more than me, then.' Sewell stood up, and the two men shook hands. 'We don't actually touch the core engine at sea. We've got glorified Haynes manuals and trouble-shooting sequences for the ancillaries - control circuits *etc.*- things which are accessible. Kockums build the sub. and manufacture the engines as well. If something goes wrong inside the engine itself it's a replacement job at the ship-yard. It's a fine company in the best Swedish tradition: every member of the crew who is involved has been shown an engine under assembly, and there are regular seminars for the propulsion specialists on how they work. I wouldn't mind hearing your version - and I'd bet most of the crew would, too. The Stirling engine is regarded as a bit inscrutable.'

One-by-one the remaining places at the table filled up. The gleaming white waiter arrived with bowls and an irresistible-smelling fish terrine. 'A lot of our business is discussed over meals. How about an impromptu seminar? The impromptu ones are always the best.' It was Hinrik.

'I could give a more easily-digested account if I could use my little visual aid. Would I be trusted to find my way back to my cabin to retrieve it?'

'Someone will go with you, sir. Lars!'

Sewell's patter had been refined by the many repetitions since he had given the non-technical explanation for Sir David Wyatt. He was part-way through fielding a string of questions when there was another arrival.

Lars stood up. 'I'm through, captain. Take my seat if you're eating.'

The man acknowledged and sat down. 'You must be Dr Sewell. I'm Captain Sjömann. Word has it that there are seven members of my crew who finally understand how our air-independent propulsion engines work. Excellent! If you are going to contribute to the running of this sub. I shall have to give you a rank. How does Visiting Professor suit?'

'Fine by me, sir.'

'The rank doesn't actually exist in the Swedish navy, but while we are at sea I make the rules. Lieut. Lundqvist . . . 'He turned to the lieutenant: 'Father Christmas until relieved of duty.'

'Sir.'

'Don't get carried away and too generous: deep recession above surface, remember.' Then: 'Lieut. Ericsson: You are Lord Mayor - for as long as you do a good job, that is.'

'Pleasure, captain. Civic dignitary is the sort of post I always . . .'

'You see how it works professor?'

'I'm beginning to catch on, sir.'

'I should be off - didn't come to eat. You and I are due for a confidential meeting some time. Can't fix it until after the rendezvous. Meantime, try to take your meals with different watches - get to know the whole crew. And keep up the seminars: no harm in having everyone

The Bridge - *a love affair*

on board know how a Stirling engine works. Santa: take the professor aft to the engine rooms. Show him all he wants to see - trouble-shooting manuals - the lot. But we are manoeuvring in two hours. Be through by then.'

Sewell followed his guide for what seemed like half-a-mile until they stopped between two cabinets, each for all the world like an oversize deep-freeze. A small, push-button control console carried the label 'Stirling engine'. Lundqvist released some latches and lifted aside a white panel. It was as Sewell had anticipated: surrounded by the immaculate array of pipes, sensors, wires, valves, pressure vessels was something buried deep inside which had to be the Stirling engine.

'Little to see, I'm afraid, sir. Not disappointed I hope. The engine itself is only part of the technology it takes to generate electric power by burning fuel-oil in pressurized oxygen.'

'No problem. I've seen this engine's brother - the P-40 - stripped down to the essentials, so I can imagine what's inside. It's just good to see a Stirling engine in service - and doing an important job. Is it running right now?'

'It is. Don't worry - everybody has to ask. If it were not virtually silent it wouldn't be installed.'

The panel was replaced, and Sewell was accompanied back to his cabin. 'I understand somebody will be along shortly to see whether you want to watch a DVD.'

Sewell had decided not to wear his watch until the time came to re-set it on arrival in the UK. If they were travelling at 20 kts. the days were nearer to 23 hours than to 24. In any case, nothing on the ship happened to his time scale. Time was measured in terms of intervals between meals: it seemed one could eat every four hours. After what might have been the sixth meal he was awoken by a sharp reduction in the level of background noise. The eerie silence might have lasted two hours. Then it was back to the routine hum, and at the next meal, Nils confirmed that they were under way - and still precisely on schedule.

'Captain Sjömann will see you shortly, sir.' It was Lars. 'When you've finished your coffee we'll pick up your little demonstrator and I'll show you to the captain's quarters.'

He was duly ushered into a cabin where the captain was sitting at a table with a man in uniform carrying a lot of braid. 'Barry, meet our resident professor, David Sewell. Sewell, this is Admiral Dundas.'

The admiral reached out a hand without getting up. 'Ah! The man who's breathed new life into the Stirling engine. Glad to meet you.'

'You too, sir.'

'The world is changing fast, Sewell. Name of the game is mobility combined with un-detectable transport. Under the ocean, in other words. This sub is brilliant - but we've got to look ahead to the next generation. They say you've cracked the problem of getting more power for given size or weight. How's that?'

'The power of any heat engine is the work per cycle multiplied by cycles per second. We get a factor of three or four times the cycles per second: all things being equal that's three or four times the power per swept volume.'

'And what about noise?'

'Noise comes largely from mechanical vibration - from un-balanced inertia forces. The horizontally-opposed configuration has just two moving components - of equal mass. If you can ensure that their respective motions at any instant are equal and opposite, then inertia forces cancel out and what you are left with is no vibration.'

'So the secret is in the synchronization?'

'Precisely, sir.'

'Why isn't everyone doing it?'

'Peak acceleration in the demonstrator I took to the States is about two thousand-times the acceleration due to gravity - two thousand 'g'. This means 35 tons positive in one assembly and 35 tons negative in the mirror-image assembly. Imagine the shaking if they get out-of-sync.'

'And what's to stop them?'

'The work of my colleague, Dr Jiménez. Predictive control - implemented by micro-computer, obviously. A single cycle takes about five thousandths of a second. Feedback on the basis of conventional real-time sampling just doesn't cut it. The management system has to be looking ahead in real time. It does it by understanding the dynamics of the internal gas process interactions and simulating them in real time - keeping a quarter-cycle ahead of the game.'

'So. Correct me if I am wrong: anyone could build one of these engines, but you have cornered the market in the management system.'

'That's the basis of the deal brokered through Canada last year: the UK keeps control of chip design and manufacture. Anyone can make the engines. Those with commodities to spare can barter for a supply of processors. Going well, apparently: the Cambridge lab. is working overtime and increasing capacity.'

The captain spoke: 'You men seem to be getting on like a house on fire. I'm on duty, but you are not. How about a tot of rum a-piece?' The admiral gave a gesture signifying that Sjömann should have known better than to ask. Before pouring, the captain turned to Sewell:

'It would be my first ever navy rum, Captain. You bet!'

Dundas downed his tot in one and nudged the empty glass in the direction of the bottle. Sewell's approach to the drink was more circumspect: he had been getting a kick out of promoting Charo's brilliant contribution, but was suddenly less comfortable. Dundas's demeanour was palpably changed. How many tots had he already downed before Sewell's arrival?

'Now understand this, Sewell. What we are talking about here - quite literally - is the security of supply chains for entire nations. Did you hear about the naval exercise off the California coast not long before Melt-down? One of these Gotlands ran rings round our navy. On the score-card it killed one of our nuclear subs. and sank a carrier - our biggest, the Reagan. Never heard it coming.'

'A YouTube did the rounds, sir. I saw it.'

'We've left it almost too late to catch up - but we've actually got to do more than catch up - we've got to leapfrog. Now, are you telling me that this controller is something that our scientists and engineers - the men and women who sent America to the moon - can't reverse-engineer if we decide to go that route?' (Had Dundas been one of those commanders whose vessel got outwitted by the Gotland? Could explain a lot.)

The captain poured - and the admiral downed. Sewell declined the offer of a re-fill.

'One thing that no-one has succeeded in doing so far - and that includes the Russians and the Chinese - is to pull off an image of what's on the processor.' He outlined the self-destruct feature.

'Then I'll come to the point: what would it take for you to return to the States and give us the processor technology? I am authorized to offer you the best . . .'

'I don't know the terms of the US agreement with Canada, sir. All I know is that I don't have the option of considering an offer - any offer. On top of that, all I contributed was the thermodynamic analysis of the gas process interactions, and the original Fortran-coded version - the numerical equivalent of the algebra. Since then, Dr Jiménez has re-coded for goodness knows how many streams of parallel processing by her custom-designed chips.'

The admiral's face was as black as thunder. 'Why have you been in the States and not this Jiménez? Are you asking me to believe that you are not the brains behind this project?'

'Admiral Dundas, I have given it to you straight. The deal was that the US should get all the ready-coded processors you were prepared to barter for. It was a contractual understanding that you didn't need to know what goes on inside them.'

Dundas jabbed his glass in the direction of the rapidly-emptying rum bottle. Sewell was glad that Charo was not part of these 'negotiations': the situation was bordering on the intimidating.

Captain Sjömann intervened. 'Barry, listen. In this job I get to know - and trust - lots of engineers. It's a profession which attracts integrity - and is unforgiving of lack of integrity: if an engineer cooks the results of a fatigue test on a material specimen for the wing spar of a 747 an aircraft can fall out of the sky. I think we can take the professor's statement of his position at face value.'

Two against one. Dundas leaned back and appeared to relax a little. 'Where do I find this Dr Jiménez.'

'After twelve months away from Europe, sir, I've no idea.' dissembled Sewell. 'Saw her last September at a conference in the UK. She left immediately the conference was over: missing her children. I went to the station to see her off - back to Spain.'

The admiral did not give up readily: 'Did she sign up to this Official Allegiance Act of yours?'

'As a matter of fact, I understand that she did, eventually - and optionally. But that's not the point: she is not a UK citizen, so the signature is almost certainly not enforceable.' Sewell was getting the measure of the situation. 'But I respectfully suggest not taking advantage, sir: she signed because she could trust herself to keep an agreement.'

'Are you in contact?'

'We have not spoken all the time I have been in North America. Right now I'm on my way home to the UK . . . ' He glanced at the captain '. . . so I'm told.'

Sjömann nodded. Dundas extended a hand: 'Here's my card. As soon as you get back see if you can track her down. Let me know the instant you do.'

Here was a man accustomed to issuing orders - and to seeing them obeyed. Sewell would have to warn Charo the moment he got home.

The captain took over. 'Thank you for helping us, Professor. Let yourself out, please: the lieutenant will have arranged for you to be escorted back to your quarters.'

His accommodation below the surface of the Atlantic was vastly superior to that of many hotels above the surface - but if a hotel room got a bit familiar it was usually possible to take a walk. Another four hours to surfacing, the lieutenant had said.

Slipping off his shoes he lay on the bunk and closed his eyes. How far had he journeyed through his life on the flight with Erwin? Ah, yes. The accident. It would be difficult to separate what he actually remembered from what Lígia and the medical staff had told him during and after recovery. He would give it another airing:

Floating into and out of awareness - and he had no idea if he had done so once a minute or once day - he had been aware of lying face-down and looking at a linoleum-covered floor. His mouth and nose were covered by a mask. Over what might have been days, the intervals of consciousness increased. From the combination of sounds and movement he eventually judged he was inside some sort of tent - but with arms outside. If he moved them slightly, the walls of the tent moved too - as if tent material and arms were taped where they passed through.

It did not matter when - or to what extent - he surfaced, someone was invariably holding his left hand and stroking the arm. He thought he heard her voice - but in any case no-one else communicated through touch like that - Lígia.

The periods of consciousness increased - as did the combination of pain and itching on his back. Long or short as the intervals might be, Lígia was always there. If she left, it was because the bed was about to be wheeled somewhere. She would be there holding his hand as he came round after the next skin graft. They were now chatting, and she was full of ideas as to what they would do when he was mobile again.

She had not given up her studies, but had organized things so as to be with him whenever he was back on the ward. And had she organized! She had talked the accommodation officer out of a room in the nurses' home. Although not fully trained, she had a medical degree, and no qualms about chatting-up a consultant (bet *he* didn't hold a gliding instructor rating). There was little effort involved in persuading the consultant that it was not best use of his time to be looking out patient notes for his clinic: she would do it for him: dig out the files for that afternoon's list, put them in order of consultation and re-file them afterwards. A clientele of three consultants yielded a profit over the cost of room and food.

Transfer to the air bed indicated the end of the skin grafts, and gave him some choice as to when he slept - or attempted to. She brought her books, and held his hand with her left while writing - and sometimes operating a ten-inch slide-rule - with the right.

It was three months before she eased him awkwardly into the car and drove home. A further month of constant care followed before he could dress and prepare food unaided. Once he was independent, however, progress was rapid.

Six months after the accident a hand-written letter arrived from Kevin Kennedy: a film crew had invaded the Dingle peninsula and set up to film *Ryan's Daughter*. They had 'borrowed' Kevin's pupils for classroom scenes where Robert Mitchum plays the schoolmaster.

'That does it.' announced Lígia. 'If you're up to it by autumn we go back. Complete the honeymoon. In the meantime we look out for *Ryan's Daughter*. It's bound to be a while yet: apparently they've got to shift filming to South Africa for the shots that need sunshine.'

He was now working at home, but on most days managing an hour in the office or lab. Lígia had caught up with her study schedule. The foreseeable future offered no prospect of involving Sewell in her passion - gliding, so when the weather favoured, Sunday was her day to drive to Bickmarsh, where she never tired of doing circuits with students.

The more adventurous of the partnership, she had seen the future of amateur flying in the new Rogallo hang-glider. He had remained an advocate of fixed-wing machines, and might have succeeded in dissuading her had a couple of club members not each bought an assemble-it-yourself hang-glider kit and taken lessons from the manufacturer.

In the conventional glider, you push the control column forward and the nose pitches down; rearward movement raises the nose. Depending what you understand by 'weight-shift', the opposite applies to the flexible wing hang-glider. Sewell had argued that the more experienced you were on conventional types, the more likely it would be that, under stress, you might push rather than pull, possibly stalling the wing.

Half-a-dozen club members had taken the two machines to the Cotswolds on a perfect day - a stiff breeze up Cleeve Hill. The machines were assembled and each pilot had inspected the fool-proof cable connections of his own glider and cross-checked the rigging of the other.

None of the five saw the stall (if that's what it was). Of all the things she could have hit, it had to be a Cotswold dry stone wall. They had clambered down to the crash scene and found her unconscious with an arm in an unnatural position and deep-looking facial wounds where the helmet had afforded no protection: those wretched machines were flown in the prone position, head forward.

By the time he had been contacted and raced to the hospital she was conscious. Concussion had been confirmed, the arm was in plaster and the duty trauma surgeons had wrought miracles on the jaw and cheek. The hair appeared to have been washed and thoughtfully dried. Those skilled, caring people had restored the face whose winning smile had melted his insides on a thousand hellos and goodbyes. Far too few MBEs got awarded to practitioners of that sort of work.

It was now Sewell's turn to do the nursing - to reciprocate. However, she was soon home. If anything, his own recovery was speeded by the pressures of multi-tasking. Maybe healing took place during sleep: he was certainly catching up on that.

Another sudden reduction in background noise transported him back to the present. With no idea of the time of day or night, he rubbed thumb and fingers through his stubble. A day's growth least since the last shave. He set about smartening up.

A knock at the cabin door was followed by a voice outside: 'Dr Sewell. Executive Officer here.' He opened up. 'I'm authorized to explain first of all that Captain Sjömann does not apologize - especially for the conduct of representatives of other services. If we can leave it at

The Bridge - *a love affair*

that, the captain invites you to join him and the officer of the watch aloft. You might like to know that we surfaced at midnight.

Sky's clear and it's boringly calm. No need for protective clothing. It's 03.00 local time and the moon's up. It's the only light apart from navigation buoys until we dock - in about an hour-and-a-half. You will probably find it all a bit un-wordly - but I think you could enjoy it.'

The X/O accompanied Sewell aloft. The acknowledgement he got from the officers already there was perfunctory - as though he had been reporting for duty - and unspoken. The submarine might have been travelling at four or five knots - and in near silence. There appeared to be distant coast-lines to both to port and starboard. Moonlight flickered in the water. At intervals a flashing buoy approached and slipped silently astern.

After an hour the coastlines had converged to two or three miles either side. The submarine commenced a right turn, heading in the direction of what was evidently a light-house. So, they were going to dock earlier than the X/O had said.

The speed reduced further, but the vessel sailed past the lighthouse and entered a channel probably less than half-a-mile wide - a slow-running river, maybe. In a matter of minutes they were passing beneath a modern concrete bridge. Why he did not ask their position he was not sure: something to do with not wishing to break the spell.

The vessel rounded a tight bend, then a shallower one, keeping in mid-stream as the banks drew closer. A further quarter of an hour and the banks both sides were high above him. Another gradual bend - and Sewell's heart seemed to stop: ahead and high above in the moonlight was . . . the Clifton suspension bridge! Little convulsions in his stomach made his breath come in jerks. He countered by swallowing hard, but his eyes were watering and there was nothing to be done about it. The crew must *not* see this!

He gripped the rail for moral and physical support, and set about bringing himself down to earth by looking for distractions: re-set the watch: it was no longer 03.00, but the minutes would not have changed. Hell! Not enough light.

The Bridge - *a love affair*

There was no possibility under the sun that they had diverted merely to give him a lift home. What business could a stealth submarine conceivably have in a port which had lost military significance centuries ago - and had seen its commercial rôle dwindle almost to zero since the Second World War. The high-value cargo Sernas had alluded to evidently re-defined 'high value'.

They were now passing beneath the bridge. Seen from directly below it had become purely functional - an enormous help in regaining self-control.

Brunel had been a ship designer. He must surely have sailed the gorge - possibly many times, and in both directions. Was that how he had selected the perfect setting? It would be easy to draw the wrong conclusion: he had proposed more than one scheme. But it was not inconceivable that he, too, had witnessed the very moonlit scene that Sewell was marvelling at right now. If so, what a tragedy not to have lived to see the bridge completed.

And what a welcome this would have been for sailors arriving after, maybe, two months from the West Indies.

Back to the other mystery: why were they making landfall in Bristol? Perhaps the question should be why London? With the collapse of the City, the capital had been emasculated as a focus for trade. Street value was no longer proportional to tonnage. What would a quick back-of-envelope sum reveal? Charo's micro-processor chips were 2 mm thick and 400 square mm. Close-stacked and without individual packaging, more than a million would fit into a cubic metre. Say £2 each in old currency and a storage space of 2m x 1m x 5m would hold £20 million-worth. The high-value cargo - if any - which had funded his trip remained a mystery, but Bristol no longer remained an unlikely port of call. He decided to focus on the once-in-a-lifetime experience of seeing the bridge glide away astern. The few minutes involved were sufficient for emotion to give way to hypnotic calm.

The submarine had slowed to a point where it could have been drifting - or maybe starting another turn. 'Would you mind going below now, sir.'

A crew member at the bottom of the ladder escorted Sewell to his cabin. 'Please keep the door closed and don't come out until you are asked to do so. The timing of the next phase is not completely under the ship's control: we draw slightly more water than your famous Great Britain - and it took an especially high tide to launch her. We've got precision depth-sounding and ocean-floor mapping. She managed with a lead line - so don't get nervous! We could be through in an hour - or it might take longer.'

Slipping off his shoes he lay on the bunk. If there isn't a woman to share an experience like tonight's, then you need one to talk to about it afterwards. When you are young it can be your mother. Might explain the origin of the expression from boarding school parlance: *It's nothing to write home to mother about*. In later life, experiences, good and bad, would normally be shared with wife or partner. It had been decades since Lígia had vanished out of his life: his own mother had survived his marriage by twenty years.

By the time the final knock at the door came he had dozed off. 'Sorry it's been so long, sir. Misunderstanding about handling facilities at the docks. Had to improvise shears. It's coming up to seven am. I doubt you'll find anywhere for breakfast ashore, sir. X/O suggests breakfast with the crew.'

With hindsight the voyage had gone far too quickly. Ship's breakfast, definitely! Postpone the parting of the ways by half-an-hour's worth of uniquely professional company. The crew were in good spirits, and those at the table insisted on individual hand-shakes and farewells. As he was helped down onto dry land and handed his suitcase there was a brief, irrational feeling of home-sickness for this magnificent, sombre vessel.

Several people were making their way in his direction on foot. He prepared himself mentally against getting button-holed by anyone who might recognize him and ask for an account of the absence.

When someone did eventually hurry towards him from the opposite sidewalk he was only too glad to stop and talk to his friend and mentor, Michael Langford. 'Thought you were off to Didcot for a couple of days. Must be a year at least since we met on the train. Still, you don't look any older.'

After being allocated something like a minute for his account of events of the previous twelve months, Sewell was impressed to hear that three further novels were waiting for printers to start printing again, and that the journal *Grenzen der Filosofie* had, that very day, notified acceptance of the latest paper *Is "A-matter-of-fact" a matter of fact?* Sewell had no need to excuse himself, being beaten to it by Michael, who had an appointment with a friend from college days. The professor was evidently running late, and was already receding into the distance calling out something about 'taking a look' at a bottle of vintage port.

He had left his house keys with Mrs Hawkes in preference to carrying them around North America. He knocked at the communal front door, which opened as if she had been monitoring his progress up the road. 'David! How wonderful! With no news I had no idea whether we would ever see you again. How long has it been?'

'About a year. And how have you been?'

'At my age I can't complain. Come through to the kitchen, there is something I have to tell you.'

'I've only come to pick up the keys, Violet. I'm back for good now, so we can get our Thursday morning chats going again and I can tell you all about my travels.'

'I'm afraid this can't wait. There's no electric at this time of day to make tea - and no gas either for that matter - but I can tell you quickly. Two things have happened, and I was wondering which to tell you first until I realized it was obvious. Storm is dead. He was as right as rain until it happened - only a matter of days ago.'

There was a pause. 'He would have been nine in November. If he didn't die of old age, do you know how?'

'You had better know the second thing, and then you may be able to tell me: about the beginning of the year the mail service got going again - one delivery a week. The post-man does the rounds on foot, and I suppose he delivers to one postal district on a Monday, a different one on Tuesday and so on. When I went into your place I always picked up the mail and put it in order behind that model steam engine thing on the hall table. Anyway, about once a month since April there has been the same sort of envelope - long, brown paper one. Ordinary stamp, not official, but always the same hand-writing - capitals - and without any of those qualifications you usually get after your name. Well, there was another one through the door last Saturday. I went to put it at the front of the pile - and all the others, all the long brown ones - they weren't there. They had just vanished.'

'It doesn't make sense yet. Is there more?'

'Well, I wasn't afraid. If it was burglars there's not much they are going to do to someone my age. But there was no sense in inviting trouble, so I put the latest one in the usual place, locked up and haven't been back. The plants have enough water for another few days. I hope you don't mind.'

'From what I have picked up so far, you did exactly the right thing - as always. So you think there may be a connection with Storm's death?'

'Perhaps they didn't know how friendly a husky can be - away from the pack, that is. Storm would have welcomed them in and shown them straight to the DVD-player in return for a scratch behind the ears.'

'So where did you find him? In the house?'

'No. He was curled up in the garden in his favourite place - for all the world asleep. Just didn't respond when I asked him if he was hungry. I left him sleeping - as I thought - then tried again.'

'We had no idea how long you would be away, so we buried him not long after he was confirmed dead - gave him a dignified send-off - but what you need to know is that there was no sign of distress: he hadn't been thrashing around in pain. Just curled up peacefully.'

'Sophisticated modern toxin. Part of a picture.'

'You know who it was?'

'Maybe. Look: if you are worried I can sleep in your house for the next week or so.'

The Bridge - *a love affair*

'If Storm was murdered then it's the people who did it who should be worried. I've been keeping Leo's machete within arm's reach, day and night, indoors and in the garden. Would you like to see where we buried Storm?'

'I certainly would - but he's not going anywhere, and I'd better take a look inside the house. Back in a quarter of an hour if that's alright with you.'

'If the power's on I'll have the kettle boiling ready for tea. I almost forgot: your friend from the Army Reserve called. Brought something heavy rolled up. I couldn't lift it. Opened your front door for him and he stood it in the hall.'

'The old sleeping bag, I expect.' Sewell lifted the keys from a hook in the hall. Closing the door behind him, he crossed the communal entrance hall and, for the first time in twelve months, put the key in the latch of his own front door.

13

Call-up papers

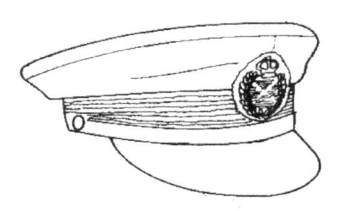

Expect the unexpected!

Silently coaxing the key into the night-latch he listened again. A tentative push opened the door by a centimetre or so. At least there was no-one inside right now: a professional on the job drops the latch so as not to be caught out by the owner's return. Withdrawing the key, he stood back, placed a foot against the door, gave a hefty shove, at the same time stepping smartly aside. Instead of the anticipated crash of inside handle against wall plaster - hardly a sound.

He waited and listened. Despite the unaccustomed onslaught the door remained only partially open. Someone behind the door - alive and in-wait - or dead, maybe? He held his breath. Still not a sound. He inched inside. Just protruding from behind the door was a khaki-coloured roll. The sleeping bag! Probably fallen after being propped against the hall table.

An ornamental walking-stick stood in a holder on the far side of the hall table. Withdrawing it silently he picked up the sleeping bag and advanced to the closest door - the lounge door. He had left all internal doors about one third open, a habit cultivated to avoid trapping Storm. Held vertically, the sleeping roll covered his upper body from head to crotch, and should protect everything vital from a bullet and the worst effects of a booby-trap. Listening for a few seconds at each door in turn he pushed gently with the walking stick. Nothing. No-one. Nothing obviously disturbed.

Inspection completed he returned to the hall. The latest mystery envelope stood at the head of the stack behind the model engine. Whoever had taken the first batch evidently didn't require more. No sign of forced entry, either. Professionals with a specific mission. Maybe the latest letter would shed light. He opened the envelope. It was from HQ, Army Reserve.

Dear Dr Sewell,

This final attempt to contact you is being sent to the address on file, as the Land Registry confirms that it remains in your name.

Assuming this eventually finds you in good health, please re-establish contact with your local Unit without delay.

If unable to comply, the enclosed, pre-paid card may be used to indicate the reason(s) by ticking the appropriate box(es).

With best wishes.

Saunders
Lt. Col.

Not a great deal he could do before evening. Top priority must be to warn Charo about Dundas. It was after 08.00, and thus after 09.00 in Spain. It took a while to look out his phone list, but he located the number and lifted the receiver. A further twelve months after Meltdown would he even get a dialling tone? A tone! So far so good! The answer was almost immediate. '914 . . . .'

'Charo. It's David - in England.'

'I'm sorry. Not Charo. This is Talía.'

'Talía - sorry: you sound so like your mother. Is she there?'

'My mother doesn't live here any more. Would you like the number?'

'Yes please. But is she alright?'

'Now she is - but many things have happened.'

He took down the number and checked by reading it back.

'It's an apartment quite close to here. Very small. Don't worry. She will tell you all about it. I see her every day - twice, sometimes. Would you like the street address?'

'Certainly would!' He wrote it down and they checked it. 'Talía. Have you taken any calls from an American recently?'

'Something like that is on the answerphone right now. It must have come very early.'

'But have you answered it?'

'I listened quickly - but I'm only just home off duty. Got here a few minutes ago and haven't had time.'

'Talía. If they ring again, ask for their number but say that you will pass it on to your mother. Don't say where Charo is. Trust me! This is important. You do trust me, don't you?'

'My mother always said you were someone she could trust. So, yes, I trust you. Are you going to tell me what this is about?'

'I could - but it will be an awful lot easier if I explain to your mother first and she explains to you. It's to do with our work together.'

'Thank you for looking out for her. Since the divorce and the illness she has felt very, how you say? vulnerable. She will tell you everything.'

'And how about you?'

'I've been lucky. Passed my consultant's exams just before the economy crashed. I get four days' full-time work a week - nights, actually, not days.'

'And Ricardo?'

'He's OK. Got a paid job in Germany. Not a permanent position - but that's good in a way. Means he gets home to see my mother quite frequently.'

'Talía. I'm going to leave it there and phone your mother.'

The Bridge - *a love affair*

They exchanged farewells and Sewell dialled the new number. This time there was a delay before the phone was picked up. After the initial exchanges of surprise he explained the encounter with Admiral Dundas. Charo sounded alright - but not the characteristic, bubbly self. 'Talía says that a lot has happened. Why don't you put her in the picture as to why I have rung. I'll call you again later for a proper chat about old times - if you want to, that is.'

'Of course I want to! But not too late in the day: I get very tired.'

He put down the phone. Poor Charo. Sounds as if she's been through the mill.

He took a more detailed look around the house for evidence of the break-in. Not a sign. He went out into the entrance hall and towards Violet's door. It was opened before he could knock. 'Storm first, or tea?' she asked.

'Can we see Storm. Then I shall probably need a cup of tea!'

A French window gave onto a paved patio. There stood a small table, and on the table a floppy white sun-hat which shielded her eyes as she read or carried out darning repairs. To the left as you faced the spacious lawn was a small rose garden, and further to the left a wooden shed which housed Sewell's workshop equipment - lathe, pillar drill and so on. The rose garden showed evidence of recent digging. 'He's right here - where I can keep an eye on him. We put him just where you will be able to see him as you are working your machines - through the shed window.'

Sewell looked on in silence. An average of three walks a day, each of about three miles for three hundred and sixty-five days a year was three-and-a-half thousand miles per year - as near as made no difference. So in five years they had covered some seventeen-and-a-half thousand miles together. What a sad and unnecessary end. Didn't everybody know that an individual husky is not aggressive - in fact, the very reverse: a touch over-enthusiastic, maybe, but not aggressive. Had they asked Storm, he would have welcomed them into the house, and like as not, given them a guided tour.

'The day I found him, Graham was going up past Rose Barton's place. You know, she used to be a horse vet. She came straight away. Said the only way to be certain would be to look for evidence of skin puncture - and doing that thoroughly would mean shaving off all his lovely fur. She thinks he was given a tid-bit laced with a drug - or drugs - used on humans. She was confident he had not suffered.

'I had been keeping some curtains from the old house in a strong cardboard box. We left one curtain in the bottom of the box and laid him out on that. And you remember how he would sleep when he could find something to use as a pillow - just like a human being? I found a small cushion - one I had embroidered years ago. Made him look comfortable and peaceful. And there was that black cap - the *Whisper* cap?'

'I know - the WhisperGen cap from the Stirling engine conference. Whenever anyone called he would grab it and shake the living daylights out of it. It was supposed to entice the visitor to play.'

'Well, I'd never seen you wear it, so we put it in the box to keep him company. And I kept his collar with the brass name-tab you made. It's on the table just inside the French window. Graham dug the grave. We waited a couple of days hoping that Michael would call by so that he could say a little blessing in that eloquent style of his as we covered him up. He didn't, but Graham brought Charlotte, and Rose came back. I think we all said our own little prayer. One thing you can be sure of is that he didn't take his leave of this world alone or un-loved.'

By now Sewell was struggling to contain his emotions. What a dear, kind, thoughtful lady. Uncertain as to whether he was going to be able to speak, he gestured towards the table and sat down in one of the three chairs.

By the time Violet emerged with the tray of tea he had composed himself. The break-in was looking increasingly like a combination of brute force and finesse - in more or less equal measure. Boris and Nikolai? 'I shouldn't worry, Violet. There's nothing in it for them to trouble you. They've got what they came for, so there's no reason for them to come back.'

'They are the ones who should worry if they do! They will have to get past Leo's machete before they can cause me problems.'

He took a last look at Storm's resting place. 'Here, I have brought you something. It's had your name on it for weeks so, Storm or no Storm, it was always yours. He pulled an envelope from an inside pocket. Open it now, because it needs a bit of explanation.'

She reached out and took the envelope. It was not sealed, and by lifting the flap she could see currency bills.

'I came by quite a few dollar bills. Those hundreds are for you. They have no fixed value in the UK - just what you can exchange them for in any given situation. Make sure you deal only with people you know and can trust. If you do, one of those bills will buy many times its face value.

'And there's another thing: my ration allocations have been accumulating during the year away. The entitlement is probably with the mail. I'll change them into disposable tokens and bring them over. I get quite a quite a kick-back from the government over this technology barter we did. So don't worry: I shall not be missing them.'

She was pulling out the bills one-by-one, looking at them in disbelief. 'A thousand dollars! David, the words won't come, but let me give you a big hug. You're not thinking of going after the people who killed Storm, are you?'

'It's more likely they will come looking for me.'

'Oh, David. Do be careful. You're one of my sons. You know that, don't you!'

Reassuring her that he remained one of her innumerable adopted sons, he returned to the main house. The rest of the day was spent pottering and contemplating the implications of retiring from the retirement from which he had retired a decade previously.

The CO of his local Army Reserve unit was Lt. Col. McNinch. As well as having been fellow officers since Territorial Army days, they were good friends. Angus McNinch lived ten minutes' walk away. Sewell consulted his watch: 7.30 pm. 'No time like the present,' he thought. 'Could do with a walk around the old patch anyway. See whether he's home.'

He fanned through the mail, picking out the envelopes likely to contain ration token entitlements. He would have to produce his passport at a post office or bank to get them changed for the disposable item. A job for first thing tomorrow. That way Violet would get her tokens by lunch-time.

He had been away for almost exactly a year, so in terms of foliage, trees, bird-song and so on, it was as if it had been an overnight absence. But certain things had changed: people who still owned property had evidently devoted their involuntary early retirements to tending lawns, gardens and the external fabric of their houses. There was remarkably little litter. Presumably the fewer the consumables the less the packaging.

Before he had left, the streets had been lined with cars whose value had dropped to zero for lack of affordable fuel. The disappearance of revenue from vehicle licensing and from fuel tax would have crippled the economy by itself without the help of the banking collapse. Some local authorities had used existing legislation to justify clearing un-taxed vehicles from the streets without consulting owners. Protests, apparently, had been few. Sewell, who welcomed any incentive to keep fit by cycling, had got a few pounds for his car some weeks prior to Melt-down. The sight of the vehicle-free streets of childhood memory he actually found quite refreshing.

He knocked at Angus' door. 'DG! Great to see you! We were about to give up on you. Where the hell have you been?'

'On Her Majesty's Secret Service. But unless you've got all evening, don't ask what that means. I've been instructed to report. How about getting it over with here?'

'I'll say so DG. Good man! Do take the weight off those legs of yours. Glass of wine? Home-made, I'm afraid.'

'What have you been using for berries?'

'I haven't: this is a pre-Melt-down bottling.' Over the years Angus' hobby had evolved into an enviable skill. Were it not for the risk of being branded a philistine, Sewell would have admitted to preferring the colonel's vintage to the majority of proprietary labels. 'But for a rather fine Riesling in Ottawa, this will be my first in twelve months. Pour away!'

They sat in their accustomed places. 'I need more bodies - particularly officers - men and women who can think, work together, formulate strategy.'

'Angus. Somebody in the system has forgotten my age.'

'If you hadn't already noticed, DG, this is a crisis. Track record and experience take priority over age. The Reserve is being lined up for unprecedented responsibilities - and in between there's endless dogs' labour to be coordinated. Let you in on some background first. Your options later:

'First of all, the Reserve has been promoted, and the TA re-formed - unfortunately under regulations which would enable a CO looking for easy options to run it like Dad's Army. There's nothing to say that we should be setting lower standards, but it's the noddy jobs which will fall to the new TA. A high priority is going to be keeping up morale.

'The Provisional Government is planning trial distributions of motor fuel. A couple of refineries have re-started limited production. Apparently the crude was a barter against a few shiploads of serviceable used vehicles. Clears the streets and yields enough fuel over and above the military requirement to get some commercial traffic flowing again.

'Quite a brisk trade, apparently - and growing, They're forecasting a margin of production for the private market. Nothing's reached the pumps in Bristol yet. Nobody seems to have a clue as to the extent of public and commercial demand, so it's chicken and egg: how do you get a production stream going when you don't know how many cars are going to be wheeled out of hibernation - or how drivers are going to pay at the pumps?'

'We could pay the garages in home-grown carrots. Hey - and this vintage of yours is something. You could ask litre per litre on the forecourt - and get it!'

'Thanks! They're so desperate for things to start moving again - not to mention tax revenue coming in - that they have drafted in every economist, mathematician, meteorologist and tarot-card reader in the land to look into it. My immediate problem is that the TA is in line to pick up responsibility for security.'

'What security issues do they see arising?'

'If only they would tell us. Storage tanks are under-ground. Pumps only work when the electricity supply is on, otherwise the fuel can't be pumped. Means garages can't function overnight - or at any time when supplies aren't connected. There is something more sinister - or somebody is scared there might be.

'Anyway, a series of exercises starts soon - too soon, and we're involved. Two units from the other side of town - we are not even told which - have been instructed to brain-storm an 'event'. All we've got to go on is that it will involve one, two or all three of the garages assigned to our protection. We have to thwart the 'event' without knowing what it is.'

'And presumably you have orders to do this on the usual budget of three shillings and sixpence?'

'Yes and no. All units get an unprecedented allocation of brand-new kit - at least it's all new to me. And that's just for the training while we adapt to the new rôle: we're to get surveillance and monitoring gear - state-of-the-art they tell me. And brand new rifles. These go 'bang' without using expensive blanks - but only if you have remembered to load the dummy ammo. Laser sights and automatic range-finder obviously - digital camera technology, I suppose. And GPS: all moulded in plastic in authentic detail and looking for all the world like latest issue to the regulars.'

'All except realistic weight and balance, I suppose.'

'Not a bit of it. Shredded scrap metal is moulded into the chassis to give exactly the right balance and all-up weight. The batteries for the two-way radio communication - encrypted, or course - make up the weight to a totally realistic feel. The lads in some trials didn't realize they had been issued with a replica until it came to pulling the trigger. No recoil!'

'Why the GPS?'

'The full kit includes a monitoring station - two, in fact: one for luck, maybe. Every shot fired is mapped in terms of time, compass direction, elevation and whether it scores a hit. Every movement. Every re-load too. The 'battle' can be re-played and analysed down to the last detail - then given a post-mortem. All that's been delivered so far is the weaponry and the recording gear - none of the surveillance stuff - although one or more of the other units may have it. Wrong priority if you ask me. Anyway, we got a delivery of weapons a few days ago.'

'When do you get to try it out?'

'I had been hoping you would say 'we'. Saturday night, between dark - about 21.00 hours - and 02.00.'

'And you want a strategy in place in time for briefings and training?'

'I've reconciled myself to the fact that it's impossible. We can't make sensible use of the kit until we know how to get the best out of it. We are going to have to play cowboys and Indians and absorb the scenario as it evolves. If you take a positive view it can be exciting territory. Will you come aboard?'

'Without telling me what's in it for me?'

'Sorry. Got carried away.' A second bottle was un-corked. 'Here - help yourself; no chance of a drink-driving conviction! You will be re-commissioned to the rank of captain. There is no pay in the old-fashioned sense - but the perks are handy. Remind me to give you a printed list on the way out. Includes a warrant giving free travel on any public service vehicle still operating. Airlines - and I know there is only one left - airlines having an un-booked seat free on a domestic flight are obliged to allocate it to you on demand. The armed services must do the same for international as well as domestic transport. You can insist - at gun-point if absolutely necessary - that the driver of any vehicle having a spare seat give you a lift - but only to a point en route to where he or she was already headed: no joy-riding!'

'The world is evidently my lobster.'

'Next parade-night is tomorrow evening, 19.00. The uniform you handed in has been re-cycled. A replacement will take a fortnight at least, but you can pick up boots and other outdoor gear for the exercise. For some bizarre reason, hand-guns issued to officers for ceremony - and for exercises - are now to be retained - kept at home: we're becoming another Switzerland. There's still a choice between revolver and pistol. The Brownings are ten-a-penny since the issue to the regulars was changed to Glock, but as they don't work when firing blanks - at least, not our blanks - they are no use except for show.'

'Are you likely to have kept my old revolver?'

'Good grief, man. This is about action, not nostalgia! You couldn't hit a brick-built toilet with that relic even if you were sitting in it. It'll be there right enough: who would want it? Tomorrow night, then. That full list of entitlements is on top of the filing cabinet.'

One of the faces Sewell did not recognize at the parade was that of a woman, anything between twenty-five and thirty-five. He did not have long to wait for an introduction. 'Capt. Sewell, this is cpl. Weissova. Joined us about six months ago.'

Sewell held out his hand. 'New recruit - and corporal already?'

'She'll make colonel before I do, sir.' He lowered his voice. 'Runs rings around the lads - no fuss. Just gets on with it.'

'Family?'

'Two daughters from a teenage marriage in Slovakia, sir. With a partner now, sir. Daughters have grown up and left home. We ran our own business. It was doing well and expanding before Melt-down.'

'From Slovakia? Read an intriguing novel about the part of the world you come from. All about an architect-designed house - with an onyx wall.'

'*The Glass Room* by Simon Mawer, sir? The house really exists. It's actually in the Czech Republic. I've visited it.'

A mind-reader, too! A soldier to be reckoned with. 'Welcome, corporal. And congratulations on your English.'

'It's been a job of work, sir.'

'Sounds as though you thrive on it.' Sewell made a mental note to bid for her for his group on Saturday.

He watched the sergeant drill his charges in handling the replica rifles. Corporal Weissova had joined them. If she hadn't handled a weapon before then he was a Patagonian parking attendant. The woman should have signed up for the Regulars. Probably hadn't got citizenship at the time.

She was also cleared to sign out a key to the armoury, and located his revolver as though she had been minding it since it had been handed in. Sewell looked at the new rifles remaining in the rack. Half-a-dozen, with a chain running end-to-end through the aperture in the chassis. 'Did the sergeant check the R/T on the new weapons?'

'I know for sure he checked the nine he used for familiarization, sir. But I re-checked the lot anyway.'

'Transmit and receive?'

'Of course, sir.'

'Do you know what's become of the old Lee Enfields?'

'Still here, sir. In the metal box under the floor - and enough blanks to re-enact the Second World-War.'

'I haven't seen how the new equipment works yet, corporal. Go check with the CO, then issue us both a rifle. Re-chain the rest, switch your weapon on and sit tight. I'm going on a walk-about. When I'm out of sight I'll call you. Then keep talking. Sounds as if your life-story should do for a start.'

He left the drill hall and walked out into the street. 'Sewell here, corporal. How do you read?'

'Fives, sir.'

'Keep talking, please.'

The R/T always exaggerated an accent, but usually not at the cost of readability. 'I left a little place back in Slovakia', she said. 'House, large garden - and a well.'

With the help of occasional prompting she kept up an engaging account as he walked around. Terminating the test he returned to the armoury. 'Thanks corporal. Crystal clear. I could imagine this sort of audio quality being a real bonus in live combat. Secure the equipment again, please.'

They returned to the drill hall together as Col. McNinch emerged from his office. 'Lieutenant!'

'Sir?'

'Separate the troops into the three groups. Mine in my office, yours in the lecture room. Captain Sewell can have the drill hall.'

Sewell found himself with two men and two women. One of the latter was Cpl. Weissova. Good start.

'You have been given an outline of next Saturday's night exercise - an outline because that's what we've got. We have to use the new kit to thwart an 'event'. No idea what it is, except that it is probably being planned as I speak. It can affect one or more of three closed filling stations. At least we have been told which three: Shell in Muller Road - that's ours - Tesco in Eastgate Road and Murco, which is way down in Hampton Road. Do you all know our pitch - the Shell station?'

There was a chorus of 'Yes, sir.'

'For the duration of the exercise I am 'Shell leader'. If you hear 'Shell' - that's you - in fact, it's just two of you - Cpl. Weissova and private Carter. Why shall I just be talking to the women?'

'Sir?'

'Why are the women working the R/T?'

'Because you say so, sir?'

'No! Two reasons: (a) all other voices will be male: a female voice instantly means *us* - Shell. There's a bonus (b) female voices are crystal clear on this equipment. You will operate in pairs, one male, one female. You will cover your partner, and your partner will cover you.

'Remember my call-sign: Shell leader. Any orders you may overhear from Tesco or Murco are for information only until/unless you are notified that I am *hors de combat*. Clear?

'Right: On being issued with your weapon you will check it's on safety, and will leave it on safe even when deployed. In other words, it remains on safe until you receive the order from me to prepare for firing. After that there are only three scenarios in which you will go to safety-off: (a) when I clear you to do so, (b) when your own life is under threat, (c) when your partner's life is under threat.

'Convince me you have taken these three conditions on board: Recite them back.'

There was a reassuring chorus.

'Any questions?'

Private Cooke's hand shot up - one of the men. 'Where do think the action will be, sir?'

'I hope it will be on our pitch, obviously. What's your prediction, private?'

'Tesco is a terrorist's paradise, sir: car park lined with stacks of scrap vehicles - four high.'

'Private, you have been thinking! Anyone else? Yes, Cpl. Weissova?'

'That makes Tesco so obvious they will expect us to focus there.'

'Come on the rest of you.'

'They'll hit Murco, sir.' It was private Carter. 'Shell and Tesco are, like: a couple of minutes' trot apart. Means both of them are covered by, like: ten of us. Murco's like: miles away: just four plus the Colonel.'

'I like the reasoning. Not sure about the prospect of like-speak over the R/T. Have a word about that later, maybe.

But why are we all thinking terrorists and a single target? There is nothing to say that this 'event' has to be hostile: the opposition are perfectly entitled to put on Oxfam badges and open a fore-court soup kitchen. Our best hope is to expect the unexpected. A good start is to get into our minds that shooting is not a priority: what's expected of us is an appropriate response - not a knee-jerk reaction. Personally I smell a rat with this exercise. But I'm confident we can expect a vehicle - or vehicles - to feature. Suppose the vehicle or vehicles need stopping. How do we do that?'

'We shoot the tyres, sir.' It was Cooke.

'Provided the vehicle is not hurtling in the direction of a school and carrying explosives that might be an option. Assuming it's not hurtling, which tyres?'

Carter and Weissover in unison. 'Front tyres, sir.'

'What sort of target practice have you had at the range?'

'Sir?'

'Stationary or moving?'

All four voices: 'Stationary, sir.'

'If a target shows up on Saturday, chances are it will be moving. Take a look at the flip chart. He drew a large circle. Below, and tangent to it, a horizontal line. That's a wheel. We can pepper it with shots, or we can use the exercise for a little scientific experiment. Which is it to be?'

'A bit of science would make a change, sir.' It was Weissova - of course.

'No matter how fast the vehicle is going - a hundred miles per hour if you like - there's always a point on the tyre doing zero miles per hour reckoned in the direction of travel. Which?'

'Sir?'

'The tread in contact with the road: the road isn't moving, so the contact point isn't moving either. There's an awful lot to be said for a stationary target: don't have to pan an unfamiliar weapon with weight on the elbows when lying low. Suppose we have the luxury of knowing the vehicle's coming. We get horizontal behind cover from where we can see a spot on the road dead ahead. We fix our aim - three or four inches above road level. We let the front tyre come to us. *Squeeze* the trigger when it lines up. Has the added advantage of killing fewer drivers and not breaking so many bedroom windows. Think about it between now and Saturday.

'One last thing. Here's a sketch of our pitch.' He produced an A-4 sheet of paper. A hand-drawn map marked the Shell station and points X and Y. 'We've got no photo-copier, so after parade get yourselves to the Black Horse next door. They dispense something they call beer - do *not* be tempted - but they've got oil lighting. The corporal will give you a sheet of A-4 a-piece and something to write with. Each make a copy. Cross-check each other's work. Before Saturday get to know every road, path, track and back-garden between X, Y and Shell like the back of your hand.

'Anyway, time's up. Final parade in ten minutes. Indulge in lots of lateral thinking in the meantime. Let me know of all the things we haven't thought of - and remember: expect the unexpected. Call by my place if necessary: let's get this one right first time.' He beckoned to private Carter: 'You are on the R/T for two good reasons - three if we include a chance for you to shine. Those who are depending on you don't want to hear that you are 'like: ready', because that can mean anything from 50% ready to 150% ready. Any like-speak over the R/T on the night and I shall ransack Regulations for a breach of discipline!'

'You won't need to do that, sir.'

'I hope not. Corporal Weissova, take the writing equipment. Issue our little squad with a night compass a-piece. Check what the other two groups want by way of kit, then lock up and get keys back to the CO's office.'

'Yes, sir. All compasses on charge since last parade. Checked earlier this evening.'

Eye on the ball yet again, thought Sewell.

14

Night op.

He spent much of Thursday night awake thinking about Storm and wondering what use the intruders had for the correspondence from the Reserve.

Sleep finally took over towards dawn, and he eventually awoke shortly after nine. He skipped shaving, dressed hurriedly, decided it was too late for breakfast and headed *via* the back door for his workshop. The bike was there just as it had been left on the return from Temple Meads a year ago. He squeezed the tyres. Soft. After a few moments to locate the pump, the machine was serviceable again and ready to take him to the post office.

The down-hill ride without the hold-all - in daylight - was a somewhat different affair from the trip twelve months earlier. In no time he was securing the bike to a lamp-pole opposite the post office. As anticipated, the queue extended out of the door, but with no option but to join it, he took his place.

Three quarters of an hour later he was un-locking the bike, pockets bulging with a year's worth of tokens. He would have preferred to take a ride around town to see how it was surviving post-Melt-down conditions. However, it was getting towards lunch-time, and preparations forming in his mind for the night exercise might take the rest of the day - maybe even run over into Saturday.

He chose a route back through Clifton which could be negotiated in bottom gear without getting off the bike. He arrived back in North Road puffing, but not in an undignified sweat. Great! No obvious reduction in fitness despite the year on North American rations.

Shortly after entering the house he emerged into the garden. Unbolting the side-gate from the inside drew attention to the pyracantha. Did these things never learn? It had received a vigorous short-back-and-sides before his visit to the States and was already re-asserting itself. Next time he would take a leaf out of the rose-fancier's book, which held that there were but two ways to prune: (1) not hard enough or (2) not nearly hard enough.

He wheeled the bike through the gate, re-bolted and carried on round the back of the house towards his shed. Violet was setting the patio table. 'Oh good! Here's David. I was just getting lunch. It will stretch to two - and you still haven't told me what you did in America.'

'Here. I've brought you these.' He put a wad of tokens on the table. 'Exchange is no robbery, and I missed breakfast. So, yes please!'

Violet explained the menu: 'Michael's oat-cake hobby is turning into a cottage industry. And somebody in Robbie's lab. is making cheese. Will cheese and biscuits keep the wolf from the door?'

'Couldn't be better. Robbie told me about the cheese. He says there's even a choice: mature cheddar or mature cheddar. Finally a spin-off from nuclear physics research we can actually use. You may never hear me complain about university research funding again!'

Violet lifted the teapot: 'It's nettle tea - but young nettles. Picked in the spring and dried.'

Over the modest lunch he recounted the highlights of the year away. His offer to help with clearing up was refused out-of-hand, so he retrieved the bike and wheeled it towards his backdoor. Still conscious of the break-in, he opened up cautiously. Finding nothing amiss, he changed into tee-shirt and shorts and went out to the workshop.

The Bridge - *a love affair*

Hanging behind the shed door was the ex-RAF Nomex flying suit which did duty as overalls. Returning outside to get more elbow room he squirmed into it, drawing the body-length zip up to the chin. Perfect kit: nothing to catch in rotating machinery.

He re-entered the shed. To the right was the wood-working department based around a handsome beech-wood bench - an import from Sweden. To the back of this he had attached a rack, from which protruded the handles of two Henry Disston panel saws and a row of chisels. To the left was the metal-working machinery - Myford ML-7 lathe, Fobco Star pillar drill and an eight-inch, double-ended tool grinder. How, he pondered - and not for the first time - did anyone keep house and home going - let alone lawn mower and bicycle - without the aid of the essentials.

A polythene sheet covered the lathe. He lifted it to see how it had survived his absence. A heavy object in cast-iron responds to temperature change very slowly: if a humid day follows a cold night it can become covered in condensation. He had always cleaned the Myford after use, spraying the un-painted parts with WD-40. Of rust - not a sign! That stuff was surely the biggest boon to mankind since the invention of the wheel.

Today was to be carpentry day, so he replaced the polythene cover and went outside. The wooden floor of the shed was set on blocks which raised it about eight inches above the ground. The space beneath was storage for his supply of rough-sawn timber. Good: it had not been raided for firewood. Withdrawing two lengths of deal, three inches square, he propped one against the side of the shed, taking the other length inside to the bench and securing it in the vise. Having located the Rabone square and his carpenter's pencil, he reached for the smaller of the two panel saws, wiped off the film of WD-40 and set to work.

Time flew, and at about four o'clock Violet came to the door. 'Kettle's just boiled!' After a couple of hours' sawing, 'delicious' hardly did justice to nettle tea in the late-afternoon sun and - as she insisted - it was full of iron and therefore good for him.

The Bridge - *a love affair*

Just once more before dark he left the shed, this time to search the spare room for a reel of sash cord. Eventually he could not see well enough to carry on, and emerged, brushing sawdust from the overalls as he walked to Storm's grave. The evening air was still and the French windows were open. His thoughts were interrupted by a voice from inside: 'You miss having him take you for the last walk of the day, I expect.'

'And shall do so for the foreseeable future.'

Stepping back out of range of the roses, he shrugged himself out of the overalls, walked to the shed and re-hung them in their accustomed place. Tomorrow night there would be little sleep, so an early night would make sense.

Saturday morning was spent in the shed putting the finishing touches to his project. On testing it on the lawn he discovered that they had not, after all, been finishing touches, but by midday he was finally satisfied with his efforts. The prospect of the night operation called for a doze in his easy chair.

The forty-five minute nap was just long enough to leave him refreshed rather than groggy. This being the first time on for the newly-issued kit, he laid it out on the bed. Shirt: clearly his size; woolly-pully: likewise; trousers - good grief! Who had she mistaken him for? Cyril Smith!? Socks (OK, one size fits all); boots: size 11, his size again, and belt. Had this been the same Cpl. Weissova who had created such an impression at Thursday's parade? Ah well, no-one's perfect.

An army belt was an army belt. Still in shorts he adjusted it to his 34-inch waist. Shirt and tie next. Getting into the trousers was like stepping into a sleeping bag. The belt took up the slack like the draw-string of a meal sack. Stylish - if you didn't mind looking like Charlie Chaplin.

An A-4 pad lay on the kitchen table. On parade at ten p.m. to get issued with kit and final briefing. Now calculate backwards: allow fifteen minutes' ride from Shell back to HQ. Half-an-hour between Shell and Tesco for a thorough snoop-around. Another fifteen to cycle from

The Bridge - *a love affair*

home to Shell. Add a further fifteen for contingency - the inevitable puncture in the dark. OK, then, set off at eight forty-five.

Making sense of position reports while looking at a map by torch-light was going to be a whole lot easier for a bit of homework. He put the waiting time to use poring over a street map of Bristol - and trying to imagine what sort of event they might be called upon to thwart. At eight-thirty he gave up. The only hope now was that Cpl. Weissova had been looking into her crystal ball. He would have to sound her out without asking directly.

He picked up the prepared length of sash-cord and left by the back door, locking it behind him. The two sacks were bulky, but not particularly heavy. Doubling the sash-cord he secured a sack to each end and began the ritual of manoeuvring the bike through side gate out to the road. He retrieved the sacks, slung the sash cord around his neck, tied the free ends around his waist and pushed off from the kerb.

His rounds were complete without the need to attend to a puncture and he arrived at HQ minus the bags. The parade was a formality, except for reinforcement, group by group, of the briefings of the previous Thursday night.

Just before eleven-thirty Sgt. Tolley drew up in the Land Rover. 'Sorry it's got no roof. But it's not raining. If it does we'll be soaked anyway before the night's out.'

Sewell could - perhaps should - have travelled in the cab with the other two officers, but if he stood in the back - it was standing room only - there would be the prospect of finding out whether Cpl. Weissova had been crystal-ball gazing.

As no-one else broke the silence, he put the obvious question to nobody in particular 'Looking forward to it?'

'At least it's not raining, sir.'

Silence returned.

'How about you, corporal?'

'Well, sir, it's the first op. I've been on without knowing whether we're going to get bombed, ambushed or entertained.'

How was it that some picked up while ordinary folk merely reacted? She had responded to a platitude - but responded with that undercurrent of engagement. It was just like talking to Lígia again. No, not talking *to*, communicating *with*. Little short of that verbal intimacy.

Wishful thinking for a 76 year old. He turned his mind to business - the possibility of ambush or entertainment - or, indeed, a combination! Now, there was an interesting possibility - and, *dammit*, a perfectly *realistic* one. Home-made fireworks, maybe. After all, no real motor fuel, so no fire hazard. And what about troops dressed as aliens - turning up in a cardboard flying-saucer. Why was his thinking so blinkered: expect the unexpected!

The Land Rover pulled into the forecourt of the Shell station. By moonlight it was even more derelict than by day. Sewell put a hand on the side of the vehicle and vaulted over.

'You are more agile than some of us, sir.'

He had made that opportunity - and she had grabbed it. Perhaps not wishful thinking after all. 'Thank you, corporal. When you hear I have finally retired from retirement you will know that you no longer need to evaluate my fitness.'

His four charges followed. Reaching back into the vehicle for their weapons, they waved the Land Rover off in the direction of Tesco where it would drop the CO and his squad. Last stop would be Murco, just a step from Sgt. Tolley's lock-up. There it should be safe until 02.00 from ambush, bombing, gratuitous entertainment - and, with luck, from the rest of the unexpected.

Sewell's two pairs headed off towards their positions without the need for further instructions - evidently having done their homework. Sewell walked to the position he had allocated himself and they ran radio checks.

Half an hour took at least two hours to drag by. Then 'Murco two to Murco leader. Sound of vehicle, sir. Heavy.'

'Report when visual.'

'Got it, sir. Truck. Coming north up - coming our way.'

'Say colour.'

Waste of air time, thought Sewell.

'We've only got moonlight, sir. Dark. Could be military - olive drab. Hey: it's a tanker, sir.'

'Shell two to Shell leader: Got it, sir: we're covering a real delivery - first in eighteen months.'

'With dummy weapons, I suppose! Maintain R/T silence until you've got something to report.'

'Tanker pulling into Murco. Stopping - no! Moving out again. Out of Murco now, heading . . towards the station.'

'For pity's sake, *which* station.'

'Redland, sir - heading north-east.'

'Shell leader to Shell. You got that? Could still be a decoy, but if we're dealing with a tanker expect it in five minutes. Listen and report: keep a look out for things which don't make a noise as well.'

Two sets of double clicks acknowledged receipt of the instruction. The next five minutes did not exactly race by. Then

'Shell two to Shell leader: Sound of vehicle, sir. Heavy.'

'Tesco one to Tesco leader. We hear him too, sir.'

Coming up the M32, thought Sewell.

'Shell one to Shell leader. He's leaving at junction 2, sir. All the way round. Slowing - could be coming east. Not indicating - into Muller Road now. He's ours, sir. Turning into Shell right now. Moving slowly towards the filling points.' Then: 'Off again, sir, driven straight through.'

'Shell leader to Shell. Wait until he's out of sight, then leg it to X-ray. See you there. Acknowledge.'

'On our way, sir. Meet you at X-ray.'

'Four of us on X-ray - north side of island. Out of sight of traffic using Tesco.'

'I know: I'm standing right behind you.'

'How did you beat us to it, sir.'

'I think the captain has been here all the time.'

'Corporal Weissova: you may stand down your horoscope skills. They're starting to un-nerve me.'

229

The Bridge - *a love affair*

The sound of rifle fire came from the direction of Tesco.

'Shell leader to Tesco. What gives?'

'Driver and co-driver hostage. Bandits hi-jacking tanker.'

Several more shots followed. 'Lay down your weapons.' Sewell turned to Cpl. Weissova: 'Corporal: grab this bag. Here - by the bottom. Do *NOT* let go! Private! Grab the cord. Leg it to the far side of the road - north side. Then get out of sight.

'Carter and Hinks: Get this bag to the opposite side of the island - south-east.' He gestured. 'Carter: hold on to the bag. Hinks: run the cord across into the car-park. Then both get invisible.'

Sewell made the short climb to the top of the island and lay flat, looking south down the exit road. The tanker was building up speed, and, in a few seconds, would turn east or west into Eastgate Road. It chose east, and the four axles in turn bounced noisily over the string of blocks.

The tanker came to a halt to acknowledge. Sewell walked towards the passenger side where the more senior person would be sitting. The window was being wound down as he looked up. 'What have you stopped us with?'

'For the purposes of the Operation, a stinger - a string of wooden blocks with six-inch nails sticking out. Actually, it's just the wooden blocks without the nails, so you have just saved the cost of a dozen or more puncture repairs. Every little helps, as they say back at the Store.'

'It's a fair cop.' admitted the officer.

'I like your style, though.' volunteered Sewell. 'Where did you get the ex-WD tanker?'

'Used to be a milk tanker. Driven into Stickley's yard eighteen months ago with only a couple of thousand on the clock. The son's in the Reserve: did the negotiating.'

'Shouldn't it be bright shiny stainless steel?' enquired Sewell innocently.

'It's a makeover: a few buckets of emulsion - fifty-fifty green with brown. The whole job took less than an hour with five of us on ten-inch brushes. Paint was twelve years out-of-date. We were praying it wouldn't rain and wash off.'

'Well done, DG. Looks like you did a more effective job than us.' Col. McNinch had walked from Tesco. They waved the tanker on its way back to the yard. Were you expecting a dummy delivery?'

'Greatest hazard by far when fuel starts flowing will be hijack. Once the stuff's in the underground tanks with power supply isolated from the pumps it needs an oil drilling rig to get at it. Up to that point there will have to be somebody riding shot-gun at every stage of delivery - probably escorts as well.'

'And you and Maj. Hurley's lot both hit on the tanker scenario by chance?'

'Unlikely: This may have been just a noddy little op. but the Ministry needs maximum value for money - if only because there is no money! They were put up to it: nothing in the scenario to say that we should be told. My guess is that some organization somewhere is already designing aircraft-type self-sealing tankers - if only to counter trigger-happy TA units.'

'David, listen. My lot took the cowboys-and-Indians remit too seriously. And my lot includes me. Noddy exercise or not, the signals from those weapons will be analysed by Monday night at the latest. If one of those shots hit the tank - or even the truck's own fuel tank - that's the end of my TA career. I'm going to cut my losses by beating them to it and resigning. In all probability you will be offered the command.'

'Angus, don't be hasty. The army has been your life - from Regulars to TA through to Reserve and back to TA. Anyway, the rules can't be bent far enough to offer the command to a seventy-seven year-old.'

'This is the brave new world, DG and not before time, too. The few jobs that come up are being offered on the strength of ability, not age. You have kept your eye on the ball with your research, your writing, your computer coding and your music. And all that cycling, squash and rowing didn't do your body any harm. What have I done

The Bridge - *a love affair*

outside the unit? Pruned roses, sorted stamps by candle-light and bottled a retirement's supply of home-made wine. I'll bet you're even keeping up your piano practice.'

'When I can get on a real instrument - or a keyboard during power-on. Best stint of piano practice recently was several feet under the Atlantic: a weapons specialist had his Yamaha P-105 with him. While he was minding his torpedoes I minded the Yamaha.'

'I hope you didn't play when the vessel was on silent watch. Getting depth-charged half-way through a rendition of '*La mer*' would not have gone down well with the Swedes - if you'll forgive a pun. Well, there you go! Will you call up the sergeant, please. Get him to stand his men down, bring the Land Rover and get everyone back to HQ with the kit. Then I'd consider it a great favour if you would walk home *via* my place. I've come by a fuel canister for the little Camping Gaz stove - and a twist of coffee. It'll stretch to two.'

'Gladly. It's 02.30. I shall be awake all night now, anyway.' And to Cpl. Weissova: 'Organize your people to re-pack those dummy stingers. Then wait for the Land Rover - on the correct side of the road.'

After accounting for all the heads, Sewell and Angus set off on foot. The latter spoke first: 'What do you make of Corporal Weissova?'

'Bit early to say. She's got something that's seriously lacking in the others. Why single her out?'

'She fits - and she doesn't fit. I get scores of pre-applications - pre-apps are now processed locally. Almost all totally unsuitable: just in it for the perks - and who can blame them. Then along comes this woman. She's got class: would have romped through officer selection. How can she afford to turn down the extra benefits? Enigma is the word you academics use when you are pontificating in your senior common-rooms.'

'Come on, Angus - you know the plot if you care to admit it. She would radiate personality through six layers of army blankets'.

They were at the front door. McNinch reached for his keys and opened up. Holding the door ajar, he pressed the switch of a battery-operated LED and beckoned Sewell inside. Once in the kitchen, he picked up a match-box and, in a practised gesture, lit a couple of candles and the Camping-Gaz stove with a single match.

'All the blokes in the section will be trying to understand her: it's the first step in getting control - and that's the very last thing she wants. Let's do what we veterans do best', suggested Sewell. 'Where's that coffee. What is it? Colombian Supremo, Kenya? roast acorn? Ah, heck - doesn't matter - this will be my first coffee on home soil for well over a year.

'Angus - about this resignation business. Presumably you invited me so that you could get a second opinion, so here it is - in three parts:

'First, you are - above all - a professional. Do as the other professionals do: when all the alarms in the cockpit go off at once, check one of them is not the stall warner, then sit on your hands and count to ten.

'Second, it's three a.m. Sunday: there will be nobody to accept or decline your resignation before Monday morning. You've got over twenty-four hours to count to ten.

'Third . . . .'

'DG, if you knew the relief that's come over me since taking the decision you wouldn't be trying to talk me out of it now. Let's change the topic: What's it like to look back on your star-spangled career? Here - let me top you up.'

'Not what you are probably thinking. Hey! This coffee's alright! There are two main sides to the job - lecturing and research - three if you include the inevitable administration. It's the teaching appointment which earns the crust, but to call it a vocation would be misleading - at least in the applied sciences: lecturing is the price paid for access to the facilities for doing the research. I'm not even convinced it deserves to be called a profession. More like a facility picked up on-the-hoof - entirely and exclusively self-taught in my case. Surviving the challenges has been a career-lifetime of trial-and-error. I was into the final five years or so before getting to grips with it.'

The Bridge - *a love affair*

'You mean there's no training for lecturing? In the military it's non-stop teaching, training and drilling - and when you're required to train others, you're drilled in how to do it.''

Sewell laughed. 'None. Zero. Full-stop. Couldn't have been further from your background.'

'So how could it possibly work in practice?'

'You were given a course and told to get on with it. No syllabus, no outline, no discussion. During my first year in the job - already struggling to run a course in which I had no background - I was given an additional course for the following year - another post-graduate course - *Mathematical methods in Engineering*. Ideal job for a mathematician, or a graduate in engineering science, or a practising engineer with experience of what the professions needed - for *anyone* but me.'

'A bit like being issued with rifle and bayonet and being told to start a military campaign, then?'

'Less chance of death or physical injury - but a cast-iron guarantee of a thorough morale-bruising.'

'Where does one even start?'

'I set two criteria and looked at some topics (a) did they look relevant to what I knew of engineering practice and (b) would I be capable of applying them in anger myself. We got through it somehow - but after the examination I remember being told *We were expecting something a bit more like numerical analysis*. Imagine being told *Train your platoon in un-armed combat* and then getting *We were expecting something a bit more like bayonet drill*!'

'How were you supposed to improve?'

'Well, if you're the slightest bit self-critical - and I suppose that's me, but more so - then one way or another you're going to get less bad. The detail's getting a bit fuzzy, but I remember some milestones - one in particular. But are you really interested in the fine detail?'

'You've wetted my appetite. Don't stop now.'

'The research had been going well and I'd been allocated a PhD student. Didn't even have a PhD myself at the time! The student

234

reached master's level - but then quit. Don't blame him. I was beginning to question the whole system - a bit late, I know - but there was a university job going in Brazil. The advertisement suggested they did things differently, so I applied, got the job and went to find out. It fitted anyway: my wife's family had been from Brazil.'

'And did they do things that differently?'

'In more ways than the job description revealed! I'd been told I could rely on everybody at university speaking English. Well, most of the professors did, but few of the students. The department allowed me the first term to prepare the course. It was post-graduate yet again - but that was a coincidence - to get the library stocked with the up-to-date English language text-books on the subject - engineering plasticity - and to get to grips with Portuguese.'

'They expected you to lecture in Portuguese - *technical* Portuguese!?'

'No. They expected me to lecture in English - but then I wouldn't have had any students. Anyway, don't be too impressed. All you need is the basics of the grammar. For technical vocabulary just tweak the English and add a São Paulo accent: plasticity is *plasticidade*, thermodynamics is *termodynâmica*, tension is *tensão* and so on.

'Anyway, I'm digressing: it turned into the only course where I ever actually had fun. I was entitled to a teaching assistant, and the one allocated was bright, responsible and hard-working - *caxias* in Portuguese. Part of his job was to check the printed handouts and to be the guinea-pig for worked examples before the students tackled them. He also marked the coursework. It ran like clockwork and everybody was a winner: by the time we'd finished he'd got a package - a complete course, comprehensively checked plus a full set of overhead transparencies. So he was set-up to take over in a subsequent year - which is just what he did when I left - and with his own teaching assistant - his own under-study. What a contrast to the UK system.'

'I hope you haven't finished, DG - this is something of an eye-opener to an old campaigner.'

'Could go on all night with the aid of this coffee of yours. I didn't say the course ran without hiccups - and in fact it caused me to start bearing in mind the maxim *Expect the unexpected*. After the first class a student came to my room asking why I was running the course before the library had any books on the subject. It turned out that one of the professors had gone off on a sabbatical tour of Europe: he had signed out every single one of the newly-arrived books. He came back after the end of term - minus the books, which he had sent back sea-mail because air-mail would have been expensive!'

'I hope he had at least read them.'

'He had - every word.'

'How on earth did you know that?'

'Because when they eventually came back - too late for my course by the way - every paragraph of every book had words under-lined in ball-pen! Library books!'

'Sounds as if you've reached the peak of any number of learning curves by - what was it? - the early nineteen-seventies. Are you telling me there was still a long way to go?'

'A hell of a long way. But it's late, so just a couple of points. They're little things, and with hindsight they're obvious - but they add up to the feeling that you've made something professional out of a do-it-yourself situation:

'The priority of a lecture isn't to impress: it's to communicate the best possible level of understanding. If an explanation is tricky, then prepare it long-hand and don't be embarrassed to read it word-for-word. Above all, practise the whole thing *on location* the night before: Why discover at the last minute that this particular overhead projector is a route-march from where there's enough light to read your notes? And if you've got a tricky diagram, and if chalk-on-blackboard's the only medium, then draw it in purple chalk before the start: you can see it - but the students can't.

'Angus: you're still awake! I'm off - but I'll call by again on Monday. Don't get up - I'll let myself out.'

236

The Bridge - *a love affair*

Pulling the door closed against the night latch he paused to look up. The full moon hung low in a crystal-clear sky. But for being in monochrome, the route home would be as clear as daylight. He had left the bike at HQ. It could stay for a day or so, so he headed for Clifton Hill on foot.

Almost asleep on his feet he allowed the matter of like-speak to re-enter his mind. Did it qualify as a dialect? There appeared to be a sort of grammar, achieved by dispensing with the conjugation of the verbs *to say* and *to do*, both being rendered instead by *he/she was lyke* . . If so, it held nothing like the attraction of Stanley Unwin's skillfully-mangled English, epitomised in his priceless advice as to how a gramophone record should be played: *Place on the turny-top and groove it*. Remote indeed from Oxford English, but as clear as many instruction manuals, a good deal clearer than most - and with a bonus beyond price: wit.

In the total silence of the moonlit small hours, mental leeway was unlimited: How had private Carter articulated it in the back of the Land Rover? *There were, lyke: three of us in the queue and we were, lyke: talking.*' He ransacked his brains for an activity which could be *like* talking without actually *being* talking - but his weary mind soon conceded defeat.

Leaving the future of like-speak to, lyke: resolve itself, he pressed on past the disused toll-booth at the eastern end of the suspension bridge. Part-way across he became aware of a figure detaching itself from the side of the walk-way.

'Dr Sewell, I presume. We've been waiting for you since the end of your - what is it called - your night operation. But . . good to see you at any time of day or night.'

The Bridge - *a love affair*

15

Expect the unexpected

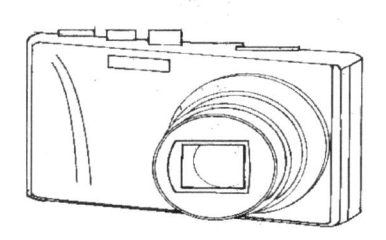

'You said "we". I see no glamour-boy. Where is he?'

'Doctor Sewell (forgive the formality - it adds that little extra to what I have in mind). And thank you for drawing your revolver - saves me asking you to do so.

'We are here, Doctor Sewell, because it is thanks to you that twenty or more Russian traitors remain at large in London rather than showing their loyalty to Mother Russia by accepting our President's invitation to return. My son Pyotr is, at this moment, being held as bargaining counter against my returning with photographs of you before and after your untimely death.'

'Well, nice to know where I stand. I asked about Boris.'

'He's setting up no-entry signs on both approach roads. Don't need an audience, do we - and sorry this is taking a moment: Moscow doesn't trust digital photography. Too much scope for editing. I shall be wanting you to pose for good, old-fashioned emulsion film - and Polaroid as well.'

As casually as he knew how, Sewell transferred his free hand to the cylinder of the revolver.

'The new recruit who issued your kit on Thursday. She enlisted while you were in the USA. She's one of us, you know. Surprised she hasn't been rumbled: they haven't let her loose on ammunition yet. But she knows how to access it. Any live round finds its way to us. Your unit gets to keep the blanks - like those in your revolver.'

Weissova! That two-faced . . And it was he who had lectured her to expect the unexpected. Boy! had she run rings around him! Still, he had invited it. Inexplicably, even in the present tight corner, he could not bring himself to dislike her.

'Play with that weapon if it pleases you, Doctor. We're almost ready.'

Focusing all his concentration, Sewell rotated the chamber, first by one click, then two. 'Is it conventional in Russia to grant the condemned man a final wish?'

'And what would be your wish?'

'An answer: it was you two who murdered my husky, wasn't it? Just tell me why.'

'We needed to get into your house.'

'Why the hell didn't you just sedate him - as you did us? Has Boris run out of lighter fuel?'

'Neuro-toxin - on a piece of cheese. Just tossed it over the hedge. Dead simple. I threw it. Boris was afraid of him.'

'Now, isn't that just typical! A thug and a bully - and a coward. You have my solemn word of honour: if you and Boris live to regret anything, it will be that you murdered Storm.' He had counted five clicks of the revolver chamber and stopped. Trying not to over-act, he snatched an anxious glance left and right.

'I hear the threat - but I don't anticipate losing sleep. Now, Doctor, we are going to kill two birds with one stone - if you will forgive an unfortunate pun. I can't let Boris loose on you by himself: he will go way over the top. I should like you to undo that belt.'

'And what makes that a good idea?'

'Because I hold all the cards: you can die cleanly and quickly - or you can die slowly and painfully. The choice is yours. The sooner I get these pictures back to Moscow the sooner the pressure comes off Pyotr.'

Sewell released the buckle of the military-issue webbing. Nikolai gestured with the pistol. 'Completely undone, if you please, Doctor - remove the belt and drop it.'

Tendentiously casting a glance behind him, Sewell obliged.

'No point looking around for assistance. No-one will be crossing this bridge until Boris removes the signs.'

Sewell let go the webbing and the weight of keys, loose change and compass in the pockets dragged the ill-fitting trousers down around his ankles. Suppose that woman had actually known *why* she had been instructed to issue oversize kit. What sort of a specimen of humanity had taken him for a ride?

Nikolai raised the heavy-looking Russian Polaroid camera to eye level with both hands, taking the pistol with it. Sewell would have to avoid being dazzled by the flash, as some seconds of visual confusion would follow. He said the shortest of mental prayers, watched the finger move to the exposure button (praise the Lord for old-fashioned technology) and shut his eyes. The flash showed bright red through the closed eye-lids. He opened again, raised the revolver and squeezed the trigger. The report echoed through the gorge, mingling with the clatter of the pistol on the walkway and cries of protest from disturbed sea-fowl. Nikolai had both hands over his eyes, blood, black in the moonlight, dripping from between the fingers.

Sewell let go the empty revolver, looked behind, shuffled the baggy army-issue trousers back to their rightful location and re-secured the belt.

He had not given himself time to take proper aim, and the improvized slug had hit the camera, or the pistol, or both, driving debris into Nikolai's face and eye - or eyes.

The victim sank to his knees, hands still clasped to his face. Blood dripped black onto the walkway.

'Pyotr. What will they do to Pyotr? Finish the job, Sewell - do it now. Please!'

'Nikolai, listen: It's you they're holding to ransom, not your son. If that shot had killed you there would have been no Nikolai to put pressure on. I'm no good at murder in cold blood, but you were about to kill me, so you obviously take killing in your stride. Tell you what I'll do: I'll continue across the bridge and leave your pistol on the hand-rail. All you have to do is grope your way along to the far end - about a hundred and fifty yards - or as many paces. Then what you do with the pistol is your business.'

'No, Sewell. It's blanks in that pistol. You've got to do it. Hurry up: Get it over with.'

'I've got no more rounds either. What was all this about having to shoot me to protect your son's hands?'

'I could never have shot you myself. I've told you: I'm an academic like you - a musician. Boris was going to pull the trigger.'

'So where is Boris. Wouldn't he need to be around if he were going to do that?'

'He's late. He's always late! And some poor innocent relative of his in Moscow is going to be paying an appalling price. Give a hand up, Sewell.'

'Stay put: you're going no-where. I'm sorry Nikolai. Deceit and double-crossing usually lead to tragedy.'

He walked round behind the Russian and swung him around so that his back was to the side rails of the walk-way. He took a look in both directions. No-one in sight. He picked up the pistol and the remains of the Polaroid and threw them over the side. Yanking the single-lens reflex camera off its strap he tossed it after the Polaroid. 'Where is your mobile phone?'

'Inside jacket pocket.'

'What's the panic button set to?'

'To Boris' mobile. Press the button. Boris is just a machine. If I tell him to finish me off he won't hesitate.'

Sewell extracted the phone. 'Have you and Boris tested it?'

'Of course.'

Sewell pressed the panic button - and flipped the phone over the side rail to join the cameras and pistol. Poor Nikolai: maybe he would not have been on this mission but for the power of

242

institutionalized blackmail. Quite possibly a perfectly ordinary guy. But one way or another he had been party to murdering Storm - and had been prepared to stand by while Boris executed him in cold blood. It would take a better Samaritan than Sewell to overlook that.

The top priority now was to make himself scarce before Boris showed up. Checking in both directions he set off towards the western end of the bridge.

He had taken barely ten paces when the sharp crack of a rifle shot sent another flock of sea-fowl skywards, wheeling and protesting.

The Bridge - *a love affair*

16

Walk to Paradise Garden

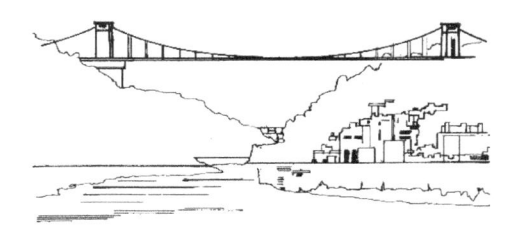

Sewell swung round, instinctively flattening his profile against the nearest upright of the structure. A bulky figure was running towards him - or, rather, was pitching forward onto its face. As the head made contact with the ground, some sort of head-gear flew off. Even by monochrome moonlight it could be one of only two things: a cleft coconut or Boris' head. Late for the party as usual. And behind, visible in the moonlight and approaching past the easterly tower, a figure hitching the sling of a rifle over the left shoulder.

They walked towards each other, the figure reaching Boris before Sewell did. It stepped casually over the inert body.

'Weissova! What the hell are you doing here?'

'Thought you might need a hand, sir. And since I happened to be passing . . '

'I'll say I needed a hand. Tell me what I am supposed to do with this corpse here?'

'It's not a corpse, sir. Just hit him in the left buttock. He's in shock.'

'You mean you aimed at the left cheek, and that's where you hit him? - and with that mediaeval musket?'

'What's the point of taking aim otherwise?'

The Bridge - *a love affair*

'We should call the emergency services. Can't just leave them both here.'

'First thing I did after pulling the trigger. Can we go, sir. If we stay we'll be filling in forms for hours - or days, and in just over an hour I've got the most important rendezvous of my life. Will you walk with me? I'll tell you about it if you like.'

'Which way, then?'

'The moonlight's bright enough to walk down the steps on the east side to Hotwell Road. We can say goodbye near the harbour entrance. It's on my way, and only twenty minutes' walk for you back up to Leigh Woods and North Road.'

'Why the trainers? Expecting the un-expected?'

'The opposite. You'll see.'

Sewell looked back and forth at the two helpless figures. Between them they had been going to kill him - possibly slowly and painfully. Finally convincing himself that they had got what was coming to them, he set off behind her towards the eastern tower. 'Can I talk first?'

'Of course.'

'A few minutes ago I was thinking things about you I would not wish to have repeated. Presumably we've ended up fighting for the same side, so tell me how you got involved?'

'I have known Nikolai for years. My partner, Bart, is passionate about hot-air ballooning. A few years back, the international championships were held in the Czech Republic. He competed, and so did Nikolai - maybe to get away from his wife. Dotes on his son instead. Anyway, Bart and he evidently hit it off and kept in touch.

'About three weeks ago Bart got a call from him asking if we could meet. Nikolai had obviously found out I was in the TA. Offered money to - as he put it - just do my job a bit more thoroughly.'

'Seems to me you already do a better job than most. What did he suggest?'

'I can't believe you are missing the point! It was supposed to look like an attempt to buy me. It would have been clumsy and

246

inappropriate, given that Bart and he are friends. But at least it was plausible.

'It just happened that money was important to us: we want to go home - as a family. Things had been falling into place, and then, out of the blue, was another piece of the jigsaw - hard currency. I had to accept or let the opportunity pass.

'All they wanted me to do - so they said - was to double-check that no-one was being issued live rounds. Since that was policy anyway I didn't see anything wrong. The way I saw it, the flimsy ruse to buy me fitted the facts - boring wife and so on. The only thing that might have meant trouble was that I was to report any live rounds to him and hand them over. As things worked out, I only ever came across one, a vintage 303 - years past its sell-by date.'

'What did you do with it? Donate it to a museum?'

'I buried it.'

'You buried it! Why - where, for Pete's sake?'

'In Boris' backside - just now. The Ministry of Defence can have it back any time they want: the shell case is still in the breach.' She tapped the Lee-Enfield. 'Just get the slug out of Boris' bum: with all that muscle they won't have to dig very deep. Then a bit of powder, fit a replacement percussion cap and it's ready for service again - or for your museum.'

'Wouldn't it be a bit battle-scarred though?'

'Still more serviceable than your improvised round.'

'What do you know about my improvised round?'

'You got issued blanks, remember, double-checked for live rounds. What did you find to ram into the cylinder of that old revolver. A ball-bearing?'

They had reached the top of the steps leading down to Hotwell Road. 'The moonlight's more than bright enough for the steps. Still want to go this way?'

'Yes, of course! No-one coming the other way, so we won't be asked to explain away the weapons.'

'No, not a ball bearing; too slippery. A lead weight from a piano key. A decent piano has weights graded all the way up the keyboard by gradually varying the diameter. I've built a small collection over fifty years.'

'Why tonight after half a century.'

'Expect the unexpected. Haven't you heard? It's the new creed. Anyway, did you take a bribe to issue baggy trousers as well?'

'They contacted Bart again about ten days ago. Would I be interested in another payment for issuing an item of kit to their instructions?'

'And you accepted?'

'Look, you know how it's been financially - and for over two and a half years now: people *dying* for lack of currency, either directly or indirectly. Anyway, I haven't finished. You got your kit, and I got to know who they were targeting. Then last Wednesday they suggested a place to meet to hand over the cash. It was an unlicensed dive. They told me to go alone, and when I got there they wanted me to drink.'

'And did you?'

'No - but let me tell you something: they had never thought to find out whether I speak Russian. Must have thought English and Slovak were enough of a brain-full.'

'Do you?'

'Well enough! The basic arrangements to hit you must already have been agreed, but they were still talking trousers with a waist-band several sizes too large. I picked up enough to know that they were not out just to embarrass you.'

In broad daylight his entire concentration would have been focused on negotiating the precipitous steps. But this was all so prepossessing he was walking on auto-pilot - and on air!

'Go on.'

'When I refused to join in the drinking Boris grabbed me. Boy is he *strong*. I expected Nikolai to call him off, but he didn't.'

'What then?'

'Stuck my fingers in his eyes, of course. She flashed her nails. I was gone - with the money - before they realized Boris was out-of-action. Tell me: when you first met him a year ago, had he got a squint?'

'If I hadn't noticed it, I'm sure my partner-in-kidnap Charo would have remarked on it.'

'Well, Bart says he has now. Blood-shot too - and how! It's possible you would have been OK on the bridge without my interference. He can't focus yet. And only the top two rounds in the clip in that pistol of his were live. He would have needed to get real close to have hit you anywhere vital. Anyway, that was all last Wednesday. I started asking around to find why you were so important to them. It didn't take long to get to hear about your part in the big grain barter with Canada. The kidnap soon surfaced - and your steam locomotive stunt, of course. You're quite famous! It all fell into place - with Nikolai and Boris as the villains.

'So now I was stuck: had accepted a bribe while on military duty - put the whole trip home at risk. So I just had to carry on and play it by ear. I had made a bad choice - but at least I knew which side I was on. Here, look . . .'

She pulled out a wad of notes. 'A hundred pounds: left over from the baggy trouser fee! Please take it. We only need enough for the trip. As soon as we get home it's back to subsistence living - vegetable garden, barbecue, kitchen table. It's finally within reach, and now I've realized it's all I've ever really wanted.'

'I'm OK for buying-power of one sort or another - but thanks all the same.'

'I've got to move fast now: it's not just Boris after me. I told you earlier that I just happened to be passing. That wasn't all small talk: I'm on the way to a rendezvous. Have you ever had the experience that everything was coming together - that the gods are suddenly smiling on you - that this must be the correct and only thing? Well, this afternoon the last link in our trip home fell into place. Before Melt-down my partner was a truck-driver. Still has lots of contacts. He has linked up a

The Bridge - *a love affair*

chain of rides. The rendezvous I told you about is with the early train - with your Tornado. From London we go with a consignment of used vehicles - part of a barter. We'll be inside one of them. In France - Calais - by Wednesday.'

'If it's going to be goodbye, please tell me your first name.'

'Alexandra, sir. Alex. I know yours. Can I call you David - just for one final half-mile?'

'That would be nice.'

She was first to emerge from the steps at road level. 'There's no traffic. Let's walk on the other side - by the river. If any flashing blue lights come we can drop the weapons in the mud bank. I want to ask you about yourself? You live alone. Were you ever married?'

'I was'

'What happened? Divorced?'

'Estranged is the technical term for it. She disappeared.'

'She did *WHAT?*'

'Disappeared. Out of my life, anyway.'

'Is it something you talk about?'

'Not with people who have enquired so far.'

'Would you tell me?'

For the first time, the opportunity talk was welcome. 'It happened over forty-five years ago - that's almost half a century! Before you were born! But for me it's not a matter of everyday chat. Convince me why it matters to you.'

'It would help me to understand you. As far as you're concerned she has disappeared every day since. Sharing a problem can be the first step in letting go. Or have you made up your mind to take this piece of ancient history to the grave?'

What had this woman been through that, at the age of thirty or so, she was effortlessly disarming a dusty old academic and teasing out personal information - and in her second - or third - language? This was not just maturity - it was something over-and-above a fully-formed human being.

'I'll give you a bit of background first. It may not even be relevant, but you see things differently and may be able to suggest something I've missed. If it gets boring, just say.'

'It can't possibly be boring. Please tell me.'

'She'd had a serious accident - we both had - and had both made a full recovery. We were back to normality - full-time work and, as far as I was concerned, happily-married life.'

They walked and Sewell talked - but now oblivious to his audience.

One day she had a late shift, so he had prepared supper. Something less than a five-star chef, he had put a chicken in the oven and set some vegetables to steam. One of her many characteristics which he admired had been punctuality. She was due to walk home, so ten minutes after schedule he had set out walking to meet her. It was still winter - a few days before Valentine's day - and dark. There was street lighting - but he did not see her.

Puzzled, he had returned home. He had barely closed the front door when there was a stamping of wet boots outside. He re-opened the door - and there she was. 'I've just been down the hill to meet you. How could I conceivably have missed you?'

She had evidently found the question irritating, as though the answer should have been obvious - the first time their relationship had seen anything other than an amicable response. Side-stepping the customary welcoming hug she walked through to the kitchen-diner and sat at the table without taking off overcoat or boots. He sat down beside her and enquired how the day had been. He was answered by a torrent of abuse about working conditions. When she eventually broke off, it was to demand to know where dinner was. Could not have been more out-of-character. She had changed out of recognition. Before he had time to get the chicken from the oven the abuse re-started - and suddenly stopped. 'I want to be alone!' She stood up and flounced out into the winter night without closing the front door.

'And you let her go?'

The Bridge - *a love affair*

'It took me a second or so to get my shoes on, but I caught up with her. I tried to reason - and failed.'

'And then she disappeared?'

'To all intents and purposes, yes. I caught the occasional glimpse of her around town, but . . .'

'So that's it?'

'Almost exactly a year later I was told she had hitched up with someone - married chap, I believe, but what was the point of pursuing her.'

'Poor David. And you never found a replacement?'

'You know what they say: there's no such thing as the perfect woman? Don't you believe it: she was perfect by every criterion I ever valued. And having known - and been owned by - perfection there's no going back - no compromise.

'Our paths crossed a few times, but she always looked the other way. Five years married and wouldn't even speak! Can't tell you what it did to me - continues to do to me. As grown-ups we survive our daily dealings with fellow humans on the strength of a life-time's worth of accumulated confidence - sub-conscious confidence in our ability to predict what response our words or actions will get. When the rules of engagement suddenly change, self-confidence is undermined. An important part of my salaried job depended on a show of self-confidence - in front of a critical audience, too. I barely survived the struggle.

'I thought a complete break would help - went to work in Brazil - same sort of job, research and lecturing. The reasons seemed relevant at the time. Maybe it looked the most likely place to find a replacement Lígia. Perhaps just to *matar saudades**. Anyway, it didn't do either. When I got back I moved to London. Having your own flat in the centre of London is a great way of getting back into some sort of social scene: the phone never stopped ringing: 'I'm at Heathrow - staying the night at yours, I hope.' I got to know a stunning Spanish

---

*widely considered un-translatable. Literally *to kill nostalgic longings*

The Bridge - *a love affair*

woman, Charo - but she had it all planned to return to Spain to marry. Even at that distance she has remained a great friend and became my most important research colleague - made it possible to turn my theoretical studies into viable engineering hardware.

'No - the nearest anyone has come since has been you, Alexandra - but there is one small detail: difference of calendar age - not to mention the fact that you are not 'available'.'

There was no immediate reply. The entrance to the floating harbour had come into view. 'Come on, David. Let's take Bennett Way across the harbour entrance and have a last look at your bridge together.'

Despite being subject to the boringly dependable laws of physics, the imperceptibly slow transition from night to dawn has a unique magic: some of the light now falling on the distant structure had made the trip from sun to moon and back, and was now mingling with light arriving directly from the sun. No doubt the company he was enjoying played a part, but the subtly changing combination now illuminating the bridge was something unlikely ever to be simulated in the laboratory or on the computer.

'Look David. She is saying goodbye to the night and hello to the morning. I can see why she means so much to you. I could feel quite jealous! It would be so easy to fall in love . . .'

He tensed

'. . . with your gorgeous bridge myself.'

He held out a hand for the inevitable farewell. Brushing it aside, she stepped forward and flung both arms around him. For five seconds - maybe more (something happened to his sense of time) - he was in a real, honest, down-to-earth hug.

Before he could make sense of what was happening she had stepped back, un-slung the rifle and thrust it into his right hand. Folding his fingers around the barrel she squeezed his hand between both of hers. 'Now, be good boy.' (The only flaw with her English was the occasional omission of an indefinite article.) 'Remember, you were seventy-seven earlier this month. Sling that rifle and see if you can cover an English

The Bridge - *a love affair*

mile without being kidnapped, or shot - or needing to shovel coal. Above all, try not to get separated from your trousers!'

She stepped back, lifted the trainers from around her neck and separated the laces. Placing them on the ground she undid the clumsy boots and kicked them off. The baggy camouflaged trousers followed, and she brushed down a light-weight, calf-length skirt which had been furled up around her waist. The shapeless woolly-pully was yanked over her head as she bent to put on the trainers. Straightening up while deftly flicking her hair back into order, she stood back a further couple of paces, transformed from drab, khaki functionality into natural female sophistication.

'Fabulous!' was all he could manage.

She stepped forward, squeezed his hand again, turned, broke into an effortless jog - and was gone.

He was paralysed. To that point his senses had been charging up to over-flowing. Whatever had been charging them was already draining away to be replaced by the all-too-familiar hollow ache.

But for the slight accent, noticeable only at the start of a conversation, she had been the living embodiment of Lígia at the time she had walked out of his life.

17

A question of solace

In a matter of a few, crucial minutes the world had changed for ever. He looked up to the suspension bridge, now catching the morning sun. The last time he had looked it had still been under the spell of pre-dawn half-light. In the hands of Kenneth Graham, the haunting magic of *Piper at the Gates of Dawn* had been allowed to wear off gradually. This morning it had been brutally snatched.

Against the background of the recent, shared experience, the soul-wrenchingly beautiful span now affirmed a Bristol more empty than he could ever have imagined it. How could a functional, inanimate object of masonry, iron and wood insinuate itself into an abstract human experience?

Twice previously he had known the shock of realizing that he was suddenly alone - and felt the accompanying sensation of panic - of nausea. In a lifetime of three quarters of a century, twice wasn't exactly a regular occurrence, but at this moment it had taken over as the only state of mind he had ever known. Evidently previous experience did not equip one with a supply of emotional anti-bodies.

The Bridge - *a love affair*

He was swallowing every few seconds and perspiring. Same old symptoms - must hold on to reality - breathe deeply - find something to focus on. He un-slung the rifle. Had there really been only the one shell - the one which had quite possibly saved his life? Was she, in fact, a supremely confident marksman?

He removed the clip: Empty! He pulled back the bolt. The lone brass cartridge case flipped out. No: he had not been dreaming.

This time there was no Steinway model K; no collection of Rachmaninov preludes to sight-read. Prevention was better than cure: that downward spiral into insomnia must not be allowed to take hold. Over the years he had found calm when reciting Dylan Thomas' *Fern Hill* - out aloud. It had served on his cycle-ride to work before a nine-o'clock lecture. By the end of the seven-mile ride all six verses of that lyrical evocation of childhood had been rehearsed several times. The effect on his frame of mind had been predictable, reliable - always salutary.

The very recollection that a therapy of sorts existed had a calming effect. He looked tentatively about. Further relief followed on realising that his breathing had steadied. Getting there, he thought.

He had lost track of time, but she must be well on the way to the station by now. Over the distant sound of an isolated road vehicle was the unmistakable exhaust beat of Tornado leaving the old Passenger Shed to join the main track. After a pause came the couple of 'chuffs' which were all it would take to reverse into the station.

He focused his imagination on the 'squeeze' against the coach brakes as the locomotive compressed the buffers. Now the fireman would be swinging the heavy link over the hook on the tender. It would take him a few seconds to wind the bob-weight along the thread to tension the coupling. Now he would be connecting the service pipes, allowing the doors to be opened. The train would soon be taking on passengers.

He waited.

Somebody must have given the all-clear for departure. Tornado acknowledged with a blast on the steam whistle. With no industrial or traffic noise it would have been audible throughout the length and breadth of the city. She would be hauling fifteen coaches as well as four freight wagons, always loaded to capacity. He pictured the driver setting the gear into full ahead for maximum steam admission, while the fireman unwound the tender brake. The powerful exhaust blasts started ponderously slowly. He counted the first six. Every six chuffs would add a further 21 feet to the growing separation.

There was still an uncomfortable detachment from reality. His mind flitted from image to image in search of a corner offering a quantum of security. Cathedrals again - those trusty edifices bridging the centuries. But when it came to looking down on the affairs of men, cathedrals did not hold a monopoly: Brunel's masterpiece had surely witnessed its own measure of emotional excursions. The haunting tune and lyrics of *Winchester Cathedral* invaded his thoughts - but with a twist:

> *Brunel's bridge at Clifton, you're bringing me down*
> *You stood and you watched as my baby left town*
> *You could have done something, but you just didn't try*
> *You didn't do nothing, you let her walk by.*

Was that the rôle of song - of music? To help externalise? Certainly he was beginning to feel somewhat less forsaken - ready even to cast around for a way forward. Self-evidently there was no future in passive acceptance. How about starting with a paraphrase of Sherlock Holmes? Eliminate the unacceptable. What remains - if anything - must be acceptable. If the previous lifestyle had led to a dead end, then he must identify an alternative. First to go must be the technical work - writing, books and papers, computer simulations - the Fortran just for challenge of de-bugging. Up to this point they had helped anaesthetise against the unremitting hollow ache day after day, week after week, month after month, year after year, decade after decade.

What about the TA? Apart from his research, the TA had been his life. With Alex gone the HQ would be sterile. Resigning immediately after taking over McNinch's command would not be on.

But did he have the onus of resignation anyway? Not in the normal course - but Sewell held his commission as a result of a succession of blind eyes having been turned to the rules. Easy. Next step: insist on working to rule and presto! End of an adult-lifetime's involvement in the military.

And there must be something to be learned from the way others had coped. One particular friend whom he admired and respected had faced a life-shattering discovery, and had dealt with it by going on a pilgrimage: she had walked the Camino de Santiago, and had gone on to clock up remarkable achievements.

On the other hand, would it be for him? What would a walk of a few hundred miles achieve for a person of no conventional religious conviction? Over the centuries many had walked the Camino in search of a cure. Sewell did not for a moment doubt the therapeutic potential - but preferred to attribute it not to miracles, but to the beneficial effects of walking *per se*: fresh air, varied weather, comradeship, horizons renewed daily. If six weeks of rhythmic physical activity, deep breathing and healthy appetite did not benefit the cardio-vascular system and lower the blood pressure, then what would? And had not St Augustine of Hippo said it all long ago? *Solvitur ambulando*: It is solved by walking.

He would walk, then. El Camino. Maybe Charo would go with him. Walking the Camino would be an allegory for life's own journey, the more so for company - the right company - Charo's company. Six to eight weeks in non-stop proximity to some people would be a job of work - but not with Charo. And who knows? - the Camino might get a taste of improvised Flamenco! The 800 miles would involve time indoors as well as out. What if he were to use some of it for writing - but of a totally different sort? His autobiography, perhaps. He would take the MacBook Air and the solar panel-driven charger.

No, hardly an autobiography! Who of sound mind would read it? A novel, then - an action story. Had he not been kidnapped by

The Bridge - *a love affair*

Russian agents, held to ransom, escaped by commandeering a steam locomotive, hitched a ride across the Atlantic in a submarine, finally being bewitched* by a woman who had entered his life, casually saved it and then, equally casually, vanished.

James Bond material - but with significant differences: Bond had been young. Escaping from tight corners was easy if you had superhuman physical and mental resources - not to mention implausible gadgets and all the dice loaded in your favour. By contrast, Sewell's very age made him human and vulnerable. His 'gadget' was a scientifically demonstrated reality. Bond had rehearsed his virility in exotic settings. Sewell's tropical paradise had degenerated into a defunct I-Max cinema. Bond had shovelled down vodka-Martinis. Sewell had shovelled coal.

Melt-down had put an end - at least for the time being - to conventional publishing, but ironically had seen a surge in demand for fiction from a readership desperate for affordable escapism. This was being satisfied through 'self-publishing', meaning that any author having the resources could make it into print. A use for all these tokens, then. And what an opportunity to take a swipe at the derisory state of higher education's provision for teacher training: a book might make an impact where any number of letters to the Ministry of Education would have no effect.

Recognizing options was part-way to being in control. Being in control was on the way to re-claiming one's sanity, and was that not the message behind the prescription for happiness offered by George Santayana?

Happiness is impossible, even inconceivable, to a mind without scope and without pause - to a mind driven by craving, pleasure or fear. To be happy you must be reasonable or you must be tamed. You must have taken the measure of your powers, tasted the fruits of your passion and learned your place in the world and those things in it which can truly serve you. To be happy you must be wise.

---

*witch: Apparently far less pejorative in Slovak than in English.

The Bridge - *a love affair*

He returned to the present noticeably more composed. Even the legs felt as if they were now ready to take orders.

The abandoned boots and trousers fitted easily into the capacious woolly-pully and left enough free material for the contents to be tied in place. He knotted the sleeves around his neck, put a thumb under the sling and hitched the Lee-Enfield into position on his shoulder.

He looked around and then at his watch. A brisk walk would get him home in time to make a pot of tea before the power was disconnected. He would invite Violet. Then sleep, praise the Good Lord for the blessing of sleep.

Yes, going back to writing was definitely an option: the fog was lifting. Had not C S Lewis said *There are far better things ahead than any we leave behind*? What about a title, then? *Expect the unexpected*? *Tornado*? Better yet: *The Bridge* - but then he'd have to do justice to Brunel and his creation. Well, you never know until you try.

He turned to take a last look downstream. The intoxicating ambiguity of the earlier luminescence had, to borrow from Isaac Watts' Anglican hymn, *flown forgotten as a dream dies at the opening day*, to be replaced by reality - not harsh reality, but stunning, sunlit reality. A bridge perfectly harmonizing the laws of physics with its purpose and unique setting.

His bridge.

The most beautiful bridge in the world.

Supplementary reading, links *etc*.

Anon 2013 BBC pay row has 'damaged its reputation'. Sky News http://uk.news.yahoo.com/ex-bbc-boss-didnt-lose-plot-pay-offs-144953527.html#gRQ0VcM

Arrow, The Productions 1997 DVD CDA914012 Straight Arrow

Belgians, famous 2013 'Impromptu survey of famous Belgian musicians' BBC Breakfast broadcast, 04 Sept.

Cupitt D 1980 Taking leave of God. SCM Press, London

Darwin C 2011 The Origin of Species. Harper Press (paper-back re-print). p 78

Epi-genetics (Lamarckism)
http://en.wikipedia.org/wiki/Lamarckism

Finkelstein T and Organ A J 2001 Air Engines ASME Press, New York

Gotland class submarine:
http://www.youtube.com/watch?v=Khaa3y0i87s

Huxley A 1963 Literature and Science Chatto and Windus, London

Huxley A 2006 Ends and Means Hesperides Press (re-publisher)

Industrial Revolution 1760 to 1820/40

Jobim A C	Lígia
http://lyricalbrazil.com/2013/05/06/ligia/

Lanchester J	2010	Whoops! Why everybody owes and no-one can pay.	Penguin

Lewis C S	(on technology)
http://www.goodreads.com/quotes/tag/technology

MacKay J C	2009	Sustainable energy - without the hot air. UIT Cambridge UK

Marshall A	1994	The Marshall Story Haynes Publishing Group

Mawer S	2010	The Glass Room. Abacus UK

Orenda Iroquois	1959
http://en.wikipedia.org/wiki/Orenda_Iroqois. See also references to the Avro Arrow.

Organ A J	1997	The regenerator and the Stirling
engine Wiley,	Chichester

Organ A J	2014 Stirling cycle engines - inner workings
and design	Wiley, Chichester

Pierce A	2008	The Queen asks why no one saw the
credit crunch	coming. Telegraph, 05 Nov. 2008

Porter-Goff R F D 1976 Brunel and the design of the Clifton suspension bridge. Proc. Inst. Civ. Engrs. Pt. 156 pp 303-321

Pugsley A (Ed.) 1976 The works of Isambard Kingdom Brunel - an engineering appreciation. Institution of Civil Engineers, London and University of Bristol

Resources of the planet:
http://uk.news.yahoo.com/world-used-2013-resources-001916409.html#ukXBU2A

Saint Exuperey A de 1984 (date of re-print) 'Airman's Odyssey', Mariner Books.

Schrödinger E 1967 What is life? Cambridge University Press

Slavery, abolition of 1833 (UK), 1856 (USA)

Stewart H happen, 2009 This is how we let the credit crunch Ma'am. Observer, Sunday 26 July

Stirling R 1816 London patent 4081

Symbiosis - blue butterfly/wasp/ant:
http://bugs.adrianthysse.com/2012/03/video-blue-butterflies-red-ants-and-an-ichneumon/

Tesco 2008 UK population estimate 2008:
http://cornerstone-group.org.uk/2008/02/25/how-many-people-live-in-britain---by-greg-hands-mp/

Zuk W 2004 The Avro story. Altitude Publishing, Canmore, Alberta

The Bridge - *a love affair*

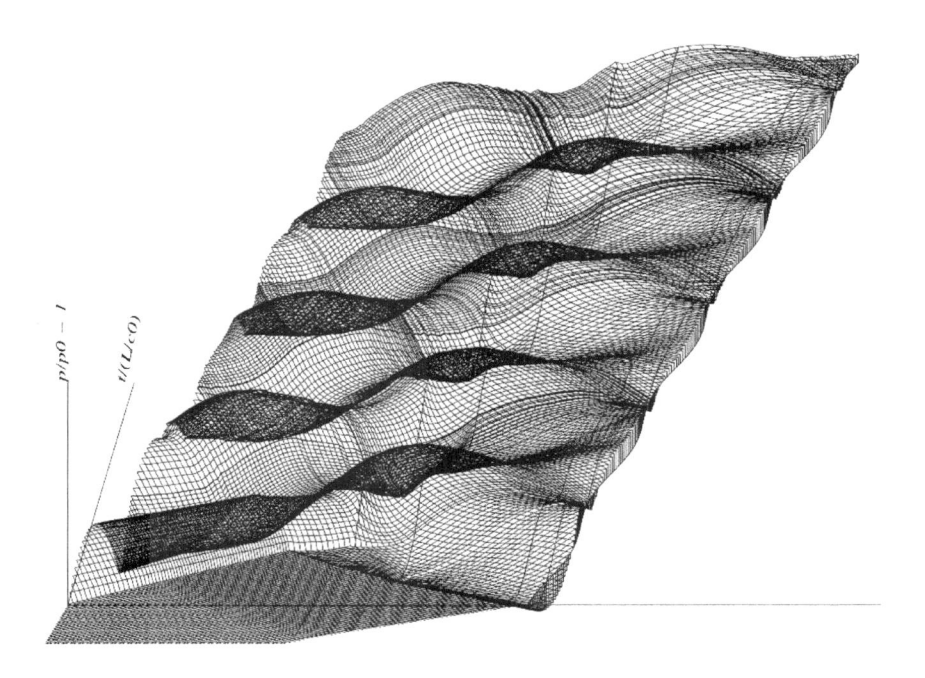

Pressure-distance-time relief generated by using Method of Characteristics to solve a problem in cyclic, unsteady compressible flow with friction and heat transfer

Printed in Great Britain
by Amazon